GOING POSTAL

"Postal inspector," Remo said.

"In a T-shirt?"

"Undercover. This is my partner, who's in deep cover."

Chiun bowed, saying, "The Japanese have my picture in all of their post offices."

"I think I've got everything under control here," the manager said. "They're on emergency sanity-maintenance coffee break now."

"They sounded pretty happy about it."

"Were they—singing?"

"Sounded like humming to me."

"My God, it works. I've got to see this."

They followed the postal manager to the back room where the entire sorting staff of the Oklahoma City Post Office lounged about drinking coffee and singing Barry Manilow songs.

"They always this chipper?" asked Remo.

"It's the Prozac in the coffee," the manager confided. "It kicked in like an adrenaline rush."

Created by
WARREN MURPHY
and RICHARD SAPIR

THE

Destr yer™

ANGRY WHITE MAILMEN

A GOLD EAGLE BOOK FROM
WORLDWIDE®

TORONTO • NEW YORK • LONDON
AMSTERDAM • PARIS • SYDNEY • HAMBURG
STOCKHOLM • ATHENS • TOKYO • MILAN
MADRID • WARSAW • BUDAPEST • AUCKLAND

If you purchased this book without a cover you should be aware
that this book is stolen property. It was reported as "unsold and
destroyed" to the publisher, and neither the author nor the
publisher has received any payment for this "stripped book."

First edition October 1996
ISBN 0-373-63219-3

Special thanks and acknowledgment to
Will Murray for his contribution to this work.

ANGRY WHITE MAILMEN

Copyright © 1996 by M. C. Murphy.

All rights reserved. Except for use in any review, the
reproduction or utilization of this work in whole or in part
in any form by any electronic, mechanical or other means,
now known or hereafter invented, including xerography,
photocopying and recording, or in any information storage
or retrieval system, is forbidden without the written permission
of the publisher, Worldwide Library, 225 Duncan Mill Road,
Don Mills, Ontario, Canada M3B 3K9.

All characters in this book have no existence outside the
imagination of the author and have no relation whatsoever to
anyone bearing the same name or names. They are not even
distantly inspired by any individual known or unknown to the
author, and all incidents are pure invention.

® and TM are trademarks of the publisher. Trademarks indicated
with ® are registered in the United States Patent and Trademark
Office, the Canadian Trade Marks Office and in other countries.

Printed in U.S.A.

For Karen Belciglio,
who should be over her obsession by now.

And for the Glorious House of Sinanju,
P.O. Box 2505, Quincy, MA 02269
[E-mail: willray@cambridge.village.com]

1

He had a face, but no one could describe it afterward.

He had eyes in his face, but everyone remembered their color differently. His complexion had texture, but no one noticed it. Some remembered his hair as red, others as yellow and still others said it was brown.

What they did remember was his uniform. Everyone noticed the uniform. No one paid any attention to the man inside.

It was not that he blended in with the early-lunchtime crowd returning to the new Wiley Post Federal Building in Oklahoma City. A few people actually flinched involuntarily as he approached the stone steps. It was the uniform that made them flinch. Yet his face was benign, his carriage unthreatening.

But no one was looking at his face as he mounted the steps.

Later a few survivors thought it was strange that he wore earphones. They remembered it as strange because they thought there must be some regulation against listening to a Walkman while making one's appointed rounds.

The security guard at the metal detector looked up, saw the blue-gray uniform and not the man and, recognizing the uniform, waved the unfamiliar face around the metal-detector line, which was backed up to the stairs.

"You're late today," the guard called after him.

The uniformed man nodded curtly and passed through the primary line of defense unchallenged. No one questioned the uniform. It could be seen on virtually every street in the nation and while it was feared by some, it was respected by most Americans.

Stationed before the elevator, where he could scrutinize all unfamiliar faces, a lobby guard made eye contact and asked, "New guy?"

"Started today," the uniformed man said curtly.

The elevator arrived, its massive doors sliding apart.

"Well, take it easy," the lobby guard said.

"Uzi does it," the man called back. In the commotion of federal workers filing through the metal detector, his exact words registered only in retrospect. People hear what they want. Just as they see what they expect.

Stepping off on the sixth floor, the man with the eagles on his uniform-jacket shoulder patch looked both ways and saw a closed door with a sign that read, Court in Session. He strode toward it, one hand dipping into his capacious shoulder bag.

Another guard was on station at the door. He suddenly blocked the way, saying, "Sorry. No admittance. Court's in session."

The man extracted an envelope from the bag, saying, "Special delivery."

The guard frowned. The envelope was addressed to Judge Calvin Rathburn.

"Okay, but try not to call attention to yourself." He opened the door to let the man enter, holding it open so he could close it quietly afterward. Judge Rathburn ran a strict court.

Reaching into his big leather bag, the man stepped in. He suddenly pivoted, and the guard saw the stubby Uzi submachine pistol in the cold, frozen moment before it snarled hot and angry at his exposed stomach.

The uniformed man snarled, too.

"Die, disbeliever!"

Crumpling to the floor, the guard watched the rest, helpless. He lived long enough to tell the authorities all he witnessed.

The man entered Judge Rathburn's court and immediately opened fire. Panicked screaming drowned out that first horrible burst. The guard recognized some of the voices. The cute stenographer he had the hots for. Lawyer Tate, who sounded as high-strung as a woman before his voice turned into a hideous gurgle. A persistent banging sounded ineffectually—the judge trying to call order in the abattoir that had become his court of law.

The gunman emptied clip after clip at random. The guard saw only one bloody slice of it from his vantage point on the floor. When Judge Rathburn's red, angry face turned to exploding blood pudding, the guard closed his eyes and, impotent with rage, shook and shook on the floor, unable to move his arms, helpless to draw his weapon.

In his ears, the screaming of the victims died as the gunman's raging voice lifted over the echoing din of gun thunder.

"Unbelievers! I drink in your disbelieving eyes! I rejoice in your misery. God is grape! He commands you to accept the deaf penalty meted out by his lawful messenger!"

No one answered. They were already beyond hearing, beyond caring.

"My God!" the guard muttered. "He's gone postal. Completely postal."

It was over in less than five minutes.

The guard sensed the gunman stepping over him, hard heels clicking down the marble hall. The ding of the elevator signaled his escape.

That was the final thing he remembered before the FBI started questioning him. It was the last clear memory he carried with him to the grave.

THE FBI WERE ON SCENE in less than ten minutes. They could have been there in five. Their local office was on the twentieth floor, but the new federal building had been constructed like a bunker. Bombproof. Bulletproof. Soundproof.

No one had heard the shooting and dying. Until the lunch crowd began filtering back to the sixth floor and the guard was discovered in a welter of his own blood, no one suspected anything violent had happened.

One look inside the half-open courtroom door changed all that.

By the time the FBI got organized and ordered the building sealed, it was far too late.

The faceless man in the respected uniform had quietly left the building and melted into the streets of

Oklahoma City. No one would have thought to detain him anyway. No one would have dared search him or his big leather bag. He was inviolate.

For everyone understood his mission. And although a tragedy had occurred, he could not stop or be stopped.

Rain or shine, snowstorm or bloodbath, the mail had to go through.

2

His name was Remo, and he had nothing against the Japanese.

He felt certain on this point, so he said it aloud. "I have nothing against the Japanese as a people or a race."

A squeaky voice hissed, "So you have forgotten Pearl Harbor?"

"Before my time," said Remo.

"What about the Bataan death march?"

"Same answer. That was an earlier generation."

"The dead cry out for retribution, and you say this?"

"Peace was declared fifty years ago. We're not at war anymore," Remo said reasonably.

"Then why did they send their vicious samurai to these shores intent upon slaughter and maiming?" asked the Master of Sinanju.

"For crying out loud, Chiun, you only lost a nail!"

"You who have no fingernails to speak of may say this. It is nothing to you to be deprived of a nail. You have never achieved correct nail length."

Remo had no answer for that. He sat on a round tatami mat in the bell-tower meditation room of his home. Remo was looking out a window. On the other side of the white-walled square room, the Master of Sinanju sat at the opposite window, also gazing out.

They were supposed to be meditating. Instead, they were arguing.

The silence lasted long enough that Remo thought he was going to get some peace. As usual, he was wrong.

"And why am I forced to endure this interminable wait?" Chiun suddenly wailed. "Why am I forbidden to rend Japanese limb from limb?"

If there was a good answer to that, Remo didn't have it, so he kept quiet.

At length Chiun spoke in a more subdued squeak. "What about their hideous automobiles, which clog the streets of this land you love so well, filling the very air you breathe with their stench?" he asked.

"If people want to drive Japanese cars, that's their business."

"Have I not heard you refer to them as rice burners?"

"The cars, yes. The people, no."

"Reverse racist!" Chiun spit.

"I am not a reverse racist."

"You do not hate the Japanese as you should. Therefore, you are a reverse racist."

"There's no reason for me to hate the Japanese," Remo insisted, an edge creeping into his voice.

Abruptly Chiun whirled to his feet, his face a wrinkled web of rage. He shook a fist.

"I am forced to wear this to hide my shame. Is that not reason enough?"

More calmly than he felt, Remo got to his feet and faced the Master of Sinanju.

Chiun stood only five feet tall, but his rage seemed to fill the close confines. He shook a fist like a yellowed ivory bird claw. Abruptly he opened it.

His extended fingers looked even more like bird talons. His nails were long and curved to glittering points. Except the right index nail. It was capped by an ornate nail protector of imperial jade.

"Only till it grows back," Remo contended, trying to keep calm.

He stood exactly six feet tall, and the only thing he and the Master of Sinanju had in common was the leanness of their limbs. Chiun looked seventy, but was a century old. His face was a wrinkled map of Korea. His eyes were hazel almonds.

Remo was white. In him, only a hint of Chiun's almond eye shape was noticeable, and then only from certain angles—a fact that Remo always denied and that never seemed apparent to him no matter how much he stared into the mirror. Remo could have been anywhere from twenty-five to forty-five. His skin was stretched tight over high cheekbones, and his dark brown eyes lay deep in the hollows of his skull. His wrists were unusually thick. Otherwise, he looked outwardly ordinary.

But he was not. Neither man was. They were Masters of Sinanju, practitioners of the formative martial art called Sinanju, from which all other Eastern killing arts had been struck, like transitory sparks off a spinning flintstone. Where karate, kung fu and *ninjutsu* had devolved into mere tournament exhibition skills, Sinanju remained the ultimate assassin's art. From the royal courts of Cathay to the Pyramids of the Pharaohs, Masters of Sinanju had preserved thrones down to this very day, where they secretly worked for America.

"You know yourself to be blessed with Korean blood," Chiun snapped.

"Yeah . . . ?"

"It is the duty of every Korean to hate the Japanese, who have oppressed their homeland."

"My homeland is America," Remo pointed out.

"Only because your most important ancestor, Kojong, stumbled to this land and took root."

Remo knew he couldn't argue with that. An exiled ancestor of Chiun's had indeed come to America. Remo was a direct descendant of Master Kojong. That made him part-Korean. And gave meaning to the historical accident that had caused his government to select him as the first non-Korean to be trained in Sinanju in order to protect America from its enemies.

"In your essence, you are Korean," Chiun continued. "And the essence of being Korean is to hate the Japanese oppressor."

"I do not hate the Japanese," Remo said flatly.

"Their vile kudzu weed is even now strangling the gracious garden that is your southern provinces."

"I do not hate the Japanese," Remo repeated firmly.

"Not even for the horrors of Yuma?"

Remo's strong face stiffened. Years ago he had been in Yuma, Arizona, when it was attacked by unsanctioned Japanese forces and overrun. It was a rogue scheme undertaken by a Japanese industrialist determined to avenge the nuking of his home-town of Nagasaki. Seizing Yuma, he began executing U.S. citizens, televising these war crimes to all of America.

He had hoped to goad the U.S. president into nuking Yuma to save it.

It might have worked, but Remo and Chiun were already in Yuma, on assignment for CURE, the supersecret government organization for which they both worked.

Although the industrialist was killed, the company he controlled had continued to make mischief.

The most recent instance had been an industrial-espionage agent sent to wreck the U.S. rail system. He'd operated in the electronic equivalent of samurai armor. Chiun had encountered him, thinking it was a ghost samurai returned from the dead to haunt the House of Sinanju. During their first encounter, the samurai's electronic sword had clipped off Chiun's right index fingernail, which only convinced the Master of Sinanju he was dealing with a supernatural avenger. Though Remo and Chiun had eventually caught up with the samurai and separated him from his head, Chiun considered the insult not fully avenged because the samurai's employers had not been relieved of their heads, too.

It was a political problem, according to their employer, Dr. Harold W. Smith. The Nishitsu Industrial Electrical Corporation was one of the most important conglomerates on the face of the earth. There was so far no evidence the Japanese government had backed any of the corporation's clandestine operations.

"Look, Smitty explained the problem," Remo said with more patience than he felt. "The Japanese government knows America employs the House, which almost every foreign government also knows, thanks to that stunt you pulled last year where you offered our services to every tyrant and thug who controlled a government treasury.''

"It was good advertising," sniffed Chiun.

"If we hit Nishitsu Corp and the Japanese find our fingerprints on the deed, we'll have an international incident.''

"Our fingerprints will adhere to no Japanese corpses," Chiun flared. "No one will know it was the House."

"Everyone will know it was the House if you flay the Nishitsu payroll to ribbons like you've been threatening for weeks.''

"Weeks!" Chiun shrieked. "It has been more than two months. Nearly three. Why, oh, why am I being denied the vengeance that is my right?''

And so saying, he faced a pristine white wall and inserted nine of his ten fingers into it. The wallboard made a sound like cardboard being murdered.

Then he dragged both hands all the way down to the baseboard, leaving nine ripping tracks.

"Tell you what," Remo said suddenly. "Why don't I check with Smith?''

In answer, the Master of Sinanju inserted his surviving nails into another part of the wall and waited expectantly.

Snapping a telephone off a taboret, Remo hit the one button. Relays clicked, initiating an untraceable call to Folcroft Sanitarium, the cover for CURE. After a moment, a distinctly lemony voice came on the line.

"Remo."

"Smitty, you owe me."

"Remo?"

Remo made his voice hard. "You framed me for a murder I never committed, railroaded me into the electric chair and buried me in absentia."

"I am still looking for your missing daughter," Smith said hastily.

"This isn't about her. It's about Chiun."

"What is wrong with Chiun?"

And Remo lifted the receiver in the Master of Sinanju's direction.

As if on cue, Chiun brought his nails ripping down again. He threw in a low moan of repressed rage.

"Is he dying?" Smith asked anxiously.

"If he doesn't get another crack at the Nishitsu Corp, someone will be," Remo said pointedly.

"I am still working on the logistics of it. I may have a safe plan of attack for you soon."

"How about we get on the road to speed things up?"

"Are you certain it is necessary?"

And Remo lifted the receiver again.

This time Chiun punched a hole in a new wall and pulled out a mass of wiring.

"My honor must be avenged!" he cried. "Why will the gods not hear my beseeching entreaties?"

"You know it's urgent when he starts invoking the gods," whispered Remo. "Normally he doesn't acknowledge any gods."

"I will make flight and hotel arrangements," said Smith.

"You'll be glad you did," said Remo, hanging up. Turning to the Master of Sinanju, he said, "We're on."

Chiun flung a nest of wiring away with such force it adhered to the wall like tossed spaghetti.

"At last. At last my ancestors will again rest in peace."

"Not to mention this descendant," Remo said dryly.

THE NORTHWEST AIRLINES flight to Osaka had more than its share of Japanese passengers, and their faces stiffened when the Master of Sinanju stepped aboard, resplendent in his apricot kimono with silver stitching.

Chiun glared at every Japanese face that dared glare at him first.

By the time the plane filled up, the cabin atmosphere was thick with glaring.

Chiun took his accustomed seat over the left wing. He wore the jade nail protector designed to protect the stub of the injured nail he was cultivating, and curled the finger in the palm of a clenched fist so it could not be noticed.

"Let's not have a scene," Remo whispered. "It's gonna be a long flight."

"Agreed. We will talk of Korea to pass the long hours until we perform this important service our Emperor demands of us."

"Feel free."

Chiun raised his voice. "Have you ever heard of the feared kamikaze warriors, Remo?"

"Yeah. What's that got to do with Korea?"

"Everything." Chiun lifted his voice to an even higher register. "It was during the era of Kublai Khan, who wished to subjugate Japan, a noble goal. Kublai had first conquered Korea, an ignoble goal, from there to launch his invasion by sea. But Kublai impressed Korean shipbuilders to build his war fleet."

All through the cabin, Japanese heads cocked to catch the words of the Master of Sinanju.

"Are Koreans good shipbuilders?" asked Remo. "I know they were excellent horsemen."

"Yes, Koreans were excellent shipbuilders—when building ships for Koreans, not oppressors."

Remo nodded. He used to listen to Chiun's accounts of his homeland with one ear. Now that he knew Chiun and he shared a common ancestry, he was more interested.

"The day came that the invasion fleet of the Khan set sail for Japan," continued Chiun, his voice growing in fullness. "Mighty were its vessels, packed with soldiers and horsemen. Fearsome was the fate that awaited Japan, the unprotected."

The Japanese passengers became very still in their seats now.

"Then a mighty wind blew out of the north," said Chiun. "A typhoon, Remo. It tossed the fleet of the Khan about. They wallowed helpless in the waves. The warships fell apart, foundered and sunk. The noble invasion was never to be. The fearful Japanese, beholding this with their own incredulous eyes, named this storm Kamikaze, which means 'Divine Wind.'"

All through the cabin, Japanese heads bobbed in agreement with the words of the Master of Sinanju.

"But in their ignorance, they never suspected the truth," Chiun added quickly.

The agreeable bobbing stopped.

"The Master of that time sunk the ships, right?" asked Remo.

Chiun shook his wise old head. "No."

"No?"

"No," said Chiun, waving his jade nail protector in the air without realizing. "That had nothing to do with Sinanju and everything to do with Japanese ignorance and arrogance. For the Korean shipbuilders who constructed the fleet of Kublai Khan did so with inferior lumber and weak nails. Any storm would have sunk the fleet. The Khan never knew this, so no retribution was visited on Korea. The Japanese never imagined this, so they believed themselves to be under divine protection, which accounts for their insufferable arrogance."

All through the cabin, the glaring of turned Japanese faces grew venomous.

"Look," said Remo, "can we get off this subject? No more Korean stories, okay?"

"If you insist," Chiun said thinly.

Chiun was silent for only a short time.

"Have you noticed, Remo?" he asked over the windup whine of the 747's turbines.

"Noticed what?"

"How much Japanese faces are improving."

"Huh?"

"Not the older generation. They are too set in their ways. But the younger ones. They are marrying outside of the islands. New blood is flowing into their veins. I do not normally approve of mixing the blood, but for the Japanese it is a good thing. Their faces are slowly improving. They are not as good as Korean faces, or even Mongol faces. But in another century, perhaps two, Japanese will not be burdened with such morose countenances."

Assorted Japanese passengers turned in their seats and looked unhappily in Chiun's direction.

"I never noticed that," Remo said guardedly.

"It is a fact, Remo."

After that, the majority of the Japanese passengers found ways to change seats with others, and the midsection of the cabin was suddenly free of Japanese glaring.

The Master of Sinanju smiled with quiet satisfaction for the remainder of the flight.

Remo just hoped it would end soon. They were only now taxiing to the Logan Airport runway. And it was fourteen hours to Osaka.

3

NYPD Patrolman Tony Guiterrez had just turned the corner of Eighth Avenue and Thirty-fourth Street when it exploded.

A hot blast of air picked him up off his feet and threw him down the side street as he was admiring the maddening swing and sway of a redheaded girl's walk. She had a nice behind. It wiggled. Normally Patrolman Guiterrez paid more attention to his surroundings, but you didn't see a lot of Anna Nicole Smith behinds on the streets these days. Women liked to keep themselves trimmer than that.

A slow smile of appreciation was tugging at Patrolman Guiterrez's lips when he felt his feet leave the hard concrete, and he forgot all about the girl and her undulating pelvis. The thunderous boom seemed to be chasing him.

His mind froze in midthought.

Explosion!

Many people's lives flash before them when they feel the cold touch of death. Patrolman Guiterrez was made of different stuff. He recognized the sound of a detonation. Even in that split second when his eardrums were being punished by the leading edges of the traveling shock wave, his mind correlated a half-dozen random facts.

The explosion was directly at his back. Couldn't be more than twenty yards away. Sounded right at the corner, too.

What had exploded? he wondered with an eerie clarity of thought.

The faces of the pedestrians Guiterrez had passed flashed by his mind's eye. Ordinary people. None had caught his observant eye.

There had been a Dodge Ram pickup truck at the corner light. Traffic on Eighth Avenue was flowing smoothly.

A car bomb! he thought. Yeah. That's gotta be it. A car bomb.

Then he was slammed into the free-standing wire trash container.

It probably saved his life, though Guiterrez didn't realize it for a while. He struck the trash barrel with such force that for three days afterward the wire pattern was visible in white against his red cheek. They bumped together in midair, then rolled. Guiterrez landed atop the rolling container, mashing it almost flat with his 215 pound body. The barrel was full of newspapers and other paper refuse. They helped save him, too.

When Guiterrez came to, he was looking at a dragon of smoke rolling across the otherwise blue September sky.

Guiterrez sat up. He hurt in so many places he didn't know where to start. He looked at his feet. Still attached—though he'd lost one regulation shoe. He noticed he couldn't feel the ground with his supporting hands, so he looked right, then left, half-expecting to see raw stumps.

One palm was skinned raw, but it was whole. He counted his fingers to make sure.

When he tried to stand up, his spinal column felt like a fracturing icicle.

But Guiterrez got up. He had to. His clearing sight showed him the corner he had just passed.

The first thing he saw was the woman on her back. Her mouth was open as if she were screaming. Something very red and uncertain was foaming up from it. Her eyes stared glassily. Guiterrez couldn't tell if she was ejecting blood or viscera or a jellylike combination, but he could tell she was all but dead.

Not far from her, a meaty naked leg lay scorched and smoking.

The silence in the aftermath of the explosion seemed to last a long time. The screaming soon followed it.

Guiterrez was running to aid the wounded by the time they were swelling into a chorus of agony.

He found the man who had lost his leg around the corner. A black man. He sat up against a building facade looking down at his missing leg. Guiterrez could tell he was seeing what had happened to him but he wasn't getting it. Not yet. Then without warning, he did. He let out a bellow like a wounded bear.

Guiterrez was barking into his shoulder radio.

"Central, send X-ray and fire apparatus. Corner of Eighth and Thirty-fourth."

The Dodge pickup was on fire. The driver behind the wheel didn't have any head. He didn't have much of anything from the shoulders down. A monster might have taken a bite out of him.

If it was a car bomb that had done this, Guiterrez realized, it wasn't the pickup.

Other cars were shattered and broken. One was
flung over on its side.

Whatever the bomb was, it had been big.

But it wasn't a car bomb. Guiterrez had seen plenty
of car-bomb footage on TV. They usually left a
smoking axle. Maybe not where it should have been,
but it always landed somewhere.

No cars had blown up. Guiterrez was positive of
that.

As the wail of sirens started up, Guiterrez went from
car to car, checking for dead and wounded, wondering what had blown up. What on earth had blown up?
He should have seen it when he turned the corner. The
corner had been ground zero. But try as he might, he
couldn't remember anything sitting on that corner.

At least, nothing that stood out. And Tony Guiterrez prided himself on his powers of observation.

THE CHIEF OF DETECTIVES for Manhattan's bomb
squad took him aside an hour later and asked, "What
did you see?"

They were on ground zero. The crater on the corner
still smoked lazily. Blood and glass lay everywhere.
Building facades at all four corners showed scars.

Guiterrez was staring at the crater. It had disrupted
the entire corner, flinging granite curbstones like
bricks. One had been discovered on the smashed re-
mains of a desk in a second-floor office on the other
side of Thirty-fourth.

"There was something there...." he muttered.

"What?"

Guiterrez banged his forehead in frustration. "I
don't know. Damn."

"A package?"

"No."

"A suspicious person?"

"Only the injured. Unless someone came out of a building. But he wouldn't have time to drop a bomb and get away intact."

The detective frowned at the crater. "Whatever blew up, it was big. Too big to carry. Too big to escape notice."

"I walked this beat every day for three years," Guiterrez was saying in frustration. "I know this corner. There was something there."

"Something out of the ordinary?"

"No," Guiterrez said dazedly. "Something that's always been there. I just can't remember what it was."

"How can something be there and you can't remember it?"

"It was something ordinary. Something you take for granted."

The bomb-squad detective was looking around. A lone EMT ambulance stood nearby, in case an unsuspected body turned up. A fire engine was pulling away, its job done. The air smelled of hot metals and warm blood.

"What color?" asked the detective.

"I don't remember that, either. Damn it, why won't my mind work?"

"Was it green?"

"Huh?"

The detective was on his knees. He waved Guiterrez to join him.

Near the pediment of a door, something had chipped at the concrete. A fragment lay on the ground. It was scorched black, but as the detective nudged it with a pen, the other side came to light. It was olive drab.

"Could be military ordnance of some type," the detective was saying.

Guiterrez shook his head slowly. "I don't remember anything military."

"A jeep? A duece-and-a-half truck?"

"It wasn't a car bomb, I tell you," Guiterrez said angrily.

The detective got up and looked around. He held the fragment of scorched olive drab metal in a clean handkerchief.

"It wasn't any guy wearing a brace of M-80s for a girdle, either," he said grimly.

AT THE FIRST AVENUE city morgue, the coroner extracted a large section of steel from the body of the woman whose pureed innards had come bubbling out of her mouth.

Patrolman Guiterrez was there to see it.

The coroner laid the piece of metal on a stainless-steel circular tray and with a thing like a tiny flexible shower nozzle, hosed it clean.

As the blood ran clear, the steel turned olive drab. And embossed on one side were two raised letters: U.S.

"Damn," the bomb-squad detective muttered. "Damn. Maybe it was an ammo box. I hope to hell we don't have militia loose in Manhattan."

"We don't," Guiterrez said slowly. "I don't think."

"You recognize it?"

"Yeah. If you search hard enough, you'll find the piece that fits under it. There'll be letters stamped on it, too."

The bomb-squad detective and the ME looked at him expectantly.

"The letters will say 'Mail.' I remember now. The thing that blew up was a U.S. Mail relay box."

The detective looked as if he wanted to cry. "Did you say a mailbox?"

"Yeah."

"I gotta call the commander. This could be big."

THE COMMISSIONER of police of New York City received the call from the commander of South Precinct Midtown at approximately 12:53.

"It was a mail relay box that blew up," the commander said.

"Damn. Anyone could have planted it, then."

"No, sir, I said a relay box. Not a postal collection box."

"What's the difference?"

"Collection boxes are blue and are for the public convenience. Relay boxes are olive drab and can only be accessed by a postal employee with a key."

"That should narrow it down, shouldn't it?" suggested the commissioner of police.

"It should, sir," the precinct commander agreed.

"So, this isn't a terrorist event?"

"It doesn't appear that way."

"Could be a Unabomber-style mail bomb that detonated prematurely. Or a disgruntled postal worker."

"Is there any other kind?" the commander grunted.

The commissioner thought it prudent not to answer that question directly. It was one thing for a commander to indulge in a little gallows humor. A commissioner had to be sober.

"I have a detective interviewing the postmaster," the commissioner said. "All mail is sorted before it's dropped off. We may develop a lead by the evening news, if not sooner."

"Let's hope we don't have a jurisdictional problem."

"I hadn't thought of that."

"The blown box is a federal problem."

"But it blew in a city street. That makes it our investigation."

"Like I said, let's hope we don't have a jurisdictional problem."

NYPD CHIEF OF DETECTIVES Walter Brown walked up the granite steps and through two of the phalanx of Corinthian columns of the General Post Office on Fifth Avenue in midtown Manhattan. It was the most impressive building in the entire city that wasn't a skyscraper. It occupied a full city block and looked as solid as the bedrock under Manhattan. Over the lintel was carved the motto of the United States Postal Service:

Neither Snow Nor Rain Nor Heat Nor Gloom Of Night
Stays These Couriers From The Swift Completion Of Their Appointed Rounds

Inside he was directed to the office of the postmaster of New York City, where he flashed his badge and announced himself.

"Detective Brown. Urgent business."

"One moment," said the secretary. A moment later, Brown was ushered through a door with pebbled glass panel and the words Myron Finkelpearl Postmaster in gilt letters. It was a substantial door, as befitted the office of the man who oversaw the flow of mail through the most important city in the world.

The postmaster waved Brown to a maroon chair.

"A half an hour ago," Brown began, "an explosion took place at the corner of Eighth and Thirty-fourth."

"I heard."

"We've determined the object that exploded was one of your relay boxes."

The postmaster turned pale. He actually wove on his feet like a drunken man. Out of his pocket came a white linen handkerchief. He ran it across his forehead, sat down and said, "Thank you for bringing this to my attention."

It was Brown's turn to look dazed. "We'll need the names of all postal employees with access to the box in question."

"Impossible."

"Don't give me that. Generate the list from payroll."

"Relay boxes are locked with what we call a master key. Tens of thousands of master keys are carried by postal workers all over the country. Any key can open any box anywhere."

"Let's start with your people."

"Sorry. This is a federal matter."

"Federal? There was an explosion!"

"Of federal property. I will launch a full investigation and relay the findings to your superior."

"With all due respect; I can't accept that answer. There are casualties. Destruction of property. Not to mention the possibility that the individual responsible may have planted more bombs in other relay boxes.''

If possible, the postmaster turned even more pale. And Detective Brown figured he'd gotten through the man's thick, bureaucratic skull.

"I will get right on it, I assure you."

Brown lost it then. "Are you crazy!" he barked, slamming a fist on the postmaster's big desk. "This isn't a jurisdictional matter. A mass murder took place not three blocks from here. It falls under police jurisdiction."

"It's federal. Now I must ask you to leave."

Detective Brown glared at the postmaster for a full minute.

The postmaster's return glare was opaque. Neither man looked as though he would budge an inch.

"You'll be hearing from us," said Brown, storming out.

AS HE CLATTERED DOWN the wide granite steps, Brown wore his face like a stone mask. The brass of that guy. So what if he was federal. Did he think he could sweep this under the rug? Already the corner of Eighth and Thirty-fourth was surrounded by news crews. By 6:00 p.m. this would be the lead story. They were already breaking into afternoon programming with updates.

Brown was pulling open the door of his sedan when he was knocked off his feet. He landed on his back, the air driven out of his shocked lungs from the impact.

He lay there dazed a moment, his ears ringing, then found his wits and his feet.

Down Fifth, a worm of black smoke was coiling upward in the aftermath of the detonation. Then the screaming began.

Detective Brown started for the sound when he heard another boom. This one farther away. Then another. Then, as if fireworks were going off, a string of detonations reverberated through the canyons of Manhattan.

Over the skyscrapers and high-rise office buildings, thin threads of smoke lifted, darkened and became a pall. All in the space of a minute—the time it took Detective Brown to reach the scene of the first explosion, cursing the delays, the bomber and most of all the postmaster of New York, who now had the biggest headache in the greatest city on earth sitting on his desk like a ticking bomb.

And it served the fucker right.

4

At Osaka International Airport all the Japanese passengers got up simultaneously, blocking the aisle. They seemed in a rush to deplane. Remo figured it might have had something to do with the Master of Sinanju's trips to the bathroom. He managed to hit every one of them. After which the doors refused to open. This led to a lot of squirming passengers and a few unpleasant accidents.

"Guess we wait," said Remo.

"*You* may wait," said the Master of Sinanju, getting out of his seat.

As Remo watched, Chiun started forward. His hands were tucked into the joined sleeves of his kimono when he started. Yet Japanese passengers began jumping back into their seats, making a path as if stung by a very busy bee.

The way clearing before him, Chiun padded up the aisle like an apricot apparition. Red-faced Japanese faces glared at him in passing. A few held themselves and looked desperate.

Remo hurriedly followed.

As the Master of Sinanju stepped off the plane, the Japanese stewardesses in their traditional geisha-style kimonos blocked Remo's way.

"You are not staying, *gaijin?*" one asked.

"Osaka is my destination," Remo pointed out.

"We are coming back to Osaka. You may stay with us. Fly back to America, then come back. We will make it very pleasant for you, *gaijin.*"

And they all smiled their geisha smiles.

"Thanks," said Remo. "But my friend will make it very unpleasant for me if I don't get off in Osaka."

The Japanese stewardesses all made pouty faces and one asked, "You know of Japanese hara-kira custom?"

"If you're trying to blackmail me into staying by threatening to commit suicide," Remo said, "it's been tried."

"It has?"

"Many times."

"Did the girls open their bellies for you?"

"I never stick around long enough to find out," said Remo, brushing past.

Remo found Chiun waiting near the baggage chute. There was no luggage. They were only staying a day. Normally the Master of Sinanju took some portion of his fourteen steamer trunks along but in this case he decided against risking even one to what he darkly referred to as "Japanese atrocities."

"Let's find a pay phone," said Remo.

"You did not stay to watch?"

"The stewardesses commit hara-kiri? No. Too messy."

"It is the one Japanese custom of which I approve," Chiun said loudly in English. "If only more Japanese would slit their bellies in shame of being born of these islands."

"Look," hissed Remo, "can we just be on our way?"

"Yes," said Chiun even more loudly. "Let us be on our way. Let us enter Occupied Japan with all its sinister intrigues."

"Japan isn't occupied anymore, Little Father."

"It is occupied by Japanese. Better it were occupied by Koreans, who would improve it. But that is not to be in my lifetime, I fear."

Remo noticed they were being followed by a white-gloved security detail so he pretended not to be with the Master of Sinanju. He found a pay phone and dialed the USA country code, then leaned on the 1 button.

"We're here," Remo told Smith when the lemony voice came over the line.

"Go to the Sunburst Hotel on Sakai-Suji Avenue," Smith said.

"No time. Chiun's already stirred up the natives. We've got to be in and out quick."

"I have not yet determined a plan of attack for you," Smith hissed.

"We can go in and kill everyone," Remo suggested.

"Technicians and salarymen are not worth our time. Go to Nishitsu Osaka. Make sure the Nishitsu executives understand we have discovered their plot to destroy our rail system and have traced it back to them."

"How?"

"You will find a way. Just be subtle. You are delivering a message."

Rejoining Chiun, Remo related the conversation, then added, "Guess we're just going to have to march in and kick butt."

"Too subtle," Chiun said, stroking his wispy beard.

"You call that subtle?"

"I have a more appropriate idea. One that will impress even thick Japanese skulls."

"You lead and I'll follow."

Remo did. First to the Osaka customs counter, where Chiun was asked if he had anything to declare.

The question and the Master of Sinanju's vituperative answer were in Japanese, and Remo didn't understand any of it. But the way the customs officials' ears turned red and their facial expressions flattened out suggested that Chiun had declared them all illegitimate sons of Japanese snow monkeys.

The security police who were hovering in the background now rushed forward.

More heated exchanges transpired.

Chiun flung hot words and brandished his jade nail protector in official faces. Someone decided it was undeclared contraband and attempted to seize it.

Instead, he seized his own crotch. Others seized other sensitive portions of their anatomies and Remo had to rush in to rescue the Japanese constabulary from the Master of Sinanju's wickedly flashing nails.

He accomplished this by sending them spinning into a nearby men's room and with his hand cold-soldering the door shut after the last one tumbled in.

After that Remo followed the Master of Sinanju to a waiting taxi.

"Why did you not come to my aid sooner?" Chiun sniffed. "You know I am nearly toothless in my present condition."

"I was pretending I wasn't with you, okay?"

"I do not blame you," Chiun said, voice suddenly dejected. "I have allowed myself to be shamed in your eyes. And in the eyes of my ancestors. I wear a horn of jade where my Killing Nail should be."

"That's not it, Little Father. I just didn't want to be made."

Chiun's eyebrows lifted. "But it's all right that I am made?"

"Look, you couldn't be more obvious if you carried a flag. I like to blend in."

"I would like to blend the Japanese shogun who stole my honor," Chiun said fiercely.

"Just keep a low profile and you'll get your wish," Remo cautioned.

Chiun gave the driver instructions and Remo spent the ride looking out the rear window in case they were being pursued.

"You know they'll be looking for us when we try to fly out of Osaka," Remo undertoned.

"I will be looking for them, too," sniffed Chiun. "They who dared covet the nail protector of Gi."

"A previous Master broke a nail?"

"Gi had weak cuticles and protected his Killing Nails when he was not dispatching enemies of the Khan with them."

"Which Khan?"

"Kublai."

"Gi worked for the Khan who oppressed Korea?"

"Gi offered his services to the Korean emperor, whose offer was far less than that of the Khan."

"Doesn't sound like much of a Master."

"He was a wonderful historian and so we revere him."

"You revere him," said Remo, "The only thing I revere is finishing this freaking assignment."

"Oh? Are Japanese bothering you?"

"They're starting to," Remo growled.

Chiun only smiled thinly.

FROM THE OSAKA AIRPORT the red taxicab conveyed them to a train yard where old diesel locomotives sat rusting and peeling.

While the cab waited, Chiun went among these and inspected them carefully, knocking on noses and sides until he was satisfied.

The Master of Sinanju haggled with the yardmaster in Japanese. Then they reclaimed their cab.

"What was that all about?" asked Remo.

"You will see."

Next Remo found himself in an airfield where helicopters buzzed overhead. Again there was haggling. Then Chiun called out, "Come, Remo we are going for a short ride."

Soon a giant helicopter skycrane was lifting off with Remo and Chiun in the cabin.

Night had fallen. Chiun guided the pilot with quick gestures. Before long they were over the train yard. A cable was lowered at Chiun's direction and the locomotive was secured by a ground crew.

"Why are we stealing a locomotive?" Remo wanted to know.

"We are not. I have purchased it at a fair price."

"Yeah? What are you going to do with a locomotive? It won't exactly fit into the overhead bins on the flight home."

Chiun examined his nails. "I will think of something."

Twenty minutes later they were approaching a great industrial complex of white buildings under blue-white floodlights. Remo looked down. He saw a tiny helicopter on a roof helipad. The helipad was in the shape of the three-moons symbol of the Nishi samurai clan, now Nishitsu Industrial Electrical Corporation.

If they stayed on course, the ponderous weight of the diesel locomotive would soon overfly the helipad, Remo saw.

"You're not thinking what I think you're thinking," Remo said.

"We have been asked to deliver an unmistakable message."

"Does *he* know that?" Remo asked, indicating the earphoned pilot in the control bucket.

"Not as yet."

"So all we have to do is pressure him to hit the cable release at the right moment?"

"No, he will never do that because he would fall into great difficulties. I will persuade him to tarry here a moment or two. Having accomplished the difficult part of the assignment, the rest will be up to you."

Remo shrugged. "Fair enough." And opening the side door, he stepped out into a wheel strut. His actions were so quick and fluid that the pilot, occupied with his flying, didn't notice.

Remo was gone almost five minutes. The skycrane started to pitch and sway. Then with an adroit parting of cable, the helicopter suddenly rose higher, freed of its tremendous burden.

The locomotive actually whistled as it fell. Its monstrous moon shadow lay over the helipad, and kept shrinking. It struck with a great booming like a peal of thunder. The chopper actually shivered.

The pilot started to caterwaul the most ungodly curses as Remo climbed back in. He hadn't noticed Remo was gone.

"What took you so long?" asked Chiun.

"Cable that thick takes time to snap," said Remo, looking at his greasy hands.

Chiun made a face. "If you have correct fingernails, your hands would now be clean."

Remo frowned.

"I thought you were off this fingernail kick?"

"I have agreed that you may wear your nails as you wish. That does not mean I am forbidden from describing other options."

In the control bucket, the sweaty-faced pilot swung his ship around to inspect the damage.

It wasn't complete, but there was a big hole where the main Nishitsu roof had been. Gone were the helipad and its helicopter. Smoke and flames were boiling up. Amazingly, almost no one reacted on the ground. Since it was evening, loss of life would be minimal.

And the Master of Sinanju leaned forward and took hold of the pilot's very red neck.

The pilot decided this was the airspace he most didn't want to loiter in. The skycrane went rattling away like a huge frightened pelican.

"Think they'll get the message?" asked Remo.

Chiun shrugged. "Who is to say? They are Japanese and therefore thick of head and slow of wit."

5

Dr. Harold W. Smith had been plucked out of the CIA data-analysis section to run the supersecret government agency called CURE for more than one reason. There were many excellent analysts in those early days of the CIA when Univac computers the size of an entire room were constantly keypunching data to be processed and analyzed.

It was said of Smith in those Cold War days that he was worth two Univacs. The raw intelligence that passed before his gray eyes prior to being fed to the big systems often never reached the keypunch stage. Smith had only to glance over it, correlate it with other data cataloged in his gray brain and inform a superior of his conclusions.

"The Soviets are about to crush the Hungarian revolution," Smith would warn.

"What makes you say that?"

And Harold Smith would reel off a list of seemingly routine troop and armor movements, canceled vacations, recalled ambassadors, increased food imports and other outwardly unrelated data in support of his conclusion. And he would be right.

At first he was dismissed out of hand.

"Leave the correlating to the computers, Harold."

But Smith was stubborn. And not blind. He kept offering his analyses, and they were on the money 99.7 percent of the time.

As punishment, Smith was exiled to a windowless office of his own. To his superior's intense exasperation, he continued predicting world events and continued memoing his superiors. And he was invariably, infuriatingly, stubbornly correct.

Finally they had no choice but to promote him to senior analyst. From then on, the agency pretended Harold Smith was just another Univac. In fact, he outperformed the Univacs, which were only brute computers whose keypunched ticker tape had to be decoded by higher-level analysts. Uncorrelated data in, correlated data out.

With Smith, they skipped two of the three steps. And saved on electricity.

Smith called the revolution in Cuba correctly. He proved conclusively on paper that the so-called missile gap was just Soviet propaganda perpetuated by Pentagon scare mongers. And by the time of the Bay of Pigs invasion of Cuba, the CIA was only too glad to see him take early retirement. A man that unrelentingly single-minded could be a royal pain in the ass.

Harold Smith did not retire. He instead went on to head an organization that CIA never dreamed existed. It was called CURE. The premise of the President of the U.S. who had created it and installed Smith as its director was staggeringly simple. The American experiment was in collapse. The Constitution lay in shreds. It was not possible to maintain order and defend the nation from the rain of threats from all quarters—and remain within the rigid limitations of the law.

CURE would operate outside constitutional and legal mandates. Smith's task—one as staggering as those faced by the early Founding Fathers—was to beat back the modern-day Huns and Visigoths who were chipping away at America's freedoms by any means possible.

Three decades later, Harold Smith was still at it, operating from the same cracked leather chair in the same Spartan office in the same cover institution. Folcroft Sanitarium, ostensibly a warehouse for the chronically ill and mentally impaired. Smith ran both organizations with a firm, unsentimental hand. Older, grayer, yet still recognizable as the supercompetent bureaucrat the CIA had nicknamed the Gray Ghost.

The only thing that had changed in those years was Smith's computer setup. Initially it was an oak desk that concealed a terminal that rose from his desktop like a crystal ball and connected to the hidden bank of mainframes in the basement, dubbed the Folcroft Four by Smith.

The Folcroft Four still hummed behind a blank concrete wall, backed up by optical WORM-drive servers and other new innovations in data storage and retrieval. But Smith's desk had been replaced by a modern desk with a black glass top. Buried under the tinted glass was a fixed monitor. Smith hated change, but this new desk was much more secure than the old.

From his chair, he stared down into the black glass. The amber letters on the screen floated as if in some dark liquid medium.

There was no keyboard in the usual sense. When Smith brought his hands close to the desktop nearest him, the thin white letters of a standard alphanumeric keyboard arrangement glowed. But there were no keys in the physical sense. It was a touch-sensitive capacity keyboard, that darkened the second Smith withdrew his hands.

Smith was scanning the vast daily stream of data that his mainframes pulled off the Net and wire-service links, collating the bulletins, discarding the trivia and saving in files those items he believed would be useful for future operations.

It was after noon. Two hours past midnight in Japan. There was no news out of Osaka. Smith had had misgivings about sending Remo and Chiun to deal with Nishitsu before he had fully identified the situation. But sometimes keeping his only employees happy was his only survivable option.

At 12:33 his system beeped, and a red light popped up on one corner of his screen. Smith brushed a flat hot-key, and an AP bulletin appeared. It was brief, indicating it was only a first, sketchy report moving on the wire.

Oklahoma City, OK—Courtroom Shooting (AP)
An unidentified gunman burst into the court of Judge Calvin Rathburn at 11:15, Oklahoma time, opening fire. Initial reports indicate more than two dozen persons wounded or killed. The gunman fled. Eyewitnesses have so far provided no description of the assailant. The attack took place in the new Wiley Post Federal Building, which replaced the old Alfred P. Murrah Federal Building, destroyed by a truck bomb more than a year ago previously in the worst case of domestic terrorism in U.S. history.

Frowning, Smith began tapping his keyless keys and dumped the report into a growing file he called Militia Threats. This was supposition on his part. But it seemed a solid one.

Not ten minutes later, the first report of the explosion at the corner of Eighth Avenue and Thirty-fourth Street in midtown Manhattan bubbled up. One glance at it, and Smith immediately consigned it to another file labeled Terrorist Threats.

Nothing about either event suggested a link to the other. Smith invariably thought in links and patterns. But no pattern or link was apparent. In fact, it never occurred to Smith to connect the two, even as closely spaced in time as they were.

Smith had gone on to his work, knowing his ever-vigilant system would alert him to significant follow-ups when, approaching 1:00 p.m., the bulletins began peppering him like thrown darts.

New York, New York—Mystery Explosions (AP) A string of as yet unidentified explosions occurred today at approximately 12:27 in Manhattan's West Side. Initial reports indicate a series of seven detonations, all in a multiblock area surrounding the Manhattan's General Post Office. Damage and casualty reports are unavailable at this hour. No link to the earlier explosion at Eighth Avenue and Thirty-fourth Street has been established.

The anonymous AP wire copywriter, bound by the rules of journalism, could do no more than suggesting a link. But not Harold Smith.

Eight explosions at a minimum, all in the relatively confined sector of midtown Manhattan.

Something was up. Something big. With a sharp pang, Smith regretted having sent Remo and Chiun out of the country. But done was done.

In their absence, Harold Smith would look into the situation. There would be time enough to bring Remo and Chiun into this when a target was established.

After all, they were assassins, not investigators.

Smith made excuses to his secretary and left his office with a shiny leather briefcase that contained his telephone-computer links to the Folcroft Four. It was a new system, one he had built to replace the old one, which had been destroyed recently. This would be a good opportunity to field-test it.

SMITH TOOK the Henry Hudson Parkway into Manhattan, noticing that the trees on either side of the parkway were being choked by wild catbrier and hops. He frowned. Someone should do something about it. Smith hated untidiness in any form. Even in nature. If he had his way, trees would grow in orderly ranks and flowers would sprout only where they were wanted.

His briefcase lay open on the seat beside him, and the computer system was up and running.

Bulletins continued to pour in. There were now nine confirmed explosions. Eyewitness accounts recounted of death, maiming and carnage. This was a big operation, one of the biggest since the World Trade Center, Smith thought grimly.

No sooner had the thought crossed his mind than the skyline of Manhattan came into view, featuring the twin towers of the World Trade Center. These were Smith's ultimate destination.

New York City was under siege. Law-enforcement agencies would be mobilizing. Security would be tight. That meant one thing to Harold Smith.

The White Room.

IT WAS NOT CALLED the White Room because it was white, although the walls were white. The door was a plain veneer panel with no lettering. The only key belonged to the commissioner of police for New York City.

The plain door lay at the end of a long corridor on a lower floor of Tower One of the World Trade Center. It was soundproof and bugproof. Its phones were scrambled.

That was why, although the police commissioner's office was only a few blocks away, in moments of greatest emergency he held crisis-management meetings in the White Room. No news leaks ever escaped the White Room. No eavesdropper ever overheard a whisper from within. The press knew of the White Room, but could not get to it. Especially in the aftermath of the failed World Trade Center bombing. All that came out was white noise. Hence the name.

It was the irony of ironies, the police commissioner thought as he unlocked the plain door to the White Room, that during the last serious terrorist crisis this leakproof office was denied to the commissioner of police because it literally stood on ground zero. No one had gotten into the White Room that day. The World Trade Center bombing had been a crisis that belonged to a previous police commissioner. Now the current holder of that position had a crisis of his own.

There was a long, buffed mahogany conference table in the middle of the White Room. It was bare except for strategically placed telephones. A Mr. Coffee stood on a wheeled cart and offered six kinds of coffee. The commissioner started the Mr. Coffee, knowing it was going to be a very long day.

The meeting had been called for two-thirty. Ostensibly its purpose was intelligence sharing and tactical coordination of the joint NYPD-FBI Anti-Terrorist Task Force, but that would be the least of it, the commissioner knew. The FBI just wanted to stake out their territory. The Bureau of Alcohol, Tobacco and Firearms would claim this as their investigation. It would be all the commissioner could do to keep his hand in. But it was his city. And his meeting.

He was sugaring the first cup when a peremptory knock rattled the door.

"Who goes there?" the commissioner called over his shoulder.

"Smith. FBI."

The commissioner of police opened the door, saying, "Your office said to expect Special Agent Rowland."

"Rowland was held up," said Smith, quickly entering.

"Well, you're early anyway."

The commissioner sized Smith up as a middle-level bureaucrat. A GS-10 at best. He wore a gray three-piece suit and had the personality of a rain cloud. His accent was lockjaw New England.

"Coffee?"

"No time," Smith said. "There is much to be done. I need to be brought up to speed as quickly as possible."

The commissioner blinked. "Is this happening outside the city?"

"No comment," said Smith.

"Damn."

"There is no time to waste on guessing," said Smith. "Who has claimed responsibility for these acts?"

"Who hasn't?" the commissioner grunted, pulling a sheaf of faxes from his open briefcase and laying them on the polished table. "Hezbollah. Hamas. Islamic Jihad. The Muslim Brotherhood. The National Front for the Salvation of Libya." He grunted. "I guess Khaddafi is out of favor among the fundamentalists these days. The Abu Nidal Group. A.I.M. M.O.M."

"M.O.M?"

"Messengers of Muhammad. Then there are the Eagles of Allah, the Warriors of Allah, the Islamic Salvation Front, Armed Islamic Group, Taliban, the National Front for the Liberation of Palestine and something called the Islamic Front for the A.P.W.U. We don't know what 'A.P.W.U.' stands for yet."

"In other words," said Smith, "every active terrorist cell looking for publicity has claimed responsibility?"

"This time we can safely discount them all."

"Why do you say that?" Smith asked sharply.

"We've determined the first explosion was a post-office relay box. A piece of shrapnel was stamped U.S. Mail. The later explosions showed the same MO. Every explosion took place on an open sidewalk. Olive drab sharpnel everywhere. I'm still trying to get a handle on the dead."

Smith was sharp. He jumped right on the money. "Relay boxes are not accessible to the public. It is virtually impossible for a letter bomber to orchestrate a series of closely spaced explosions in relay boxes and have none of the devices go up in postal-service hands or at the destination address. We may be dealing with a postal employee.''

"Exactly. Some letter carrier gone postal.''

"That theory does not fit the psychological profile of postal offenders,'' said Smith.

"What doesn't?''

"Postal employees invariably direct their anger at their superiors and co-workers, not the general public.''

"There was an incident a few years ago up in Boston. A disgruntled postal clerk grabbed his AK-47 and buzzed the South Postal Annex in a stolen light plane, sniping at random.''

"Exactly,'' said Smith. "He fired at his place of employment.''

"And everything else in sight,'' the commissioner countered.

"I assume you have the names of the postal employees who had access to the destroyed boxes?''

"They're stonewalling that.''

"Who is?''

"The postmaster.''

"What!''

"Won't take my calls. Says it's a federal matter. I don't suppose you FBI boys have any pull with the postal service?''

"I will get back to you on that,'' said Smith, picking up his briefcase and storming to the door.

"What about the briefing?''

"I have had my briefing,'' said Smith, slamming the door.

THE HEAD of the port authority arrived ten minutes later and accepted a cup of black coffee and a seat. Then came a knock at the door.

"Who is it?" asked the police commissioner.

"FBI."

"Smith?"

"No, Rowland."

The commissioner threw open the door and said, "Smith told me you couldn't make it."

"Smith?"

"Special Agent Smith. You know him?"

"Do you have any idea how many Smiths there are with the Bureau? What did he look like?"

"He was—" the commissioner frowned "—gray," he said.

"That fits a lot of Smiths, too."

"Over sixty. Banker's gray. Gray eyes. Rimless glasses. Gray hair. Thin as a rail."

Special Agent Rowland looked doubtful. "That doesn't fit any of the Smiths I know. You certain he was with the Bureau?"

"That's what he claimed."

"Claimed! You saw his ID, didn't you?"

The commissioner of NYPD blanched. "I—he didn't show any."

"You didn't ask for ID?"

"It slipped my mind. Christ, he could have been—"

"Media."

"My God, if the media has penetrated the White Room, I'm going to look like a fool."

"Let's concentrate on the crisis at hand before we start worrying about job security," said FBI Special Agent Rowland, flint in his voice.

The commissioner of police sat down like a log dropping. He wore the approximate expression of a crosscut tree stump—flat and spinning in concentric circles.

6

When the helicopter skycrane landed in an Osaka field, the pilot jumped out and came at the Master of Sinanju with a knife.

"Don't do it," Remo said in English.

"It is too late," said Chiun, stepping out. "I have been challenged."

"I was talking to the idiot," said Remo.

The Japanese pilot lunged for Chiun's midriff. Chiun separated his hands as if to clap them together. Then he did. They came together flatly, with the thrusting steel blade between them. Chiun twisted both wrists, redirecting the knife thrust. The pilot's wrists were carried along for the ride. The hapless pilot, too.

Chiun left him holding the broken bits of his blade in his hands and a stupefied expression on his gaping face.

"You know," Remo said as they walked away, "I don't blame him for being upset. They're going to hang this on him."

"Let him commit hara-kiri, then. I do not care. It is nothing to the pain inflicted upon my august person."

They found a cab with a red light in the windshield

indicating it was free, and Chiun got into an argument with the cab driver before they were under way.

"What's he saying?" Remo asked Chiun.

"He is saying the airport is closed at this hour. I am saying it will be opened for us."

"Little Father, they're going to be waiting for us."

"Good."

"To arrest us."

"That they will never do."

"What say we crash for the night and figure out something in the morning?"

"What hotel did Smith say he secured for us?" asked Chiun.

"The Sunburst. Knowing Smith, it's probably the cheapest fleabag in Osaka, too."

Chiun relayed that information to the taxi driver, and they were off.

They were cruising the neon-bedazzled streets of Osaka not long after. Like Tokyo, the city might have been a gigantic laboratory for company logos. Every building and tower seemed to shout a name in English and Japanese.

Seeing little police-cruiser activity, Remo relaxed slightly. "Looks like the manhunt has quieted down," he told Chiun.

Then Remo saw the Sony Jumbotron TV screen mounted high on an office tower overlooking the heart of the city—an artist's composite sketch of the Master of Sinanju was being telecast to all of Osaka, if not Japan.

Remo lowered his voice. "Little Father, don't spook the driver, but your face is on the giant TV screen up there."

"Where? Where?"

"I said don't make a fuss," Remo hissed.

Then Chiun did.

Catching a glimpse of the face shown in full, Chiun's own face collapsed in anger. "That is not me!"

"Chiun!"

"Look, Remo, they have desecrated my face with a mustache. I wear no mustache. And those eyes! They are Japanese, not Korean. How dare they! We must sue for satisfaction."

And switching to Japanese, the Master of Sinanju called for the driver to stop.

Chiun got out, walked to the sidewalk opposite the giant image, which had receded into a floating graphic beside the head of the Japanese network anchorman, and frowned up at the colossal screen.

"They have insulted me."

"Look, people are going to notice us," warned Remo, looking around warily.

Catching a passerby, Chiun took him by the back of the head and directed his face to the Jumbotron screen.

"Is that me?" Chiun asked in English.

The Japanese looked up. Chiun directed his head at his own face, then redirected it back at the screen.

"Is it?" Chiun demanded.

The Japanese man began shaking his head no. Vigorously.

"See, Remo. Even he does not see the likeness."

"That's because he doesn't understand English and you're shaking his head for him," Remo argued.

"I am not," said Chiun as the hapless Japanese's tongue began wagging like a dog's tail. His eyes rattled like crazy dice.

"You are. He's trying to get away."

"Then I will grant him his wish," said Chiun, releasing the man.

The Japanese stumbled away, holding his head and staggering off like a salaryman full of saki.

"There is the proof," said Chiun. "If he thought that wretch was the Master of Sinanju, he would have called for my arrest."

"Right now all he's calling for is a doctor."

Chiun glared at the image on the screen. "Remo, have you any coins?"

"Sure, why?"

"Never mind the why. Let me borrow the largest."

Remo dug into his pocket. "A Kennedy half dollar do?" he asked.

Chiun accepted the fat, gleaming coin. "It is perfect."

Flipping it, Chiun made the coin bounce and sing. He flipped it several times. Each time the coin spun higher, singing at a higher pitch.

On the fourth flip, the coin shot up, then angled across the street, as if suddenly pulled by a giant magnet.

Before Remo knew it, the Jumbotron screen winked out, leaving a tiny hole that smoked.

"There," said Chiun, satisfied. "Now we will go to our hotel."

"You're going to get us tossed in the local pokey if you keep this up."

But Chiun padded on, serene in the knowledge that he had righted a severe injustice done to him.

In the neighborhood of the hotel, Remo started noticing people walking around in what appeared to be thin blue pajamas. The pajamas all had the same sunburst crest over the blouse pocket.

"What kind of outfits are those?" Remo asked Chiun.

"Pajamas."

"That's what I thought. This a new Japanese custom? Wearing pajamas at night?"

"I do not know."

When they found their hotel, Remo noticed the sunburst pattern on the marquee.

Through the open door, men came and went in the identical blue pajamas with the sunburst monogram.

"I don't like the look of this."

"Do not fear, Remo. To Japanese eyes, all Koreans look alike."

"Not what I meant," Remo muttered.

Inside they had to leave their shoes and put on paper slippers. Since Chiun did this without complaint, Remo followed suit.

When they checked in, they were given keys.

"We are on the fifth floor," said Chiun as he led Remo to the elevator where more men in pajamas waited. They had the sleepy look of hotel guests, not employees.

"Casual establishment," remarked Remo.

"Customs are strange in this occupied land."

Stepping off on the fifth floor, Remo at first thought he had stepped into a morgue.

The walls were beige, and there were no doors recognizable as such. Instead, spaced along the walls were hatches like the drawers in a morgue, set in twos, one atop the other.

"You sure he said fifth floor?" asked Remo, looking at his key.

Chiun nodded. "Yes. The fifth."

"Our rooms must be down the hall. *Way* down the hall."

But in fact, they were just around the corner. Remo's key number corresponded with an upper hatch. Chiun's the lower.

"Must be storage lockers," said Remo.

"Yes," added Chiun with a frown.

But as they looked around for the corresponding room door, a Japanese in blue pajamas walked up to a wall hatch, unlocked it with his key and calmly crawled into the lighted tube, shutting it after him.

Soft music floated out of the sealed hatch.

"Did you see what I just saw?" Remo asked Chiun.

Remo went to his hatch and opened it.

Inside it was like a morgue drawer except there was bedding. Soft fluorescent lights illuminated the six-foot-long tube. On the bed lay neatly folded a pair of the blue pajamas, sunburst monogrammed pocket side up. There was a TV screen recessed into the ceiling directly over the short white pillow at the far end. On one side was a control panel for lights and TV.

"I'm not sleeping in this!" flared Remo.

"Nor am I," huffed Chiun. "It is an insult!"

They turned back, heading down to the lobby. The clerk patiently explained in English that they had no rooms. Only "capsures."

"What's he saying?" Remo asked Chiun.

"Capsures," repeated Chiun.

"I heard that. What's he mean?"

"This capsure hoteru," the clerk said briskly. "No rooms."

"We want our money back," said Remo.

"Sorry, you open hatch. Room is rented. No refund."

"It's not a room," Remo retorted. "It's a freaking drawer."

"You open, you rent. Sorry."

"I have not opened mine," proclaimed the Master of Sinanju, slapping his key down with a flourish.

"You may reave," the clerk allowed.

"Not without refunds," insisted Remo.

"If you insist, I wirr summon porice."

"Yes, call your constables," flared Chiun. "We refuse to knuckle under to your barbaric customs."

"No, don't do that," Remo said hastily. And lowering his voice, he whispered urgently, "We're wanted. Remember?"

"I am not wanted. Some mustachioed impostor is."

Remo rolled his eyes.

Turning to the stone-faced clerk, he asked, "Look, can you recommend a good hotel?"

"Yes. This one very good."

"Other than this one," Remo said wearily.

"We have branch in Shinsaibashi District."

"It have rooms?"

"Sunburst Hoteru chain never offer room. We are budget hoteru. Offer exerrent economy for weary traverer."

"Remind me to extract Smith's fingernails one by one when we get back," growled Remo, collecting his shoes.

DAWN WAS BREAKING at the Osaka International Airport.

"So how do we pull this off?" said Remo. "Disguises?"

"I do not require a disguise," said Chiun. "They are seeking an impostor, not me."

"Count on them rounding up every Korean they can lay hands on and sorting them out later. You're not out of the woods yet."

"Nevertheless, I intend to board the next aircraft leaving this hateful land, with or without you."

Remo looked concerned. "Maybe if we go in separate entrances . . ."

"Chicken," sniffed the Master of Sinanju, who padded toward the glass doors.

Remo hung back. It wasn't that he feared for Chiun's safety. The Master of Sinanju could probably take out the entire Osaka airport-security force unassisted. But doing so would create an international incident—exactly what Smith didn't want.

The automatic glass doors parted, and Chiun passed into the sprawling complex of glass and steel.

Remo counted forty-five seconds by his internal clock and followed.

When the doors hummed apart, he expected to hear the sound of gunfire, or at least screaming. He heard neither. A frown touched his strong face. This was too easy.

Taking the escalator to the Northwest concourse, Remo kept his eyes open and his other senses alert.

He got to the top of the escalator, then looked both ways.

A flash of apricot caught his eye. There was Chiun walking through the metal detector cool as could be. The security guards barely looked at him.

Shrugging, Remo decided it was going to be easy after all.

At the magnometer frame, a guard began gobbling at Remo angrily.

"I don't speak Japanese," Remo said calmly.

The guard spit out more gobbling words. Another chimed in. Remo was quickly surrounded.

"Look, I have a ticket," said Remo, reaching for his ticket, which was stuffed into his back pocket. It was a mistake. They thought he was reaching for a weapon. They drew theirs.

Remo tried to bluff his way through. Throwing up his hands, he said, "Look, I'm unarmed. My ticket's in my back pocket. Okay? Ticket. Back pocket. Don't shoot."

One guard evidently knew a little English.

"Freeze," he said.

"I'm frozen. Friendly. Okay?"

"Freeze!" the guard repeated.

"I am frozen," Remo repeated.

"Freeze!" the guard snarled a third time. Others joined in. They started to remind Remo of Japanese prison guards in old World War II movies Remo used to watch. Faces flat and harsh, they looked ready and willing to shoot him on general principles.

And deep inside Remo, a growing anger took root.

"Look, I said—"

"Freeze!"

That did it. Remo took the one-word guard out with a hard slap to his jaw. Pivoting, he kneecapped the one at his back with one heel of his Italian loafers. The third guard took two steps back and snapped off a single shot that Remo evaded without thinking. His return blow was calculated, however. Remo came in, grabbed the slide of the automatic with one hand and rammed it back hard.

The guard staggered back. Remo stepped back, relinquishing the weapon. The guard recovered his composure and raised his weapon. That's when he saw he had no hammer. The slide had broken it off.

Remo walked past the frustrated man who kept pulling his trigger over and over again. In exasperation, he threw the weapon at the back of Remo's head. The pressure of air advancing before the thrown weapon signaled Remo that he should bob his head to the left, so he did. The gun sailed harmlessly past him and went skating along the polished floor.

Remo found the Master Sinanju calmly seated at a gate.

"What do you think you are doing?" he demanded hotly.

"Waiting for my flight, of course."

"I've been made."

"But I have not been," Chiun huffed. "Please do not sit near me. I am not with you."

"You're joking."

"I am not wanted. You are. Shoo."

"I wouldn't be here if it wasn't for you."

"That is your misfortune, not mine," said Chiun, suddenly leaving his chair and disappearing into the men's room. The door shut and then opened a crack. Remo spotted one hazel eye regarding him warily.

Down the corridor, hard footsteps on marble warned Remo of an approaching security force.

"Damn." So Remo decided to board his plane early.

He found an exit door, pried it open and discovered it looked out over a thirty-foot drop. Obviously a jetway-ramp door. But there was no jetway. Remo dropped down anyway, bending his knees and straightening like a double-springed puppet upon landing.

The Northwest 747 stood out on the tarmac, a set of air stairs off to one side. The hatch was closed, but Remo wasn't going to let that stop him.

Slipping up on one of the wheel struts, he examined the wheel well. Most aircraft could be entered by a number of avenues. Including maintenance hatches. Remo knew there was one in the wheel well, so he climbed it, loosened the screws with a very hard and slightly longer than normal right index fingernail and eased the access panel open.

Slipping up, Remo replaced the panel the hard way, by turning the screw threads with his fingers.

When he was inside, he pulled up a big piece of luggage and used it for a pillow. The Japanese security police would never find him in a million years. And if they detained the Master of Sinanju, that was his own fault.

Remo knew he was home free when the big turbines spooled up and the 747 began moving. Soon the takeoff rumble of tires on tarmac ceased, and the big aircraft was climbing hard.

Raising his voice, he spoke up in Korean, "You there, Little Father?"

"I am not with you," said Chiun in a normal tone of voice that only Remo could hear.

Satisfied that the Master of Sinanju was safely aboard, Remo went to sleep.

AT LOGAN AIRPORT, Remo was the last one off the plane. He was surprised to find the Master of Sinanju waiting for him at the concourse.

"I trust you enjoyed a pleasant voyage," Chiun stated in a voice as bland as his expression.

"Remind me never to visit Japan again," growled Remo.

"Why do you say this?"

"I hate the Japanese."

"My son," cried Chiun, his wrinkles breaking into a rapturous expression.

7

Harold Smith took the Twelfth Avenue West Side Highway back to midtown.

The General Post Office was on Fifth Avenue, behind Madison Square Garden. Smith fought the congestion of ubiquitous white mail trucks and yellow cabs to Fifth Avenue, thinking that these days Manhattan traffic consisted chiefly of cabs and assorted mail, UPS and Federal Express trucks, all fighting for the privilege of moving the people and packages that made the big city hum.

Smith found a parking lot on West Thirty-fifth and grudgingly paid the hour rental fee. During the four-block walk, he passed three different post-office relay boxes.

Prudently he crossed the street three times to avoid being caught in the probable blast radius should one of them go up. None did. He noticed other pedestrians doing the same thing. In fact, he noticed fewer people on the streets than normal. They were only a few blocks from the afflicted area.

Police helicopters throbbed through the haze of cordite hanging over midtown. It stung the nostrils. Sirens came and went, not rushed, just nervous. When the wind was right, it brought the unmistakable tang of fresh blood.

Smith mounted the granite steps of the General Post Office two at a time, despite his arthritic knee. Time was of the essence.

His gaze skated across the carved postal-service motto, and an unaccustomed chill took hold of his spine.

The secretary to the postmaster of New York began, "Mr. Finkelpearl is unavailable," but Smith flashed his postal-inspector ID card.

"One moment."

Smith waited standing. In a moment, he was ushered in.

The postmaster of New York wore a sheen of sweat under his receding hairline. He had an open but worried face. It was about as worried as only the face of a man under the gun could be.

"Reilly?" he asked Smith.

"Smith," Smith returned.

"What happened to Reilly?"

"Delayed."

Postmaster Finkelpearl looked at his wristwatch. "He's due any minute."

"Then let's get started. I require the names and home addresses of all USPS personnel who had keys to the relay boxes in question."

"We've already narrowed it down to one man. The relay driver. Al Ladeen."

"Address?"

"Seventy-five Jane Street, in the Village."

"Has Ladeen shown any signs of psychotic behavior?"

"No. His supervisor tells me he's a perfectly rational man. Passed all the mandatory Dale Carnegie and stress-management courses. He was very excited to get a relay route last month. For some reason, he didn't like working indoors. We can't understand it.''

"What measures have you taken to ensure that other relay boxes have not been rigged to explode?"

"Other—?"

"Get on it," said Smith.

"Look, we have to move the mail. We can't halt the mail stream for one—''

"Massacre?" prompted Smith.

"Yes, not even for a massacre. The mail must go through. You know our motto—Neither Gloom Of Night—''

"I am expressly ordering you to take all measures to ensure that the relay boxes in this city are secure."

"Do you have any idea the number of boxes we're talking here? Over three thousand. Three thousand boxes."

"Then you had better start immediately," Smith said sharply. "I will be in touch."

With that, Harold Smith left the postmaster's office.

Down in the ornate lobby, he passed a man who had postal inspector written on his stern face. Reilly hardly glanced in Smith's direction as he strode to the bank of elevators.

By the time he reached the postmaster's office, Smith would be unfindable in the canyons of New York.

JANE STREET WAS OFF the Twelfth Avenue Highway, and Smith found it easily. Number 75 was at the Hudson end of the street, tucked in a row of aging but well-maintained brownstones.

There were three apartments. The top button was labeled Al Ladeen. Smith pressed it, not expecting an answering buzzer. He was correct. Smith then tried the other button.

Apartment 1 answered. "Yes?"

"Smith. Federal Bureau of Investigation. Are you the landlord of this building?"

"I own it, yeah."

"I would like to speak to you about a tenant."

Smith was buzzed in at once.

A black-bearded man in an open-necked white shirt met Smith at the door. He looked as if he'd last shaved during the Carter era.

"What's this about?"

"When did you last see Al Ladeen?"

"Al? Is he in trouble?"

"Please answer my question," Smith said firmly.

"Two days ago. He comes and goes. I don't pay much attention."

"I would like access to his apartment."

"You got a warrant?"

"I will not require one if you will cooperate."

The landlord scratched his curly beard and squinted his right eye, then his left, as if weighing the pros and cons with both hemispheres of his brain.

"If I just knew what this was about . . ."

"It may be connected to the midtown explosions."

"Jesus, don't tell me Al's a terrorist!"

"I said nothing of the kind," Smith said sharply.

"Isn't that what this is about?"

"Mr. Ladeen is a postal worker," said Smith.

The man clutched the doorframe. "Whoa. I didn't know that. You sure?"

Smith nodded. "A relay driver."

"Damn. All this time, I never suspected. Damn, that is scary."

"The overwhelming majority of postal workers are nonviolent," Smith explained.

"Yeah. Well, I read the papers and watch TV. You ask me, they're all slowly going bug-fuck nuts. This keeps up, it won't be long before they'll be replacing Nazis as the bad guys in the movies."

Smith cleared his throat.

"Let me get the key," the landlord said hastily.

THE APARTMENT WAS sparsely furnished and ordinary, except the walls in every room were green. They were all the same green, too. Not a tasteful avocado or an eggshell green, but a uniform lime green.

This seemed to be news to the landlord.

"Jesus, look what he did to the walls. Isn't green the color of madness?"

"No. Purple."

"Thought purple was royalty."

"Royalty and madness," said Smith. "I must ask you to wait in the hall."

Smith closed the door in the landlord's curious face and moved about the six-room apartment, not touching anything or turning on any lights lest he leave fingerprints.

In an alcove of the den stood an ordinary IBM-clone PC on a folding card table, the keyboard covered by a dust protector. On the wall behind it was a bumper sticker that said Save Jerusalem.

Smith frowned. He had never heard that slogan before.

The computer was running. That was not unusual. Sometimes people left them running, although it struck Smith as a frightful waste of electricity. Easily twelve cents per 24 hour period. On the other hand, the stress of powering up and down often wore out a system faster than continual running.

As Smith bent to examine the monitor he saw a screen saver was in operation. Another waste of money, as Smith saw it. Modern monitor tubes no longer retained burned static images if left on too long.

The screen saver featured a long building on a low hill against the backdrop of a blue bay. Nothing seemed to be happening. Then up the lone access road came a truck, trailing dust. As it approached a guard box, the truck accelerated. A uniformed guard jumped out and opened fire, his tiny M-16 making ineffectual electronic pops.

The truck ran him over on its way to crashing into the long, low building, which blew up into red-and-yellow fragments to the accompaniment of more electronic explosion sounds.

After the dust settled, the sequence started up all over again.

There was something familiar about the scene. Smith decided it must be some kind of child's game he had once seen advertised on TV.

A quick turn around the green apartment brought nothing unusual to light.

Smith had all but decided to leave the apartment untouched and was walking to the door when the computer abruptly beeped.

A thin, high voice lifted, calling out. *"Allahu Akbar!"*

Smith froze. The voice was familiar. He had never heard it before, not that particular voice. He had heard one just like it many times. In the Far East. In news reports from the Middle East and documentaries.

It was the sound of a Muslim *muezzin* calling the faithful to prayer.

"Allahu Akbar!"

"Allahu Akbar!"

The keening cry petered out, and a female voice spoke lightly in what Smith recognized as Arabic. It repeated in English.

"It is time for the afternoon prayer," the voice said.

Smith rushed back to the monitor. He had noticed the rug that was stretched out to one side. Now he saw it for what it really was. A Muslim prayer rug. It faced a blank wall. Smith didn't have to reflect long to understand it also faced Mecca.

The screen saver was still cycling. Smith looked closer, his gray eyes squinting. He pulled up the chair and sat down.

Face stiff, Smith watched the cycle again. This time he saw the flag atop the long, low building before it was destroyed. It was an American flag.

"The Marine barracks in Lebanon," Smith said in a low, stunned voice. "This is a reenactment of the truck bombing of the U.S. Marine barracks in Lebanon."

The stunned expression on Harold Smith's ashen face lasted less than a minute. When he stood up, it was stone.

Powering down the system, Smith unplugged it. Setting the useless monitor and keyboard off to one side, he gathered up the beige plastic case containing the hard drive itself and tucked it under one arm.

Lugging it and his ever-present briefcase to the door, Smith had to call ahead.

"Please open the door. My hands are full."

The door obligingly opened. Then the landlord saw the system under Smith's arm.

He said, "Wait a minute! Can you just take that?"

"I *am* taking it."

"Legally, I mean."

"It is material evidence in the commission of an act of terror against sovereign United States soil," Smith said harshly.

That impressed the landlord, who staggered back and lost facial color. "What happens if Al comes back?" he asked.

"He will never come back."

"Didn't one of the nuts who blew up the World Trade Center come back for the damn deposit on his Ryder truck?" the landlord puffed, following Smith down the gloomy staircase.

Smith blinked. "If he comes back, do not alarm him. Notify the FBI at once. Ask for Special Agent Rowland."

"Gotcha. Man, I can't believe it. He's a terrorist. That's worse than a postal worker, isn't it?"

"Far worse."

The landlord opened the entrance door for Smith, who turned and asked a question he should have asked before.

"What is Ladeen's first name?"

"Allah. But everybody called him Al."

"I was never here," said Smith, hurrying down the stairs.

8

The first thing Remo Williams did upon returning to his Quincy, Massachusetts, home was check the message machine in the downstairs kitchen.

He expected a blinking red light. There was no blinking red light.

"Maybe Smith hasn't gotten word about Osaka," he told Chiun.

The Master of Sinanju made a dismissive gesture with his jade nail protector. "Smith and his oracles see all and know all."

"Maybe the Japanese are hushing it up for now."

"Smith would know this, too."

"Well, he hasn't called," said Remo. "Could be he's not mad at us."

"Why should he be angry? We only executed his royal decrees."

"We created an international incident. Your face is probably in every post office in Japan by now."

Chiun stroked his wispy beard. "I would not mind gracing a postal stamp. Assuming my countenance was not marred by unwanted facial hair."

"I meant on Wanted posters."

Chiun's smile disintegrated. "The Japanese would doubtless fail to pay me my hard-earned royalties, knowing their ilk," sniffed Chiun.

"Might be a good idea to check the news," said Remo. "It's almost six o'clock."

"Yes. We will watch Bev Woo."

"Which one?" asked Remo.

"The substantial one, of course."

Remo frowned. "You mean the dumpy one?"

"She is substantial, not dumpy. Only obsessive Western eyes like yours would call the gracious Bev Woo that awful word."

"I like the other Bev Woo. The one on Channel 7."

"The Channel 5 Bev Woo is the only Woo worth watching."

They were mounting the staircase to the bell tower, Chiun hurrying ahead in order to be the first to the big-screen TV. There were TVs all over the house, but the one they watched together was in the bell tower.

"At least she isn't Cheeta Ching," said Remo.

"Do not mention that name in this house."

"Sorry," said Remo.

Cheeta Ching was a sore spot with the Master of Sinanju. For most of the '80s, he had been secretly enamored of the national network anchorwoman. It had not been a problem as long as Chiun worshiped her from afar. But when he attempted to pursue his feelings, it had brought Remo and Chiun in repeated contact with the voracious anchorshark.

As a result, Chiun had fallen out of love with Cheeta Ching, just as he had earlier gotten over his infatuation with Barbra Streisand. Since then, there had been no similar figure in the Master of Sinanju's life.

Beverly Woo was not the object of Chiun's affections. She had been a long-time reporter on the local

Channel 5. Until recently Chiun had hardly paid any attention to her.

Then the rival Channel 7 had hired another Asian anchorwoman, coincidentally also named Bev Woo. The second Bev Woo was young, slim and Remo found her passably attractive. It wouldn't have mattered much except Remo had once remarked to Chiun that the new Bev Woo was an improvement over the old.

Chiun had retorted, "Are you mad! The new Bev Woo is scrawny and underfed!"

"The old Bev Woo is dumpy and round."

"At least you cannot count her ribs through her clothes, like the new Woo."

"The old Woo is built like a Mack truck."

"The old Woo is built to bear babies, as a woman should. This new Woo is a mere slip of a girl."

"I'll take her over the old Woo."

"You cannot have her. I forbid it!"

"For crying out loud, I don't want her, Chiun. I'm just talking."

"You are babbling. To compare this new, upstart Woo to the wise and substantial Woo of old—"

"Look, I don't want either Woo. But if I'm going to watch one on TV, I'd rather the new Woo."

"From this day forward," Chiun had proclaimed, "I forbid the face of the new Woo on my TV screen."

And from that day on, Remo had made a point of tuning in to the new Bev Woo whenever possible, even though he would have much preferred the brunette on Channel 4. But this was a matter of pride. He was a grown man and a Master of Sinanju, besides. He would watch whomever he wanted to watch.

Reaching the top of the stairs, Chiun dashed into the bell tower and snatched up the remote control.

He aimed it at the screen. On came Channel 5 and the old Woo in all her doughy glory.

Laying the clicker on the hardwood floor as he sat down, Chiun watched the newscast intently.

Remo took his place beside the Master of Sinanju. Chiun's attention was focused on the big screen.

Surreptitiously Remo's hand took up the clicker.

"If you point that device at the old Woo, I will break it," warned Chiun without looking away from the screen.

Remo thought about that a minute. They had been through all this before, but Remo wasn't about to give in so easily. It was a matter of pride. After all, it was his house, too. And his TV.

Willing his forehead to perspire, Remo waited until the sheen of his forehead was reflected in the dark parts of the TV screen.

Then he said, "I'll promise not to point the clicker at the TV if you promise not to break it or change the channel for the rest of the evening."

"Done," said Chiun.

And holding the clicker so it pointed at his own shiny reflective brow, Remo pressed the 7 button. The infrared signal hit his forehead and bounced back.

The channel flicked over to 7, and the pretty face of the new Woo appeared.

"What is this! What is this!" Chiun howled.

"Must have pressed the button by accident," Remo said, face bland.

"You changed the channel."

"I didn't point it at the screen," Remo said quickly.

"What white talk is this? Change it back this instant."

"I'd like it the way it is, and don't forget your promise."

Chiun's hazel eyes narrowed suddenly. "Why do you perspire?"

Remo shrugged. "Why not?"

Chiun's eyes squeezed almost shut. His papery lips thinned. "You tricked me!"

"I outwitted you. Maybe. Now settle down. I want to hear what she's saying."

Redirecting his attention back to the screen, Chiun made a sour face. "How can you stand that thin, pasty face?"

"It's makeup, and her face has a nice shape."

"She has the head of a turnip. And she is sunken of cheek and hollow of eye."

The graphic over the new Woo's head showed an explosion. The words Bomb Scare labeled the explosion in scary, shattered red letters.

"Hold on. This may be it," said Remo, reaching for the clicker to turn up the volume.

"Remember your promise," hissed Chiun.

"Oh, right," said Remo.

"And I will not be silent until I have the old Woo back in all her oblate glory."

"Chiun, this is important."

"So is the correct Woo."

"How about we compromise and watch Channel 4?" Remo suggested.

Chiun hesitated. "I may be willing to compromise as long as I am spared the horrid sight of the new Woo," he allowed thinly.

"Good," said Remo, lifting the clicker again.

"No. I must do it. You have made a promise."

Remo hesitated.

"I have promised," said Chiun. "And you have promised. We are prisoners of our promises."

"Okay," said Remo, handing over the remote control.

The Master of Sinanju changed the channel with a quick flourish.

Instead of the expected brunette, there was a new Asian female reporter doing a remote stand-up on Channel 4.

"Who is she?" Remo blurted.

"*Aiiee!* A Japanese!" shrieked Chiun. "Change the channel."

"I can't. I made a promise."

"So have I," gasped Chiun. "Is there a fourth channel?"

"There's CNN, but you hate them worse than Woo."

"Not more than Japanese."

"What's with this mania for Asian news reporters all of a sudden?" Remo wondered aloud. "Channel 5 had Bev Woo, so 7 countered with their own Bev Woo. Now 4 pulls out this one. What's her name anyway?"

The graphic under the reporter's face said she was Tamayo Tanaka. She was standing against a backdrop of the Manhattan skyline, hazy with a low-hanging cloud of smoke.

Chiun lifted an apricot kimono sleeve to shield his eyes and said, "I will listen to the strident voice, but not suffer the sight of Japanese countenances."

Remo decided that was okay with him as long as he caught the newscast.

Tamayo Tanaka was saying, "At this hour, the death toll stands at forty-three in midtown Manhattan, where a string of terrorist-style bombings took place during the noon hour today. Authorities are being tight-lipped, but at least thirteen separate explosions took place within a large radius between Pennsylvania Station and the Jacob Javits Center. According to FBI sources, several Middle Eastern terrorist groups have claimed responsibility, but informed sources insist that while they cannot at this time discount a Middle Eastern connection, they are focusing their investigation elsewhere."

"Sounds like militia crazies," said Remo worriedly.

"This is good," said Chiun from behind his sleeve.

"It is?"

"Yes. If terror has gripped this nation, Emperor Smith will have work for us."

"How is that good?"

"He will have no time to fret about Japanese complaints."

"Hadn't thought of that," said Remo, leaning toward the screen.

"Tragedy is not limited to Manhattan on this busy news day," Tamayo Tanaka was saying. "In Oklahoma City, an unknown person stormed into a packed courtroom in the new Wiley Post Federal Building and opened fire, killing at least two dozen people. No motive for the massacre has been determined at this hour, but Oklahoma City police are seeking a possible disgruntled postal worker for questioning. It is not known if this postal worker is a suspect or a witness to the killings."

"Sounds to me like the disgruntled postman is a good bet," Remo said dryly.

"We are doubly blessed," said Chiun.

"I don't consider all those innocent victims a blessing," said Remo.

"We did not dispatch them. They are dead. We cannot bring them back. Their lives are wasted. Why should we not enjoy the bitter fruit of their wasted existences?"

"I'm not that cold-blooded."

"At least you despise Japanese."

Remo grunted. The brunette anchor took back the show and said, "Stay with 'News 4' for more on the events in New York. We are the only Boston station with a reporter on-site in Manhattan."

"I wish someone would explain why local reporters have to cover national stories," Remo complained. "That's why we have national news."

Ten minutes into the broadcast, there was a brief mention that the Japanese ambassador to the United States had been recalled for consultations.

"That usually means they're upset with us," said Remo.

"Not as upset as we are with them," Chiun countered darkly.

"Maybe this will blow over after all," said Remo.

The telephone rang during the weather report, and Remo shot to his feet, saying, "That's gotta be Smith."

"Convey regrets but not apologies," said Chiun.

"What's the difference?"

"Sinanju does not apologize, but we are not above expressing regret on suitable occasions. Such as this."

Harold Smith's voice was vaguely breathless when Remo picked up the receiver.

"Remo, I am glad you have returned."

"We're glad to be back, too."

"I need you and Chiun here. At once."

"Why?" Remo asked guardedly.

"Because the Master of Sinanju understands Arabic, and I cannot get the Arabic-conversion program to work."

"Huh?"

"Please hurry, Remo. This situation is urgent."

The line went dead.

"We're wanted at Folcroft," Remo told Chiun as he replaced the receiver.

"I heard," said Chiun, rising from his tatami mat like a puff of fruity smoke.

"Then you also heard that Osaka didn't even come up."

"No doubt Smith intends to ambush us with all manner of complaints. We must concoct a story he will believe, Remo. Something properly grandiose, but plausible."

Remo suppressed a sly grin. "How about the dog ate our assignment?"

"What dog?"

"We'll buy one on the way down."

"You are not making sense."

"Look, Smitty sounded worried. And he said something about needing you to translate some Arabic. Osaka's probably the furthest thing from his mind right now. Let's get shaking."

"Very well. But if we are in trouble with our Emperor, it will be your responsibility as Apprentice Reigning Master of Sinanju to fall on your sword."

"I don't have a sword," said Remo, shutting off the TV.

"We will purchase one on the way to Fortress Folcroft," Chiun said blandly.

"I didn't have a sword," Chiun replied. "No, I'm setting off the

"We will find one other one when we get to Parrise," Co- thon." Chiun said. but.

9

Dr. Harold W. Smith was swearing softly under his breath. New Englanders are a salty class by temperament, and Harold Smith, of the Vermont Smiths, educated at Dartmouth, was as New England as they came. But he had long ago suppressed the urge to curse. Profanity was a wasteful expenditure of breath, he believed. It was impolite. It accomplished nothing. And most of all, it was unseemly. Especially in mixed company.

The last time Smith had cursed aloud and in anger had been a few years before when he had read that his old college song, "Men of Dartmouth," under pressure from a campus women's group, had been changed to "Alma Mater" and all gender-specific references neutered.

Smith had read this in the alumni newsletter in the gray privacy of his living room.

"God damn their bones!" he exploded.

His wife, Maude, had almost fainted in her overstuffed chair. The Smiths had long ago ceased sitting on the sofa together. Mrs. Smith was watching "Jeopardy" while Harold read. This was their version of sharing quality time.

Mrs. Smith had severely lectured Harold on his language, and Smith had stiffly apologized. Inwardly he was embarrassed at the loss of self-control, and the next day firmly resolved to cut his annual donation to Dartmouth exactly in half.

As he now sat at his Folcroft desk with the late-afternoon light streaming in through the picture window of one-way glass at his back, Smith started cursing softly.

"Blast their souls!"

He had his desktop system running. On the desk was the captured system of Allah Ladeen, United States postman and suspected terrorist bomber. A cable snaked from the PC system into the kick space of Smith's desk, where it connected to Smith's own system.

Smith had downloaded the entire hard drive onto one of the Folcroft Four. Normally he should have been able to access the contents by a brute-force mainframe attack on the encryption system. Unfortunately the system was configured to the Arabic language, a fact Smith had discovered after a full hour of fighting what he thought were scrambled codes but was in fact flowing Arabic script.

Smith's mainframes were configured for English. They had other-language capability, but this was limited to Latin-based languages and Cyrillic Russian. He could not decode Arabic.

Reaching out to cyberspace, Smith had found and captured an Arabic-to-English automatic conversion program from Yale University's Language Department. But it was bulky. His only hope lay in the Master of Sinanju, and so Harold Smith cursed low and feelingly under his breath as he waited with the afternoon sun sinking at his hunched back.

"Damn their eyes!"

OUTSIDE THE CLOSED DOOR to Smith's office, the Master of Sinanju suddenly halted and said, "Hark, Remo. Listen."

"Damn their eyes!"

Chiun's hands fluttered with uncharacteristic nervousness.

"That is Emperor Smith's voice, and he sounds very angry."

"He sounds more like a pirate with his peg leg caught in a knot hole," Remo said.

"Perhaps he is angry with us," squeaked Chiun.

"If he is, we'll just have to take our medicine."

"Blast their cursed bones!" came Smith's voice, twisted and low.

Abruptly Chiun got behind Remo and started pushing with both hands. "You go first, Remo."

"Why me?"

"Because you are half-white, like Smith. He will not turn on one of his own."

"Here goes," said Remo, pushing open the door.

Harold Smith looked up sharply from his work. No trace of relief touched his patrician features.

"I am glad you are here, Remo," he said in a voice that contradicted his words.

"A mastiff ate our assignment!" called Chiun in a loud voice. "We are not to blame."

"What is this?"

"Chiun's making a joke, Smitty."

"I need you both."

Noticing the blind system on Smith's desk, Remo asked, "Computer crash on you?"

"I am attempting to enter this captured system."

"Captured? Who captured it?"

"I did," said Smith.

"No kidding. Who'd you capture it from?"

"If I am correct, the perpetrator of the rash of bombings in New York City."

"Anyone who would dare bomb one of your most famous cities is indeed rash," proclaimed the Master of Sinanju, stepping into the room. "Greetings, O Smith. How may we be of assistance?" And Chiun bowed formally, his hazel eyes peering upward to assess Smith's reaction.

"What did you say about your assignment?" asked Smith.

"Went off without a hitch," said Remo.

"Good," said Smith.

"Don't you want to hear about it?"

"Later," said Smith, tapping his keyboard with frustrated fingers.

"We dropped a locomotive onto Nishitsu headquarters in the middle of the night. Nobody killed that we know of. Message delivered."

Smith said nothing.

"The hotel accommodations were really special," Remo added. "You must have a saved a bundle, you old skinflint."

Smith nodded his gray head absently and addressed the Master of Sinanju. "Master Chiun, is your Arabic up-to-date?"

"It is impeccable," said Chiun.

"Please join me on this side of the desk."

With a low smile of satisfaction, the Master of Sinanju bustled up to Smith's desk and took a position beside his emperor. His eyes, meeting Remo's, were bright and taunting.

"I dropped the locomotive, but it was Chiun's idea," Remo continued.

Chiun's eyes turned venomous. A low hiss escaped his papery lips.

"We figured Nishitsu'd realize it was the American response to all those train wrecks, and rethink their global marketing strategy," continued Remo.

"Emperor Smith and I have no time for your prattle," said Chiun quickly. "We have important work to do. Why do you not take a walk?"

"Where would I go?"

"There is a short dock at the water's edge. It is a good place for a long walk," said Chiun blandly.

"No, thanks. I want to watch. This should be interesting. The hard-of-hearing leading the near-sighted."

Throughout this exchange, Harold Smith continued tapping away furiously. He seemed to have registered none of it.

"The owner of this system configured it for the Arabic language," Smith started to explain. "I cannot read Arabic. But I have a program that will convert it once I am inside."

"Inside what?" asked Chiun.

"The system," said Smith.

"What system?"

Smith pointed to the humming hard-drive case on the desk.

"Impossible!" squeaked Chiun.

"There is no system I cannot enter once I bypass the security firewalls."

Regarding the bright plastic case, Chiun said, "If touched by fire, that box would melt quickly."

"That's not the kind of firewall he's talking about," offered Remo, taking a seat on the green vinyl divan across the room. "He means the system is password protected."

"Ah. Now I understand. You seek the password?"

"Yes," said Smith, squinting at his desktop monitor, which was displaying a changing sequence of gibberish. "I believe it is asking me for the password. But I cannot tell."

"Allow me to gaze into this oracle's innermost recesses," said Chiun, bending to peer into Smith's desktop. "Yes. It is asking for the secret word."

"It says 'Secret word'?"

"Yes," said Chiun, laying his jade nail protector against the black tinted glass. "You see this script? It says, 'Secret word.'"

"I don't see a colon."

"Arabs retain their colons within their bodies unless put to the sword. But it is asking that you inscribe the secret word in that space."

"Damnation," said Smith. And Chiun shrank from the soft vehemence of the unexpected word from his emperor's lips.

"What is wrong?" he asked.

"My password-attack program takes hours to run. Sometimes days, with a particularly obscure password. The additional step of converting its data base of likely passwords into acceptable Arabic would take weeks—perhaps months with the transliteration problem."

"Then why not simply guess the secret word?"

Smith shook his gray head savagely. "That could take years. Only a sophisticated computer system has the brainpower to enter a protected system without knowing the password in question."

"Why do you not seize the owner of this device and wrest the secret word from him?"

"We have yet to trace him. And I have the system, not the owner here. And I am determined to crack it."

"You say the owner of the box is an Arab?"

"Yes."

"A cattle or city Arab?"

"I have no idea. His name is Al Ladeen."

"Ah, a cattle Arab. Bedouin are very colorful in their language."

"There is no telling what password he employed. It could be a name from the Koran or *The Arabian Nights* or anywhere at all."

"Could the secret word be more than one word?"

"Yes, it could."

"Inscribe *'Iftah ya simsim,'*" said Chiun, slowly stroking his wispy beard.

"What?"

"*'Iftah ya simsim.'* Cattle Arabs have employed it for centuries in their secret intrigues."

"Hah," said Remo. "Fat chance this is going to work."

"Hush. You know nothing of these matters, counter of ribs."

"I am willing to try anything," said Smith. "Please spell the phrase, Master Chiun."

Chiun did. Smith input the English approximation, activated the conversion program and in a moment the Arabic script equivalent to the words *Iftah ya simsim* appeared in the wake of the blinking amber cursor, which moved right to left, the direction Arabic script was read.

The screen winked out. Instantly music emanated from the system.

"What is this?" asked Chiun.

"It's a song," said Remo. "Sounds like harem music."

"It is of no importance," said Chiun. "For we have succeeded in our task."

Remo shot out of his seat. "What? This I gotta see!"

"Hold," said Chiun. "Emperor Smith has not given you leave to join us behind his royal table."

"Remo may join us," said Smith.

"If you deem it fitting," said Chiun in a thin voice. He eyed Remo unhappily.

Remo stared into the desk. "Don't you get neck strain from looking into this thing all day?" he asked Smith.

Smith didn't reply. He was eyeing the black screen expectantly as the hauntingly familiar music tinkled.

Abruptly a new screen appeared. It showed Arabic script for several seconds, then changed.

"What did it say?" Smith asked Chiun.

"It said, 'Here dwell the secrets of Al Ladeen. Infidels and idolators turn back before it is too late for you.'"

"That name sounds familiar," Remo said.

"Yes, it does," Smith agreed.

"I have heard Western tongues mangle the worthy name 'Al Ladeen' into the corrupted 'Aladdin,'" Chiun offered.

"Al Ladeen—Aladdin?" Smith blurted.

"Yes."

"Obviously a false name," Smith said.

"No," Chiun said. "'Aladdin' is the false name. 'Al Ladeen' is correct."

A new screen appeared.

"What is this?" asked Smith.

Chiun read the screen. "Verses from the Koran. The prayer Muslims call the Fatiha—or the Opening."

"Is it 'Muslims' or 'Moslems'?" Remo asked.

"'Muslim' means 'believer,'" said Chiun. "'Moslem' means 'cruel.' Muslims are very sensitive about being called Moslems."

"I'm going to have to remember that next time someone tries to blow up the Holland Tunnel," Remo said dryly.

That screen lasted nearly a minute, then a third screen came on. It was a thick forest of Arabic.

"What is this?" asked Smith.

Chiun frowned like a mummy drying. "It is not words."

"What do you mean?"

"The script has no meaning. It is only gibberish."

"It must mean something."

Remo looked at it, then pulled back. "You know, from this angle it looks like someone's made a pattern."

"I see no pattern," said Smith.

"Nor do I," said Chiun.

"Well, I do," said Remo.

"What is it?"

"A bird's head."

"I see no bird," sniffed Chiun. "You are imagining things."

"Sure, see the beak? Looks like an eagle."

Smith said, "I see nothing like a beak."

"That's because you have the imagination of a toothpick. See—this is the beak. This is the eye. And this dark area here is a kind of frame for the eagle's head."

"I see no eagle," said Smith, adjusting his rimless glasses.

"Take it from me," said Remo. "That's an eagle."

"It is a hawk," said Chiun. "I see a hawk."

"Eagle. It's the national bird."

"And it is composed of Arabic symbols. Therefore, it is a hawk."

"I see an eagle, and nothing you can say will make me change my mind."

"Let me see if I can convert this to English," Smith said thoughtfully.

"Don't waste your time, Smitty. It's a graphic."

Smith ran the program. The script soon converted into a meaningless nest of English letters with no meaning.

"Do either of you see a pattern now?" asked Smith.

"Well, it's fuzzier than it was, but I still see an eagle's head inside of a rectangle," said Remo.

"It is possibly a falcon," said Chiun. "Falcons were employed by sheikhs of old for sport and hunting."

"If that's a falcon, I'm a toad," Remo said firmly.

"You are a toad who peeps nonsense," scoffed Chiun.

Smith squinted at the screen thoughtfully. "A hitherto-unknown terrorist group called the Eagles of Allah claimed responsibility for today's bombings."

"According to the news, they're discounting the Arab-terrorist theory," Remo argued.

"They have good reason to," said Smith. "The bombs appear to have been planted by an employee of the U.S. Postal Service."

"Yeah? Now, that makes sense to me. Muslim terrorists can't bomb their way out of a soiled diaper, but I wouldn't put anything past a disgruntled postman."

"The man who owned this system was a postal worker," said Smith.

"Well, he's gotta be one thing or the other but not both, right?"

Harold Smith ignored Remo's question. "This system appears to be hung up on this screen," he muttered.

"Try the secret word again," suggested Chiun.

Nodding, Smith began inputting the command.

"What is this secret word anyway?" Remo asked Chiun as Smith worked.

Chiun fluttered a casual sleeve. "That is for me to know and you to find out. When you are Reigning Master, I may share this important information with you, which makes the Master of Sinanju more intelligent than the mightiest oracle."

"It sounds like *simsim salabim,* but that can't be it."

"I do not know that phrase," said Chiun, face puckering.

"You grew up before cartoons," said Remo. "Hey, Smith, don't look now, but I think something's happening."

The eagle graphic suddenly exploded, clearing the screen. In its place were columns of filenames. They were in English.

"What's this stuff?" Remo asked.

Smith scanned the columns. "Standard-data processing and Net-access programs. I do not recognize these columns."

"These are the names of the books of the Koran," said Chiun.

Smith pulled up a file at random.

"Yes, the Koran," Chiun said. "These are verses. And this portion is a list of the ninety-nine names of God."

"'God the Avenger'?" said Remo, reading one aloud.

Smith closed down the file. He tried others. They were books of the Koran, as well.

Frowning, Smith leaned back in his chair. "It appears to be empty of useful information."

"What I want to know is what's the secret word?" asked Remo.

Smith appeared to be intrigued by the same question. Inputting the word in a fresh file, he accessed his conversion program.

"'Open sesame,'" said Smith. "Very clever, Master Chiun."

Chiun beamed at Remo as if to say *I am smarter than you.*

"You wish," Remo whispered back.

Abruptly Smith said, "Perhaps there are files stored on Ladeen's e-mail server."

Smith brought up the Net-connection program and waited for the system to dial in. It took only forty-five seconds, and the speedy right-to-left cursor traced a skyline out of *The Arabian Nights,* complete with lofty minarets.

A flowing legend read Welcome To The Gates Of Paradise.

Once again Smith was confronted by a password prompt.

"*'Iftah ya simsim'* has worked so far," suggested Remo.

Smith input the phrase, hitting Enter. He got a "login incorrect" message.

"We are stymied," he said.

"That's your cue, Chiun," Remo suggested.

The Master of Sinanju made a face.

"Try 'Aladdin,'" said Remo suddenly.

"That will never work."

"It can't hurt," said Smith, who typed the name "Aladdin" and hit Enter.

The system hesitated, the screen went blank and they held their breaths in unison.

Then an e-mail menu appeared.

"It worked," Smith said in surprise.

Behind his back, Remo stuck his tongue out at the Master of Sinanju, who looked away from the rude display in disgust.

Smith keyed his way through the corridors of the e-mail files, finally reaching a list of folders that included Saved Mail, Sent Mail and Messages. He placed the cursor on Messages and opened the electronic file folder.

The incoming messages were logged in numerical order by date, sender, user name and subject heading.

"Jihad Jones?" said Remo, reading a name at random.

"Obviously a pseudonym."

"No kidding," Remo commented. "Are you sure?"

Other names were equally unlikely. There was an Ibrahim Lincoln, a Yassir Nossair, a Mohamet Ali, a Sid el-Cid, a Patrick O'Shaughnessy O'Mecca and others just as odd. Only one name seemed plausible at first glance. Remo pointed to it. "Try that guy. Yusef Gamal. He looks like he might be real."

"Pah!" said Chiun. "It is obviously false."

"What's phony about the name 'Yusef Gamal'?" asked Remo.

"That is for me to know and you to ponder, wild guesser."

"'Yusef' is the Arabic equivalent to the Christian 'Joseph,'" Smith explained. "The last name I confess strikes me as familiar, as if I have heard it before."

"The only thing it reminds me of is 'camel,'" said Remo.

Chiun became very still.

Remo and Smith hit it at the same time. Their eyes met and they said, "Joseph Camel?"

"Argh," said Chiun.

"Well, we know one thing," said Remo. "No terrorist with all his marbles is walking around the U.S. of A. calling himself Joe Camel."

"That would seem to be inescapable," Smith said unhappily.

"Yes, for once Remo is correct," Chiun chimed in. "There is no such person as Yusef Gamal."

10

Al Ladeen cruised the streets of the capital of idolatry, New York, blending with the flow of traffic. Here, mixing with the other vehicles emblazoned with the fierce eagle of the United States Postal Service as they jockeyed to outperform their hated foes—the Federal Express, the UPS, Roadway, DHL, and others—he was all but invisible to searching police eyes.

The coils of black smoke that he had authored with his well-placed bombs were graying now. Soon they would be but sweet, acrid memories. The tumult that was to go down in the history of the world as the last works of the brave martyr, Allah Ladeen, was subsiding.

It was sad. But at least the dead were still dead. They would never stop being dead.

And now it was time to make more dead.

As he turned onto Fifth Avenue, and the tall gray teeth of the General Post Office came into view, Al Ladeen drew in his last breath of victory and wrapped about his lower face a green checkered *kaffiyeh*.

It was the appointed hour. Time for the last great blow Allah Ladeen was destined to strike in his life.

Pressing the accelerator to the floor, he urged the white mail truck to hurry. It raced past the traffic-choked side streets, oblivious to the red lights, unheeding of the blaring cars and cursing pedestrians who scrambled from its careening path.

When he came abreast of the great granite temple from which he had left on his appointed rounds that morning, he flung the wheel to the left and with a glad cry of *"Allah Akbar!"* Allah Ladeen sent his blessed steed crashing into the immovable granite face.

And, Allah be blessed, the immovable granite moved!

But Allah Ladeen was ignorant of the miracle. He had already been catapulted into Paradise.

Although, the truth be known, his body parts were scattered all over Fifth Avenue.

11

The postal manager of Oklahoma City was in his office when the first sketchy word came in.

"There's trouble in the new federal building," the assistant manager gasped out.

"Jesus Christ!" Postal Manager Ivan Heydorn said, at first thinking the worst. "It's not a bomb. Tell me it isn't a bomb."

"It's a shooting," said the assistant manager.

Manager Heydorn relaxed in his executive chair. "Of course. It can't be a bomb. We'd have heard a bomb, now, wouldn't we?"

"Someone walked into open court and opened fire with a machine gun."

"Terrible, just terrible," the manager said, visibly relieved. He had been sitting in this very seat when the old Murrah building had been blown to kingdom come. What a god-awful day that had been. His chair had tipped over on its casters, throwing him backward. He had come off the floor thinking an earthquake was shaking the building.

An earthquake would have been a blessing. An earthquake would have been an act of God. In the early hours after the terrible truth had come out—that the Murrah Federal Building had been demolished by a truck bomb—the talk had naturally turned to Muslim fundamentalists.

It took three days for the truth to begin trickling out. That Americans had done it. It was unbelievable. Staggering in its enormity. The real enemy dwelled within the heartland of America.

"How many are hurt?" the manager asked his assistant, shaking off the dark, claustrophobic memories.

"No one knows. But they're calling it a massacre."

Hearing this, the manager buried his face in his hands. It was unreal. "How much pain can this poor town absorb?" he said shakily.

For an hour, the bulletins crackled over the office radio.

An unknown assailant. No one had seen him. Or if they had, they hadn't noticed anything unusual about him. He had mingled with the returning lunch crowd and shot up the courtroom and everyone in it. It was senseless. Brutal, senseless carnage.

By three in the afternoon, they were reporting a survivor. Someone had seen something. The FBI was being tight-lipped about it and had imposed a media blackout. The FBI had come in because a federal building had been targeted. Everyone assumed it was a deranged claimant shooting up a court that had done him wrong.

No one in his right mind would attack the new federal building in Oklahoma City.

At exactly 3:15, the desk intercom buzzed, and his assistant manager's voice said, "FBI Agent Odom to see you, sir."

"Send him right in," the manager said, snapping off his office radio.

The man was as big as a refrigerator and to-the-point. "Special Agent Odom."

"Have a seat."

"I'll just need a moment. This is about one of your carriers."

"My God. He wasn't caught in the shooting over there?"

"No, he wasn't."

"Is he the witness they're talking about?"

"No. We think he might be the perpetrator."

"Perp— You can't mean the killer!"

"A security guard lived long enough to say the man who walked into the courtroom and massacred all those poor people was wearing a postal-service uniform."

"That can't be. It just can't."

The agent flipped open a pocket notebook. "Description as follows. Five feet seven, dark eyes, curly brown hair, prominent nose."

"How prominent?"

"Very."

"Sounds like Camel."

The agent began writing. "'Camel' as in 'dromedary'?"

"Yes, yes. But this makes no sense to me."

The FBI agent was unmoved. "First name?"

"Joe."

"Joe Camel?"

"Yes."

"You have a letter carrier named Joe Camel working for you?"

"Well, I didn't name him. Oh, good Lord, it sounds phony, doesn't it?"

"How long has he been with you?"

"Less than a year."

"No sign of psychotic behavior before today?"

"He was perfectly normal."

"Except that his name was Joe Camel," The FBI agent said, grimacing.

"Look, I know how it sounds, but that was his name."

"Do you have a photograph of the subject, Camel?"

"No. But he shouldn't be hard to locate. Not with that nose of his."

"I'll need to see his personnel file."

"You have it, Agent Odom," said the postmaster of Oklahoma City, buzzing his assistant manager. "Sherry, pull Joseph Camel's file. And get the PG on the line."

Special Agent Odom cocked an eyebrow. "The PG?"

"The postmaster general. I have to report this."

"You might want to wait," Agent Odom said, flipping his notebook closed. "I think he has his hands full today."

"What do you mean?"

"Didn't you hear about the bombings in New York City this afternoon?"

"Bombings?"

"A string of relay boxes exploded all at once. They're looking for a postal relay driver. Guy named Ladeen. I think his first name was Al."

"Al Ladeen ... That sounds familar somehow."

"I thought the same thing myself. Can't place it, though."

The assistant manager walked in at that point with a manila file folder and said, "The line to the PG is busy. Shall I keep trying?"

"Leave a message that I called. I understand the PG is having a very bad day."

THE POSTMASTER GENERAL of the United States was having fits. He kicked over the office wastepaper basket. He rammed his chair against a wall so hard it bounced back and took a bite out of his heavy desk, knocking over a desktop sign that said "Protect the Revenue."

It was three-thirty in the afternoon, and the urgent calls and faxes had been coming in since 1:00 p.m.

First it was the postmaster of New York.

"We have a serious problem up here, sir."

"I'm listening, New York."

"Er, it appears that one of our relay boxes—"

"Out with it."

"—has exploded."

In the steady hum of his ostentatious office in the City Post Office adjoining Union Station in Washington, D.C., the postmaster general of the United States blinked rapidly.

"Exploded?"

"That's correct. The FBI has been here, demanding our cooperation."

"Stonewall them!" the postmaster general roared.

"I thought you would want it that way, and that's what I did do."

"Good. You're a good man, whatever your name is."

"Finkelpearl, sir."

"Take no calls, Finkelpearl. I'm sending a man. His name is Reilly. Talk to no one until you talk to him."

"Understood, Mr. Postmaster."

The postmaster general hung up, muttering, "This is all the service needs."

Ten minutes later, Finkelpearl was back on the line. "Sir, it's happened again," he croaked.

"Another bomb?"

"Thirteen relay boxes have exploded. All in a narrow radius of this facility. It's a reign of terror."

"My God. Is someone attacking the postal service?"

"I cannot speak to that, Mr. Postmaster."

"Or has one of your employees gone off the deep end?"

Postmaster Finkelpearl cleared his throat. "That's not impossible, as you know."

"Wait for Reilly. And remember the watchword. Stonewall. Stonewall. Stonewall."

"I'm stonewalling as best I can."

After New York signed off, the postmaster general was dictating a preliminary statement for the benefit of the media when the incoming calls began coming in a barrage.

"The director of the FBI, on line 1."

"I'm in conference."

"The commissioner of police for New York City. Line 2."

"Tell him to liaise with the FBI. I talk only to federal agencies."

"Yes, sir."

"Postmaster Finkelpearl on line 1."

The postmaster general hesitated. "Patch him through."

"Mr. Postmaster, this is Finkelpearl."

"I know. Out with it."

"Did you send a postal inspector named Smith to interview me?"

"Smith? No, I told you to await Reilly. He's en route."

"An Inspector Smith just left my office. He showed an inspector's badge. Then Reilly appeared."

"Did you talk to him?"

"I—I'm afraid he managed to get a name out of me."

"What do you mean, a name?"

"They think the bombs were made by one of ours."

"Is that possible?"

"We've had employees shoot other employees, take hostages, steal the mail and destroy it. Just last month, we were breaking in a new man on an optical reader here. The damn fool couldn't punch in the zip codes fast enough to keep pace with the mail stream, so he would stuff postcards into his mouth, chew and swallow them whole."

"That's disgusting."

"Pressure will do that, sir."

"We're not the only game in town any more. Federal Express and UPS are eating our lunch. If we don't get competitive by the end of the century, we'll be reduced to shoveling junk mail. There's good money in junk mail, but it isn't enough. We need more market share, especially in the lucrative express niche. Business won't trust us with their overnight packages until we demonstrate unrelenting reliability in the first-class department."

"I understand the problem, sir. What do I do?"

"What name did you give him?"

"Al Ladeen."

"Al Ladeen. Al Ladeen. Do I know him?"

"I don't see how. He came on board only last year."

"Finkelpearl," said the postmaster general.

"Yes, sir?"

"I think you may have given up one of your own to a federal agent in disguise."

"That's what Reilly thinks."

"We're really screwed now. This is no longer an internal USPS matter."

"What shall I do?"

"Stonewall your end. I'll stonewall my own. If we're lucky, Ladeen is at this moment a face-cancel case."

"Sir?"

"Sucking on the muzzle of a smoking .45."

"Let's hope so."

"You know the drill.... They all go that way in the final sort."

Hanging up, the postmaster called out to his secretary, "Tear up that press release and get in here. We're starting over."

The paper went into a waste basket and the postmaster general began again. "In an enterprise as large as the USPS, as in any military organization that depends upon conscripts and volunteers, there are always bad apples," the postmaster general began. He stared up at the office ceiling. Washington traffic hummed outside. Making a mouth, he wrinkled his forehead into fleshy gullies. "Add some boilerplate from my last speech, throw in a sprinkling of happy horseshit. And don't forget to end with 'We deliver for you.'"

"Yes, sir," the secretary said, rising.

After the door had closed, the postmaster general of the United States of America leaned back in his chair and groaned, "What next?"

That was when the call from Oklahoma City came in.

"This is Heydorn. Manager, Oklahoma City."

"Is there a problem, Oklahoma?"

"We've had a shooting here."

"And you call me with that?" the postmaster general exploded. "If I had to field every call when a postal employee went nuts, I wouldn't get any work done." Lowering his voice, he added, "Look, can you keep a lid on this a day or two? We have a pony-distress situation up in New York City."

"Mr. Postmaster, the shooting was not in this building. It was in the new Wiley Post Federal Building."

"A postman was shot?"

"No, the postman did the shooting."

"That makes it tougher to media manage. Damn."

"He massacred an entire courtroom full of people. Including the judge."

"Federal or local?"

"Federal."

"That may be a good thing. Maybe I can pull some strings. Get it swept under the rug or something."

"The FBI has already been to see me."

"You didn't give the bastard up?"

"I handed over his file."

"You utter clown! Who do you think you're working for?"

Manager Heydorn's voice tightened. "The United States Postal Service."

"And who are you answerable to?"

"Why, you, sir."

"Don't you understand the table of organization? Have you ever heard of chain of command? You don't talk to other agencies first. You clear it with *me* first. What's gotten into you?"

"But, sir, this is Oklahoma City. We've had more than our share of tragedy out here."

"Don't snivel! I can't stand sniveling. No one snivels in my outfit."

"I understand, sir. But we have a rogue letter carrier who's wanted by the FBI for mass murder."

"For which I plan to hold you responsible, Oklahoma. Didn't you read my directive about anger management?"

"We painted all the walls a soothing pink, as directed."

"Including this man's cubicle?"

"He's a letter carrier. He has a route. He can't deliver the mail if he's staring at a pink wall all day."

"What about the premium coffee?"

"Er, I haven't felt the need to deploy it. My employees all seem pretty levelheaded. Their psychological tests all came back good. No undue stress. This isn't the big city, you know."

The postmaster general's voice became low and urgent. "I hereby order you to declare an emergency-sanity maintenance coffee break. Understand?"

"Yes, sir."

"Until you hear from me, say nothing, give up nothing and above all, we haven't had this conversation."

"I understand, Mr. Postmaster."

"Remember, loose lips sink ships."

The postmaster general hung up furiously. "Two in one day. God damn the bad luck!"

When his secretary buzzed him again, he was tempted to ignore it. But then, maybe it was good news this time.

"An Inspector Reilly on line 2. It sounds urgent."

"I'll take it."

Reilly's voice was twisted like a bent paper clip when it rattled out of the receiver.

"What's wrong?"

"Sir, I just came from the General Post Office."

"You knock that fool Finkelpearl in line?"

"He understood his responsibilities, sir. But I'm afraid there's more bad news."

"Not more blown boxes?"

"No."

"A shooting?"

"No, it's—"

"Out with it!" the postmaster general roared.

"I'm trying. I left the building not fifteen minutes ago. Took a cab to my hotel. Then I heard it. It was the damnedest sound I'd ever heard in my life. Like an explosion, a sonic boom and an earthquake all run together. I'm looking west from my hotel-room window now. All I can see is a column of smoke."

"What are you trying to say?"

"It's gone."

"What is?"

"The building, sir. It's been obliterated."

The postmaster general of the United States slowly came to his feet, his mind racing. He was thinking, *He can't be talking* about *his hotel. He's calling* from *his hotel. He can't be calling about any old building, because I don't care.*

The postmaster general swallowed so hard his Adam's apple went away. "Say you're not going to tell me I've lost a post," he croaked.

"Sir, you might want to turn on CNN."

The postmaster did. The office TV was recessed into a cabinet. He used a remote.

CNN was live with the story. They were remote telecasting an aerial shot of midtown Manhattan. Madison Square Garden was in the shot. On the Hudson sat the glass puzzle that was the Jacob Javits Center. It looked as if a thousand mirrors had dropped out of a million frames.

But east of it lay a pile of smoking ruins that occupied an entire city block. Stone rubble. And among the smoke and fires, the postmaster general of the United States could see the broad, cracked steps like something out of ancient Rome, and tumbled and broken all over them lay the remnants of the twenty Corinthian columns of the General Post Office, the largest postal facility in the entire nation.

At that exact mouth-drying moment, the intercom buzzed and the secretary's hushed voice said, "The President of the United States on line 1."

12

The sun was sinking behind Harold Smith's back when his system beeped without warning.

"What's that?" asked Remo, who had returned to the green vinyl divan. The Master of Sinanju hovered behind Smith, reluctant to relinquish his honored position beside the man he called Emperor.

"Incoming bulletin."

Smith logged off the e-mail files and brought up an AP bulletin.

New York, New York—General Post Office Explosion (AP)
A massive explosion rocked midtown Manhattan at 4:44, demolishing the General Post Office and Mail Facility on Fifth Avenue. Rescue crews are on the scene. Casualty figures are unknown but the loss of life is feared to be great.

"My God!" croaked Smith.

"What's up, Smitty?" asked Remo, coming off the divan.

"The General Post Office in New York City has been demolished by an explosion. The explosive force must have been tremendous."

"Is that the big place on Fifth Avenue with all the columns?"

"It was," Smith said dully.

"What the hell is going on?" asked Remo. "Why would anyone want to blow up an entire post office?"

"Perhaps to show that it can be done."

"Huh?"

"At the very least, the person or persons responsible for the mailbox bombings have just covered their tracks in the most absolute fashion possible."

"Are we fighting Muslim terrorists or the U.S. Postal Service?"

Smith logged off the AP bulletin, and his eyes were stark.

"I believe we are fighting both."

"Both?"

"This e-mail account strongly suggests a terrorist network of Muslim fundamentalists. Al Ladeen is clearly of this group. And he was an employee of the post office."

"Yeah . . ."

"It is possible that others of his cell are also employees of the post office."

"You know, that could explain a lot of things. All these mailmen going postal, for example."

"Postal?" asked Chiun.

"That's what they call it." said Remo. "When a mailman goes nuts and starts killing other mailmen, they call it 'going postal.'"

Chiun stroked his wisp of a beard, his narrowing eyes turning reflective.

"In the days of Alexander, messengers often arrived crazed with thirst and exhaustion. It was very common for them to lay the message that they carried at the feet of their king and expire on the spot."

"That's because they had to run barefoot three or four thousand miles to get the word out."

"In those days, it was not so far," Chiun sniffed. "A certain Greek scribbler once said of the messengers of Persia that neither darkness nor cold nor rain could deter them from their duties."

"Isn't that the motto of the post office?" asked Remo.

"Adopted from Herodotus," said Smith.

"Yes, that was the Greek," said Chiun.

"According to these files, this cell has been operating for less than a year," Smith added.

"So why are they acting up only now? What do they want?" asked Remo.

"Unless I am misreading the events in Manhattan, they are making a statement."

"A statement. Of what?"

"That they exist. That they can strike us with impunity."

"That's what the fanatics behind the World Trade Center bombing thought. Look where they are now. All rotting away in a federal pen, including the Deaf Mullah."

"I must inform the President of our findings," said Smith, reaching into a desk drawer. Out came a cherry red telephone, a standard desk model, except that its blank face lacked a dial or keypad. He placed it on the desktop.

"My guess is he's already gotten word," Remo said dryly as Smith picked up the receiver and placed it to one ear.

Smith waited. The dedicated line activated an identical telephone in the Lincoln Bedroom of the White House by the simple act of Smith lifting the receiver. The line rang audibly in Smith's ear. And rang. And rang.

At length, a female voice came on the line. "Who is it? Who's at the other end of this thing? Is this Smith? Speak up. I know you're there. I can hear you wheezing."

"We are undone!" Chiun wailed. "It is the meddlesome queen!"

Coloring, Smith hung up. "Evidently he is not in the residence," he said nervously.

"Probably on the campaign trail, trying to scrounge up a few last votes," grunted Remo.

"He will have to return to Washington," said Smith. "This is too important."

"It will be too late to save his doomed presidency," intoned the Master of Sinanju.

"What makes you say that?" asked Smith, turning.

"Because those who squat on the Eagle Throne are by their nature doomed. I have dwelt in this mighty land many years now. I have seen the Presidents come and go, like untrustworthy viziers. I know them by heart. The Unshaven President. The Pretender. The Peanut Farmer. The Jelly Bean Eater. The Inarticulate One. The Glutton. Say but the word, and we will dispense forever with this succession of fools. Do not deny that your loins yearn to occupy the Eagle Throne in all its pomp and circumstance."

"We stay out of elections," Smith said flatly.

Chiun made his voice conspiratorial. "You have the power to abolish them."

Face puckering in a lemony frown, Smith returned to the e-mail.

Remo whispered to the Master of Sinanju, "Don't you ever get tired of trying?"

"He who ceases to try engineers his own defeat. He who never gives up cannot be defeated."

"He who hectors his Emperor to distraction may find his silken skirts on the street."

Chiun stiffened. "He would never—"

"We're all expendable on this bus," said Remo with a thin grin.

Face tightening, the Master of Sinanju took his right wrist in his left hand and his left wrist in his right hand. His kimono sleeves slid along his forearms and came together, concealing both hands and the jade nail protector that Chiun wore like a badge of ignominy. He composed his features into bland inscrutability.

A low growl from Smith's throat caught their attention.

"Find something interesting?" asked Remo.

"This appears to be a recipe for a homemade ammonia-fertilizer bomb similar to the one that destroyed the Alfred P. Murrah building in Oklahoma City."

"Big surprise there."

"A bomb whose chief stabilizing ingredient is junk mail," added Smith.

"No kidding."

"And here are plans to fill up a mail truck with the concoction."

"A mail-truck bomb?"

"Yes. And I would wager such a weapon was responsible for the disaster at the General Post Office."

Smith's eyes suddenly jumped behind his glasses. "My God!"

"You keep saying that. How many times can you be surprised at what these guys are capable of doing?"

"I am looking at one of the claims faxed to the FBI in the wake of this afternoon's mailbox bombings."

"So?"

"Several were received. Some came from the usual terror and jihad groups. A few were organizations never before heard from, such as the Eagles of Allah and the Warriors of God."

Remo looked to Chiun. "W.O.G.?"

The Master of Sinanju shrugged. "Are messengers of Allah not usually wogs?"

"It is very likely that these new groups are in fact one and the same," Smith went on. "It is common practice among Middle Eastern terrorist groups to operate under multiple names in order to confuse the issue and make themselves seem more numerous and threatening than they really are. One new group called themselves the Islamic Front for the A.P.W.U. This is the name on this fax file."

"What's 'A.P.W.U.' stand for?"

"See for yourself."

Remo did. He looked. Then looked again.

"Isn't that—?"

"The eagle graphic we saw before, yes. I recognize it now. It is the new emblem of the United States Postal Service. But look below it."

Remo's eyes went where Smith's bony finger pointed. He read aloud. "'Islamic Front for the American Postal Workers' Union.' A terrorist group has infiltrated the postman's union?"

"No, it is far graver than that."

Abruptly Smith turned in his chair. It swiveled to the big picture window. Smith looked past them at Long Island Sound, which was turning fiery orange in the dying afternoon light.

"A terrorist cell has infiltrated the United States Postal Service," he said, his words like flint being scraped. "That means they could be operating in every city and town and village in the nation, unknown and unsuspected. Wearing mail-carrier uniforms, they can enter any public building unchallenged and unquestioned, from the most public office building to the most secure federal facility. No one can question a mailman. I doubt if many security guards bother to ask them to walk through metal detectors. Certainly no one can look into their bag. The mail is protected from casual scrutiny."

Smith's voice was hollow. He was staring into space, looking at nothing. He was talking, but not to them. It was more as if he was thinking out loud.

"There are an estimated four hundred thousand postal employees in the nation. In some towns, the postmaster is the only representative of the U.S. government. Virtually every town and city has its own post office. There are more post offices than military bases in this country. These terrorists have theoretical bases in every corner of the nation. They have government vehicles at their disposal. On virtually every street in America, there are relay boxes just like the ones that exploded today. And these devils have the power to booby-trap any one of them. No one is safe. No building is secure."

"So what are we waiting for? Let's get them."

Smith snapped out of it. "How?"

"Can't you trace them through the Internet?"

"They communicate through an automatic anonymous server, which relays their communications to the final server site, this Gates of Paradise entity. All these e-mail files are stored there, not in the systems the terrorist cells used to access them."

"Can you trace this server?" asked Remo.

"I already have. It is near Toledo, Ohio. But I cannot follow the audit trail to the Gates of Paradise host site without accessing the Toledo site."

"So let's get a move on."

"I have already instructed the FBI to get on it. I need you for the serious work that lies ahead."

"Just point us in the right direction, and we'll do what we do best," said Remo.

Chiun made a grandiose gesture with the ornate jade nail protector. "Yes, O Smith. You have merely to instruct us, and Muslim heads will fall at your feet like so many pomegranates, and equally as red."

"No doubt Al Ladeen was the driver of the mail-truck bomb that destroyed the General Post Office, covering his tracks and killing himself in the process. That is what these people do. It is one of the others who will act next."

"Yeah. If only we knew their real names."

The system beeped again, and Smith leaped on the keyless keyboard.

"Here we go again," said Remo.

The bulletin was a follow-up to an earlier one. Smith scanned it, instantly judging it as not mission critical.

"It is just more on the Oklahoma courtroom shoot-out," said Remo.

Smith scanned the text with eager eyes. "We may have a lead," he said.

"What do you mean?"

"According to this, the shooter in Oklahoma City is believed to be a disgruntled postal employee."

"Not another one."

"They have all gone mad," said Chiun.

"This could be a simple case of one postal worker going over the edge," Smith said tightly as he worked his keyboard. "It may not be connected to the events in New York."

"Doesn't fit the MO," agreed Remo.

"If we are fortunate, the preliminary findings of the FBI have been logged into the computer in the Oklahoma City branch office of the FBI."

"Would they work that fast?"

"Everyone files on computer these days."

"Except you and I. Right, Little Father?"

Chiun sniffed, "I will have no truck with machines that beep at one like a nagging wife."

Smith was keying so furiously that his fingers, tapping the flat white letters and numbers on the desk, caused them to flare briefly.

"I have something!" he said hoarsely.

They crowded around.

The screen displayed an FBI computer form that had been filled in. Their eyes raced down the entries. Almost at the same time, they alighted on the same line. It was headed Suspect Name.

The name typed on the glowing amber line was one they all recognized: Joseph Camel.

13

It was perhaps inevitable that Yusef Gamal would come to be called Abu Gamalin—"Father of Camels."

Even as a boy, he had shown the strength of his namesake, the camel. He possessed camel shoulders. His curly hair was reminiscent of a camel's thick coat as well. And perhaps not as noticeably, he had the prominent nose of a camel.

A mighty nose it was, too. It was the first thing one noticed about Yusef Gamal, eventually to be known as Abu Gamalin.

So it was not strange that in his early years, the other Palestinian boys nicknamed him Al Mahour—"the Nose."

"That is not a bad *nom de guerre,*" his father had told him.

"It is not a warrior's name," Yusef lamented.

"There are worse things to be called," said his father in a strange tone of voice. He was looking at Yusef's face when he spoke those fateful words. And if he was looking at his face, Yusef remembered thinking, he had to be looking at his nose. It was unavoidable. Like looking up at the sky and seeing the sun.

By the time Yusef turned thirteen, his voice had yet to break and the hairs on his lower body were thin and unimpressive. By then, he had killed several men, for this was what Palestinians of his age did in those days.

For the *intifada* was in full cry in the Occupied Territories, where the Zionist entity was most vulnerable. His skill at killing Israelis came to the attention of Hezbollah, and Yusef had been summoned to Lebanon, making contact with others of his kind. There on the banks of Nahr al-Mawt—the River of Death—he was trained in the lethal arts, wearing fatigues and a checkered *kaffiyeh* over his face.

They were glorious days, filled with bloodshed and maiming. Through it all, Yusef fully expected to die. He longed to die. He prayed to Allah the Compassionate that he die in mortal combat, for he had been taught that the gates of Paradise could only be opened by breaking them down with Zionist skulls.

Yusef was responsible for denuding of flesh many Zionist skulls in the hellhole that his kind had made of Beirut.

When the tide turned inevitably against the Palestinian cause, and the PLO had sold out Hezbollah and embraced the Zionist enemy, Yusef found himself not dead but very much alive. He was disappointed. He wanted to die. He yearned to die. He had been taught by the religious leader of Hezbollah that to be martyred was a thing to be embraced wholeheartedly.

"A martyr is automatically granted entrance to Paradise," Yusef was assured. "In Paradise there is no toil, no cold, no pain. Every man wears green silk, and the sweetest grapes are always within reach."

"What about women?" Yusef asked.

"In Paradise the blessed are each allotted seventy-two virgins, untouched by man or jinn. These are called *houris*. And they belong to the martyr exclusively."

"Seventy-two?" asked Yusef, brightened by his prospects.

Thus, finding himself in a PLO detention camp, still living for his unkissed *houris* awaiting him in Paradise, only compounded the matter. Here he was no longer the feared Nose, but only Yusef Gamal, out of bullets and out of hope.

"I will never dance with my *houris* rotting away in this place of pestilence," he complained to a fellow Hezbollah freedom fighter.

"I hear there are great opportunities in Afghanistan," said his fellow Palestinian.

"Afghanistan?"

"Yes. The godless Russians have been driven out. It is jihad."

Yusef had visibly brightened. "Holy war! Killing Jews!"

"There are no Jews in Afghanistan."

"What is the glory in that?" Yusef complained. "Afghan skulls will not break down the gates of Paradise."

"That is not what the mullahs and imams are saying."

Yusef shook his head vigorously. "No, it would take too many Afghan skulls to gain me entrance to Paradise. I do not have all my life in which to martyr myself. What good will I be to the compliant *houris* if I am too old and feeble to adore them? These women are expecting certain manly duties of me."

"If you change your mind, speak to Muzzamil. He will see that you get to Afghanistan."

Eventually boredom got to Yusef Gamal, and he made the acquaintance of the mysterious Muzzamil.

"I am interested in Afghanistan," Yusef explained. "I understand the opportunities for martyrdom are very great there."

Muzzamil had a very thick beard and flashing opaline eyes, which immediately fell upon the exact center of Yusef's visage.

"You have an interesting nose."

"Thank you, but what about Afghanistan?"

"It is a very Jewish nose."

And hearing this insult, Yusef Gamal seized the insulter by the throat and attempted to squeeze his head off.

Others came and clubbed him off Muzzamil.

"He is a hothead, forgive him, O Muzzamil."

"He is Palestinian. That is the same thing," Muzzamil said as the good color returned to his dark, bearded face. His voice sounded squeezed, but his tone was without fear or anger.

"It is sometimes good to have a Jewish nose," Muzzamil told Yusef, who promptly threw off his compatriots and took another lunge at the hateful Muzzamil.

This time Muzzamil was ready for him. Yusef, who was used to fighting with Kalashnikovs and RPG's, did not expect something as lowly as a fist to lay him out. In truth, he never saw the fist that connected with the stubbled point of his chin.

When he regained consciousness, Muzzamil was bending over him. "Your nose is not broken. That is good."

"My jaw feels like broken glass," Yusef muttered dazedly.

"It will heal. For what lies ahead, you will need that Zionist nose of yours."

"I go to Afghanistan?"

"No. That is for cannon fodder and other fools. For you, I have special plans."

That night Yusef was spirited out of the camp. A long series of journeys by Land Rover, by boat and camel brought him to a city of minarets he did not recognize.

"What city is this?"

"Tehran."

"I am in Iran!"

"Yes."

"You are a Persian?"

"Yes. My true name is Aboof."

Yusef Gamal frowned. It was true that the Persians worshiped Allah and their leader the ayatollah was a devout Muslim. But they were Persians, not Arabs. It was a very different thing.

"For the work that lies ahead, you will need a new name."

"Abu Gamalin," Yusef said quickly.

"That is a good name for waging terror campaigns and issuing communiqués and threats, yes. But I was thinking of a contact name for our files."

"It will not be a name that I use?"

"No, it will be for internal use only."

"Then I do not care what I am called," Yusef snapped.

"Good," said Aboof the Persian, who told him his code name would henceforth be Yusef the Jew.

The only thing that stopped Yusef Gamal from throttling the despicable Persian on the spot was the presence of the armed Revolutionary Guards.

"You will go to America," said Aboof when Yusef had calmed down.

"I will never go to America. It is an un-Islamic place."

"There you will apply for U.S. citizenship."

"Never! I would rather burn in Hell first."

"You will get a job and you will sleep," continued Aboof the Unflappable.

"What manner of orders are these for a warrior?"

"The job will support you until you are called. The sleep I speak of will be the sleep of a sleeper agent."

"How long must I sleep?"

"Until you are told to awaken."

"What will my duties be at that time?"

"Whatever is decided then. For you may sleep a long time."

IT WAS, in fact, six years. So long that Yusef the Jew had wondered if he had been forgotten by the lordly Persians. The *intifada* had ended. Many had been martyred. The Gulf War had also passed. Yusef had missed out on all of it. Worse, he was a lowly American citizen driving a cab in New York City, unmartyred and unfulfilled.

It was a terrible destiny. All of his friends, he had heard, were dead and already in Paradise, safely in the arms of Allah. And he was stuck fighting treacherous traffic and conveying Jews to their destinations like some camel driver of old.

The call came in the middle of the night, six months after the World Trade Center bombing.

"We are assembling an army," the soft voice said.

"Who is this?" Yusef asked sleepily.

"Aboof asked me to contact you."

"Aboof! Where is he?"

"In Paradise."

"He is lucky. For I am living in Hoboken. A place worse than Hell itself."

"Come to the Abu al-Kalbin Mosque in Jersey City, Yusef the Chosen."

"Why?"

"Because we are creating a secret army to smash the Great Satan."

Now Yusef knew for sure he was speaking with another Persian. For only Persians spoke of the Great Satan. But he agreed to go anyway. Driving a cab in New York City was slowly driving him mad.

The Abu al-Kalbin Mosque was a storefront mosque in the heart of the dirty place called Jersey City, not very far from city hall. Yusef took the PATH train to the Journal Square stop and walked as instructed along Kennedy Boulevard.

The neighborhood was unpleasant, but such was the lot of Muslims who came to dwell in America. There was no justice. Never once had the taxi company Yusef worked for given him his Fridays off or allowed him to pull over and face Mecca for his daily prayers.

At the door, he was greeted by an Egyptian face he did not know. But the man's dark eyes exploded as if in recognition. Then they narrowed in anger and disgust.

"Go away, Jew. We want none of you here."

"I am no—"

The plain door slammed in his face.

Annoyed, Yusef knocked again.

"Go away, Zionist entity," he was told.

"I am no Jew, but Abu Gamalin the Feared."

"Liar."

"It is true. I swear by the beard of the prophet."

"If you speak truly, state your secret code name."

"I told you. I am Abu Gamalin."

"I have no such name on my list, Jew."

"I am not a Jew. I am sometimes called Al Mahour."

"I have no Al Mahour here. Perhaps it is some other mosque you are trying to infiltrate, Jewish dog."

"For the last time, I have come as summoned. Do not turn me away to drive the Hasidim around until I am mad with craziness."

"And for the last time, I ask you the code name you were given if you were given one."

Insulted to the bone, Yusef Gamal would have turned around and gone home. But he had slept so long. He did not wish to sleep any more. He wished excitement. He wished to feel young again. He craved the strong hardness of a Kalashnikov in his hands and the stink of infidel blood in the wind.

So he stood on the stoop of the Abu al-Kalbin Mosque, racking his brains. What was it he had been code-named? It had made his blood boil with rage when he first heard it. He was so offended by the very sound, he drove it from his memory. Now he beseeched Allah to unlock his memory again so he could speak the despised words aloud.

Then it came to him.

"I remember!" he cried through the shut door. "I remember now! I am called Yusef the Jew! Do you hear? It is Yusef the Jew. Open up."

"You admit to being a Jew?"

"No, I am called Yusef the Jew. It is my code name."

"No Jews are allowed in Allah's holy temple. This is a holy place. Go away or we will smash your teeth in your foul mouth."

Then a new voice came. Deeper, vaguely familiar. After it had spoken, Yusef placed it. It was the telephone voice.

"He is expected. Let him in."

The door opened. Yusef peered in cautiously. Shadows lay thick.

The voice said, "Enter, one who has slept too long."

And Yusef Gamal entered.

The room was ill lit. It was night. No candles burned.

"You are the last chosen one who is expected," said the voice. "Enter, Seeker of the Light, and follow."

"I follow."

Other shadows huddled around. Yusef could feel hard eyes on him. On his nose, actually.

"Is a Jew allowed to meet the mullah?" a suspicious voice asked.

"He is not a Jew, but only called that," said the voice from the telephone.

"His nose is Jewish."

"His nose is his ticket to Paradise. Be envious of it, ye of lesser noses."

"I prefer to be called Abu Gamalin," Yusef said, squaring his shoulders.

A voice hooted. Another called him Gamal Mahour.

Yusef would have taken offense, except that he did not know these men, and at least "Camel Nose" was better than being called Yusef the Jew.

They were escorted to a room where thin light fell from a skylight that was obscured with muslin to foil prying eyes. Prayer rugs were pointed out, and they took kneeling positions of supplication, including the tall shadow whose voice Yusef had heard over the telephone.

When all was still, a candle was lit. It guttered, its sickly yellow light showing a screen. The shadow of a seated man was visible behind the screen. The figure was rounded, the head fringed with a full beard.

"True Believers, we will speak English here because some of you know Farsi and others Arabic, but not both."

The voice was strange in its accents. Musical, the vowels odd. Yusef, who knew few Persians, decided it must be the accent that made the English so sickly sweet to his ears. Or perhaps it was the contrast to the nasal English of New Yorkers, with whom he had dwelt for so long.

"The sight of my holy countenance must be denied even to you, the faithful," the voice began. "To cast eyes upon me is *haram*—forbidden. My true name will never be known to you. Some called me their mufti. Others imam. Some of you here have heard of me by a name bestowed upon me by the intelligence organs of Egypt, Iraq and the Great Satan. This name is the Deaf Mullah."

A gasp raced around the supplicant men.

Yusef was impressed. All True Believers knew of the Deaf Mullah, a Persian cleric reviled in the West for his exhortations against all things Western. It was said he had personally constructed an infernal device intended to destroy the Egyptian puppet, Mubarak, but that it had exploded in his hands. His survival was considered a gift from Allah and a sign of his holiness. For the mullah had lost only the hearing in one ear entirely and the hearing in the other but partially.

More impressively it was the Deaf Mullah who had organized the enterprise that nearly brought down the World Trade Center, as well as demolishing the Lincoln and Holland tunnels, except for certain unfortunate misadventures that resulted in the capture of the conspirators, incidentally landing the Deaf Mullah in a federal prison.

As he reflected on these tales, Yusef noticed that the man behind the screen held an ear trumpet in one hand. It was the Deaf Mullah. Truly.

"You who have slept in this infidel land are now called upon to awaken. For an army of the faithful is being mustered, and you will be its soldiers."

"Praise Allah," a man said fervently. It was the telephone summoner, Yusef realized.

"Praise Allah," another man vowed.

"Yes, praise Allah that you have lived to see this day," the Deaf Mullah said. "You all have been selected for your devotion, your ferocity, your courage and your ability to exist in an enemy land unchallenged. You all are U.S. citizens. This is important. When this plan was created years ago, it was not understood how important. But becoming citizens of the United States is a necessary step to joining the army that will break the American spine in many places.

"For you all to understand your task, it is necessary that you all understand the state of things as pertains to the march of Islam."

They listened attentively.

"You all know that the first attempt to bring jihad to America ended in abject failure. The one who served me before failed. They brought disgrace to Islam through their base ineptitude. They made mistakes. They failed to destroy the twin towers of the World Trade Center. They did stupid things for which they were caught. Others of their cells also failed in executing important tasks, such as the destruction of the bridges and tunnels and other lawful targets. As a consequence, many laughed at our cause, derided us as stupid. No more. Those days are done with.''

"Praise Allah," another man said.

"We are done with being mocked. For we have found another, truer path. One that will lead us to victory over the infidel. You are not alone among True Believers. Our numbers increase. Even the American media have noted that we Muslims outnumber the Episcopalians and Presbyterians. In a few years, we will outpace the Jews. But we cannot wait for that day. We must begin to strike at their soft underbelly.''

"How, O Holy One?"

"Yes, we are with you."

A broad hand was raised. "Patience. My tale is not done.''

They settled down, their bodies leaning forward in their eagerness. Their breathing became audible.

"More recently a building was destroyed in the city called Oklahoma. For this, we were blamed, though we were truly blameless.''

"It is a sign of the anti-Islamic virus that infects America!" Yusef exclaimed.

"No, it was a good thing that we were blamed. For although it is an insult and an affront to Allah, whose children we are, it is more important that the infidel fear us. But in time it was discovered that infidel elements were themselves responsible for this outrage."

"It is not an outrage if it afflicts the infidel," a man suggested.

"It is an outrage that infidels are more successful in striking at infidel targets than us, who have been anointed by Allah to do this thing."

Murmurs around the room agreed that this was in fact an outrage.

"Long I have pondered this conundrum. Much thought have I put into this problem. The infidel no longer fears us. How, I asked myself, could I strike fear into the craven hearts? More importantly how can we strike at the heart of the Great Satan when they have hardened their hearts against us?"

"They will never embrace Islam!" Yusef spat. "It is a waste of time to convert them. Instead, they must be put to the sword!"

"The hearts they have hardened are not their false hearts beating within their breasts, but the hearts of their government. Their federal buildings. Their courthouses. These places of wickedness that are denied us."

"Oh," said Yusef, who now understood.

"How to enter these places that we might destroy them from within was my thought. Long I prayed Allah to enlighten me. It came to me that even you, who wear faces that enable you to blend in with the infidel's base, corrupt civilization, were not equal to the task."

"We are equal, Holy One."

"We are greater than equal. We are Muslims."

"We are ready to die."

"Yes, you are ready to die," said the Deaf Mullah. "But are you prepared to succeed?"

"Yes, yes."

"Good. For the next step lies before you."

"What is this?" Yusef asked.

And the candle was snuffed out by a quick movement of the hovering ear trumpet, and a curtain was drawn before the dark shape of the Deaf Mullah.

Lights came on. They hurt the eyes. When Yusef looked down, there was a pen and a sheaf of papers resting before his crossed legs.

"What is this?" he asked aloud.

"It is called an exam. In order to take the next step, you must pass it."

Yusef picked up the papers. Reading, he frowned. "I understand the words, but the questions are hard."

"Yes," another said. "It is harder than passing the test for citizenship. You must memorize all manner of godless notions."

"Nevertheless," said the melodious voice of the Deaf Mullah from behind the curtain, "you will do your mightiest."

Yusef raised a hand. Then he realized the Deaf Mullah could not see him, so he said, "I have a question, Holy One."

"Ask it."

"Can we cheat?"

"Yes. Cheating is allowed by Allah, who has blessed this enterprise."

And Yusef and the others grinned. As long as they could cheat, success was possible.

It was at that point that Yusef got a good look at his fellow worshipers. Fear touched his eyes. These men did not look Arabic or even Persian. They were too white. Even the Egyptian, seen in a clear light, looked wrong. His hair was as red as a Crusader's. Two men were black, not the coffee black of Libya, but the ebony of lower Africa.

Noticing that the eyes of the others were looking back at him strangely, Yusef blurted, "I am not Jewish. Really, it is just my nose. I am a Semite, as are many of you. It is a Semitic nose, not a Jewish one. There is a very great difference."

That night everyone took the exam, and though they cheated their mightiest, as Allah would wish them to, no one passed.

"Have we failed?" asked the flame-haired Egyptian.

"No," returned the Deaf Mullah. "This is not the true test, for that can only be given by the generals who control the infidel army we seek to infiltrate."

"What army is this?"

"The most dreaded army in this hateful land."

Yusef said, "It is the Marines. They are the most feared."

"The Marines were crushed and broken in Lebanon," the Deaf Mullah reminded.

"It is the Navy," said another. "For the Navy have warriors who are called sea lions and can swim underwater like fish and steal up from the very waters to do evil, un-Islamic things."

"You will not become Navy SEAL," intoned the Deaf Mullah from behind his curtain.

"Then what will we be?" a man wondered aloud.

"We cannot be Army men. For all know the Army is composed of pigs."

"They are called grunts," said the Deaf Mullah. "Not pigs."

"What army, O Imam?" they beseeched him.

Then the uniforms were brought out.

They were blue and gray. Down the gray pant legs ran a very military blue stripe. And on the breast and shoulder was a patch showing a striking eagle's head.

"We are Air Force!" he cried.

"Shut up, Jew," a man cried sourly. "These are not Air Force uniforms."

"They are blue and they show an eagle. Unquestionably it is Air Force that we will infiltrate."

"These are not the uniforms of the United States Air Force. Note the patch. What do the initials say?"

"USPS," a man said slowly.

"We are paratroopers!" Yusef exclaimed. "We will jump out of airplanes and strike at will! Allah be praised."

"Your brains are in your nose," the sour voice of the fiery-haired Egyptian spat at Yusef.

"May Allah change your face," Yusef retorted hotly. The two men jumped up and squared off.

The Deaf Mullah clapped his hands sharply. "There will be no fighting in this holy place. Remember that 'Islam' means 'peace.' We are men of peace when dealing with one another."

"But men of death when dealing with the infidel," said the Egyptian who had been about to punch Yusef in his camel-like nose.

"You will not be paratroopers," the Deaf Mullah said quietly. "For the initials USPS stand for United States Postal Service."

A hush fell over the room. The men looked at one another, their faces contorting with confusion and doubt.

"We will be mailmen?"

"You will be the Messengers of Muhammad," the Deaf Mullah announced, standing up.

"A *boustajai?*" asked Yusef.

"No uniform is more feared!" the Deaf Mullah proclaimed. "Nor more respected. Wearing these colors, you will be admitted freely into the holiest of holies of the infidel nation. No one will question you. No one may challenge you. For their mail is sacred to the infidel. You will swear allegiance to the mighty postmaster general, but in reality you are answerable only to your imam and Allah the Compassionate, the Merciful, on whom all praise must fall."

"I cannot be a postman," Yusef complained. "I am a Palestinian. It is a demotion in the eyes of Allah."

"As a Palestinian, you are a fierce killer?"

"Yes. Many enemies have I slain."

"Tell me, O brother, who do you fear?"

"No one."

"Do you fear the Israeli?"

"Never! I have killed Israelis like dogs."

"If I placed you in a room with two doors and told you that you could have any weapon at your disposal and that you must escape through one door and one door only, which door would you choose? The one behind which stands an Israeli soldier or the one behind which stands a United States postman?"

"Both are armed?" asked Yusef.

"With Uzis."

Yusef hesitated. "If they are both armed with Uzis, I might be able to kill the Israeli first. Or trick him by pretending to surrender and slaying him when his guard is down. But the postman, if he is armed that means he has gone crazy. Who can defeat a crazy man?"

"Exactly."

"A crazy man is crazy. He will not listen to reason, but only shoot without discrimination. Even at his own."

"Yes," said the Deaf Mullah. "The postal worker is feared because he has been driven mad by the stern demands of un-Islamic living. He will kill anyone or anything without compunction."

"This is my point exactly," retorted Yusef.

The Deaf Mullah lifted his voice to address them all.

"Today. In the West, if an American was walking down a dark street and was confronted by one of you wearing a *kaffiyeh* over your face and a postal worker carrying a gun, the American would throw himself on your mercy because he knows from the wild look in the postal worker's eyes no mercy is to be found there. That is why you will wear this feared uniform. This is how you will infiltrate the buildings that are denied to us by increased American security. This is how we will bring down the towers of the infidel so that the minarets of our own pure and thrice-blessed culture may rise to the very stars."

Yusef Gamal looked at the uniform with strange eyes and asked, "Do they not carry great leather bags?"

"You will all be given leather bags large enough to conceal the deadliest weapons. You will be scattered to the compass points of the infidel nation until you are activated. Also you will have to join a union. Some of you will join the American Postal Workers Union, others the National Association of Letter Carriers. A few, the National Rural Letter Carriers' Association."

"It is a small price to pay in order to insinuate ourselves into the bosom of the infidel," Yusef proclaimed.

"You must also change your names so that you may further blend in with the ones you will destroy."

"American names?"

"Yes. Of course."

A man stood up. He struck his chest with his fist. "Then I will be Al Ladeen."

"And I Jihad Jones," said the fire-haired Egyptian.

"I insist upon being Abu Gamalin," said Yusef.

"You cannot be Abu Gamalin," said the Deaf Mullah.

"If that one can be Jihad Jones, I can be Abu Gamalin."

"I will allow you to retain your true name, if you are careful. To us, you will be Abu Gamalin. But to the Americans, you will be known as Joseph Camel."

And for reasons unknown to Yusef, the others softly laughed in the Abu Al-Kalbin Mosque.

"It is better than the other name," he said, mollified.

YUSEF GAMAL TOOK the postal-service exam, passing only through the coaching of the Deaf Mullah and by wearing a shirt whose green patterns in fact were imprinted with key answers in Arabic script—which was unreadable to stupid Western eyes.

This was in the state of Oklahoma, in the city of Oklahoma, as prescribed by the Deaf Mullah and ordained by Allah. Yusef's job at first was to place mail in canvas bags and in pigeonholes. It was very tedious work, and the bosses were hard taskmasters, which made Yusef understand why some of the workers went crazy from time to time.

"It is not just because they have turned their face from Allah," he told the Deaf Mullah via e-mail, the secure method of communications they all used. "It is the mindless tasks they are forced to perform that unbalance them."

"But you are getting along with the Godless?" the Deaf Mullah wrote back.

"Some think I am a Jew. Jews are not plentiful here, so I am singled out in this way."

"This is good, for when the appointed hour comes, they will remember you as a Jew and not Abu Gamalin."

"When will the hour come, O Imam? I chafe and fret among these infidels."

"Soon, soon. Have patience. First, you must be given a route."

"I am trying very hard, because these pigeon holes are driving me to distraction. They have recently painted the walls a hideous pink."

"Think of Islamic green."

"I am thinking of green. But I see pink. Everywhere I look, I see pink."

"Contain your rage. Store it. When the time comes, it will be unleashed."

"That is the problem," typed Yusef. "The more I see pink, the less angry I become."

"Think green. Paint the walls of your home green so that you can at night dispel the pink influence of Christianity."

The hour at last came, and Yusef received his instructions.

"But the federal building is not on my route," Yusef protested.

"It does not matter. Your uniform will gain admittance for you. Go forth and slaughter those who inhabit the court of Judge Rathburn."

"I hear and obey."

"When the slaughter is complete, fly to Toledo in Ohiostan. You will be met there by your brethren."

"Then I am done? After only one slaughter?"

"No, for your slaughter will inform the infidel that his much-protected federal building is vulnerable to us. That the messengers of Muhammad are as mighty as their own militia. After this and other deeds are done, we will embark upon our true mission."

"Which is?" Yusef asked eagerly.

"For you to know in Toledo. Go now, Abu Gamalin. And do not forget to shout the slogans you have been taught."

"God Is Grape!"

"'Great.' The English for *Allahu Akbar* is 'God Is Great.'"

"Yes, yes, I will remember."

"And do not forget to tell the dying Americans that they are suffering the deaf penalty."

"The death penalty, yes."

"No, 'deaf.' Not 'death.' The deaf penalty."

"What is the difference?"

"None whatsoever," the Deaf Mullah replied.

It was easy, Yusef discovered. With his Uzi in his leather letter bag and ear protectors, he had walked into the Wiley Post Federal Building, took the elevator to the court of Judge Rathburn and killed all within.

No one questioned him going in, and no one stopped him on the way out. He was well out of town when a search was organized for him. But he was not the usual mailman on that route, and all who saw him saw the uniform, not the man.

It had been perfection—and proof the enterprise had been blessed by Almighty Allah.

14

The President of the United States was in the middle of a whistle-stop stump speech in Charlotte, North Carolina, trying to hold on to the slipping South when his press secretary attempted to convey an urgent message.

Deep into his exhortation, the President was oblivious to the raised finger in the wings, which turned into a circling finger, indicating that he should wrap it up quick.

The President wouldn't have been aware of the finger if it had been jammed up his nose. Besides, his handlers were forever giving him the circling finger.

The President was reading off the twin Teleprompters—two Lucite electronic screens set at eye level to the left and right of the portable podium emblazoned with the presidential seal. A traveling liquid-crystal line of text, visible whether he faced left or right, told him what to say.

"'Make no mistake, this election is about change,'" he read. "'This election is about...an explosion in midtown Manhattan'?" The President stopped reading. The crawling blue letters had turned red. That was the signal that he wasn't to read what followed. Red letters were the stage directions such as "Gesture with fist à la JFK," or "Stay behind the podium, your fly is open."

The President paused. The red letters crawled along: "No further information available . . ."

"I have just been told," the President said, recovering quickly, "that there has been an explosion in Manhattan."

The crowd made a little murmur like a wave breaking and muttering in the sand. The blue letters returned, and the President resumed speechifying. He wondered why his handlers had bulletined him in the middle of his speech about an ordinary explosion. And why hadn't they said what had exploded? A car? A building? The Statue of Liberty? Coney Island?

The President was into paragraph fifty-seven of his ten-minute speech—now running twenty-five minutes overlength—when the blue crawl once again turned angry red.

"AP now reporting multiple explosions N.Y.C. . . . cause unknown . . ."

The President decided not to communicate this to the crowd. Another ten minutes, and the speech would be over. He had to pick up the pace. A few people were already nodding off. One heavy-lidded man actually swayed on his feet, but an alert Secret Service agent caught him and shook him back to attention. This was a constant problem on the campaign trail. The President wondered if his supporters weren't afflicted with some new kind of attention-deficit disorder.

"Some say the ideals of the '60s are dead. They're not dead. They're only a prisoner of the Republican Congress. Reelect me and help preserve the legacy of the past from those who—"

"Courtroom massacre in new federal building Oklahoma City..."

The President blinked. His stricken eyes chased the red letters off the Lucite screen. Did it say Oklahoma City? Damn, he thought, wishing there was a replay button. There was no replay button. No freeze-frame, either.

As the crowd watched patiently, he cleared his throat and charged on. He was going to finish this speech if it took all day.

Casting his gaze back and forth to make eye contact with the two wings of the crowd, the President awaited the next string of blue letters.

They never came. Instead, another crawl of red marched past: "For God's sake, Mr. President! Please cut short your speech. This is an emergency!"

"In conclusion," the President said, shifting gears, "a vote for continuity is a vote for electoral balance, and a vote for electoral balance is a vote for future and lasting change."

Three minutes later, the crowd was applauding and the red, white and green balloons—some advance man had screwed up—went up to the sky.

Surrounded by a diamond of moving Secret Service agents, the President rushed to the waiting armored limo. Or was rushed by them. Sometimes it was hard to tell.

The Secret Service agents looked nervous. More so than usual. The President wondered if they had read the bulletins, too.

They clapped the door shut on the presidential limo, and a running roadblock of armored Secret Service sedans escorted the careering vehicle to the Charlotte airport.

In the back, the press secretary offered the Chief Executive his choice of secure telephones.

"What's this?"

"Director, FBI. On the explosions."

Indicating the second cellular with its light on, the President asked, "Is that for me, too?"

"Bureau of Alcohol, Tobacco and Firearms."

"What do they want?"

"I think they want to beat FBI to your ear."

"Are they fighting again? Damn!"

"Which do you want first?"

The President hesitated. "You decide."

"I can't. You're Chief Executive."

"Hell, hand 'em both over." And the President clapped both cell phones to his head, one to each ear.

"This is your President," he said in his best authoritative voice. "Consider this a conference call between FBI and ATF."

"Damn," a small voice said.

"Which one of you said that?" the President demanded.

No one answered. They figured he might not be long for this political world, but couldn't chance offending him.

"FBI, bring me up to speed on these explosions."

"Yes, Mr. President," said the right-hand cell phone. That meant it had been ATF that had cursed. "First, at approximately 11:20 Central Time, an unidentified gunman burst into a federal courtroom in the new federal building in Oklahoma City. He killed everyone in the room except a court officer who is now talking."

"Who did it?"

"I'm coming to that."

"At 12:10 Eastern Standard Time, an explosion took place at the corner of Eighth Avenue and Thirty-fourth Street in midtown Manhattan. It was determined that a postal relay box had exploded. Then at 12:20 EST—note the time—several other relay boxes also detonated in midtown."

"Eleven-twenty in Oklahoma and 12:20 Manhattan time are the same time, aren't they?"

"Accounting for the time difference, yes. There's more. The relay boxes can be opened only by a postal employee with a master key. The Oklahoma City court officer claims a letter carrier committed the massacre."

"What are we looking at here?"

"On the surface, disgruntled postal employees."

The President looked doubtful. "What about under the surface?"

"If I may get a word in?" ATF began to say from the opposite cell phone.

"Hold on. I'll get to you."

"Damn," the ATF head whispered.

"Well, Mr. President," the FBI director resumed, "disgruntled postal workers haven't to date operated in concert. Certainly not coordinated across state lines as this situation appears to suggest."

"They just flip out and shoot at anything that moves, right?"

"That's what my Violent Postal Worker Task Force behavior team says."

"You have a Violent Postal Worker Task Force?"

"Postal crimes have quadrupled in the last five years, sir."

"What gets into these people? Is it the uniforms? The routes? Paper cuts? All of those zip codes they have to remember?"

"We're still working up psychological profiles on that, Mr. President," FBI continued. "In any event, these are clearly federal crimes, and FBI would like the authority to take the tip of the spear in this early investigatory phase."

"Objection! Objection!" said ATF, who suddenly sounded like a lawyer. Ever since the O.J. trial, a lot of federal employees had gotten into the habit of shouting objections.

"You can object later. The President and I are talking," FBI told ATF, apparently using the President's head as a sound-conducting medium. "This is a federal matter. It falls under FBI jurisdiction."

"Don't hand me that. Explosions are ATF."

"Courtroom shootings are FBI. And these events are connected. FBI had suzerainty over ATF in this instance."

"Then we work together," ATF insisted.

"Not a chance," said the President, realizing the last thing he needed a month before his possible reelection was another Waco.

"Very well," the ATF head said. "You must decide, Mr. President."

Thinking that the next last thing he wanted to do before the November election was make an important decision that could backfire, the President clapped the two cell phones together and said, "You two work this out. I have a better idea."

Air Force One was suddenly visible ahead. The President was astonished at how much ground they had covered.

Exiting the presidential limo, he hurried up the air stairs with his entourage and when he entered the gleaming 747, was immediately handed a thin sheaf of papers.

"What are these?" he asked.

"Updates on the incidents in Oklahoma and New York."

His press secretary then offered what appeared to be a block of white wood.

"What's this?"

"Text of your next speech, sir."

"Cancel it."

"All of it?"

"We're headed back to Washington."

The press secretary looked as if he'd been summarily fired.

"Mr. President, we have the Washington vote all sewn up. We can't."

"And get me the postmaster general on the line. What's his name again?"

The press secretary looked blank. The chief advance man looked blank. Everyone looked blank.

"Doesn't anyone know who the postmaster general of the United States is?" the President demanded.

"Is he important?"

"If what I hear is true, he may be the most important man in America today."

And the President rushed to his private cabin to hide before the White House press corps surged onto the plane like a human tidal wave in search of quotes and free pretzels.

They were in the air when the presidential press secretary knocked once and poked his head in.

"Damon Post on line 1 for you."

"Who?"

"The postmaster general."

"Oh, right. What do I call him—'Mr. Postmaster'? 'General'?"

The press secretary looked startled. "I don't know. Should I pull the etiquette book?"

"I'll wing it," said the President, picking up the secure cabin phone.

"Damon, this is the President. I hope you don't mind if I call you 'Damon.'"

"Call me whatever you want, Mr. President."

"Damon, I've been been brought up to speed on these incidents. What can you add?"

"We have people on the Manhattan matter."

"And Oklahoma City? What about that?"

"I have no comment on Oklahoma City."

"No comment? What kind of answer is that to give your President?"

"A politic one, Mr. President. It did not involve a postal employee." And from the tone of the postmaster general's voice, the President of the United States understood that he was calculating the odds of not having to deal with executive-branch interference until after the election.

"What do you mean, it didn't involve a postal employee? A dying witness described the assailant as a mailman."

"No, he described an assailant dressed in a USPS uniform. There's a big difference. Anyone can steal a uniform."

"What about the Manhattan explosions, then? The American people want to know if their mailboxes are safe."

"We are investigating the possible theft of master keys by non-postal-employees."

"In other words, you're saying your people aren't responsible."

"I have no hard evidence to support that theory at this hour, Mr. President."

"I'm going to be getting back to you on this," the President growled.

"Feel free," the postmaster general said. "We appreciate your business."

The line went dead.

"'We appreciate your business'?" said the President, staring at the receiver. "Who the hell does that guy think he is?"

As *Air Force One* screamed toward Andrews Air Base, the President slowly replaced the receiver. He was thinking of another telephone receiver. A red one.

With the FBI and ATF struggling over turf and the postmaster general stonewalling, the President planned to cut the bureaucratic red tape the same way his predecessors had for the past three decades.

If this wasn't a CURE matter, he didn't know what was.

He just hoped that damn Smith agreed. The President who had created the organization had included a fail-safe in its unwritten charter. The President could suggest missions, not order them. It would be up to Smith to make the decisions, a situation for which this President was grateful. He hated making decisions. There were always consequences.

"Coffee or tea?" asked a voice through the door.

"Surprise me," said the President.

15

Harold Smith knew the President was upset from the instant he heard his raspy voice.

"Smith, this is your President speaking."

It wasn't the hoarseness of the President's voice. This President was naturally hoarse. It wasn't the breathlessness indicative of his sudden return to the executive mansion, and the dash he'd made up to the Lincoln Bedroom and his end of the dedicated CURE line.

It was the utter silence in the background. Almost every time Smith had spoken to the President in the past, Elvis music had played in the background. Smith couldn't actually tell—he assumed it was Elvis. All popular music recorded since World War II sounded pretty much alike to Harold Smith, who'd stopped listening to popular music around the time swing gave way to post-war bebop.

This time there was none of that. This more than anything told Smith that the President understood the gravity of the situation.

"I am listening, Mr. President."

"You've heard about the mailbox bombings in New York?"

"Yes, and the court shooting in Oklahoma."

"I think this may be only the beginning."

"You are correct. It is only the beginning."

"That's not exactly what I wanted to hear," said the President, suddenly realizing that being right in this case was not as useful as being wrong.

"That is not a guess on my part," Smith continued. "Someone just demolished the General Post Office in midtown Manhattan."

"How serious is that? We're just talking about a mail-processing center, right?"

"One that occupies an entire city block in the heart of Manhattan and greatly resembles the U.S. Treasury in size and design."

The President could be heard swallowing hard. At least, a distinct gulp came over the dedicated line.

"My God, it's as if postmen everywhere have gone crazy."

"The correct term is 'decompensated.' "

"So you agree with me?"

"No, I do not. This is not a case of a handful of postal employees experiencing a psychotic break or suffering from episodic explosive disorder."

"Why not? It happens all the time. I remember reading about a New Jersey postal worker who up and killed his co-workers just so he could steal enough money to pay his back rent."

"This is true. But psychotics do not operate in concert. They are loners. Antisocials. You would have a better chance of organizing squirrels to program network television."

"I think it's been tried," the President said distractedly. "Look, I just spoke with the postmaster general, and he's stonewalling me. You don't think this is orchestrated, do you?"

"I am afraid that it is."

"By whom?"

"Mr. President, if you are not sitting down, I must ask you to do so."

"Go ahead, Smith."

"A Muslim fundamentalist terror group has infiltrated the postal service with the intention of waging a war of urban terror against the nation."

"Infiltrated? What do you mean, infiltrated?"

"I mean," returned Harold Smith in a bitter, lemony tone, "that virtually any letter carrier, postal worker or USPS truck driver might be a secret terrorist intent upon wholesale destruction."

"My God. How many of them are there?"

"I have developed information that suggests over thirty terrorists are in this cell. But there may be other jihad cells. We do not know."

"Thirty? Even thirty can do a lot of damage."

"I assume the carnage of today is the work of one or two, or at most three terror agents. Thirty terrorists could do incalculable damage."

"Do you—do you think this is meant to embarrass me just before the election?"

"I doubt that, Mr. President. This is clearly a first strike. The cell has demonstrated its power. Assuming there are no more incidents today, we must await a communiqué of their demands or intentions."

"How can we counteract them?"

"Short of shutting down the mail system, I do not know."

"Can I do that as President?"

"That is between you and the postmaster general."

"Is that what you're recommending here? Shut down the mail until we get a handle on how deep the postal service has been compromised?"

"Events may or may not force you to that decision, Mr. President, but for now I have my people on it."

"What are they going to do?"

"They are on the trail of the Oklahoma City terrorist."

The President's voice was startled. "You know who he is? Already?"

"Yes. He goes by the name of Yusef Gamal, alias Joe Camel."

"Did you say Joe Camel?"

"I did," said Harold Smith.

The President's voice dropped to a low, conspiratorial tone. "You don't suppose the big tobacco companies are behind this, do you?"

"Muslim fanatics, Mr. President."

"Because if there's any chance—any chance at all—that the tobacco companies have funded these people, it would be a useful campaign issue."

"I would not advance in public any theories that might backfire," Harold Smith said thinly.

"I don't know which is worse," the President lamented, "Muslim fanatics, tobacco companies or disgruntled postal workers."

"Muslim terrorists in the guise of disgruntled postal workers."

"Why are they disgruntled? Were they ever gruntled? Is that even a word?"

"I will be back to you, Mr. President," said Smith, thinking it had been a long four years of service at the pleasure of this particular President. Another four was not something to look forward to.

HAROLD SMITH HAD RETURNED to his terminal and its silent, keyless keyboard.

The global search for Yusef Gamal, a.k.a. Joseph Camel, turned up the fact that he was a naturalized citizen of the United States and had been with the postal service less than two years. There were no indications of credit-card purchases of airline reservations or transportation in the recent past that would indicate a premeditated escape route. Smith had hoped for such an audit trail.

Working quickly, he input some of the other cover names—Ibrahim Lincoln, Yassir Nossair and others. It was too much to hope something would turn up, but Joe Camel had panned out despite all logic to the contrary.

While he waited for results, Smith logged on to the FBI central data base in New York City, hopping from desk terminal to desk terminal, seeking activity related to the day's events.

He caught something almost at once. A clerk or agent was inputting the just-developed information that the vehicle-identification number of the exploded vehicle found in the rubble of the Manhattan General Post Office positively identified it as a USPS relay truck.

A suicide bomber, as Smith suspected.

As he watched, Smith saw another piece fall into place. Dental bridgework found at the scene matched the dental records of one Allah Ladeen. That closed the books on one terrorist.

Then his computer began spitting out the whereabouts of the other suspected terrorists.

Jaw dropping, Smith saw the names and addresses of Jihad Jones, Ibrahim Lincoln, Yassir Nossair, Mohamet Ali and most of the others start scrolling before his incredulous gray eyes.

Picking up the telephone, he began calling FBI district offices, starting with Chicago.

"This is Assistant Special Agent in Charge Smith, calling from Washington headquarters. You are ordered to pick up the following subjects in connection with the terroristic events of the day."

No one questioned him. If they called back the Washington number he gave them for verification, they would get Smith's Folcroft line. But no one called back. Virtually every district branch had had dealings with ASAG Smith in the past.

16

It was the indignity of indignities. It was ignominy. It was shame.

But it was necessary, and so Yusef Gamal, alias Abu Gamalin, endured the shame.

He had made his escape to the airport and the flight that awaited him to the city of Toledo in Ohio. It was a good city name, Toledo. There was a Toledo in Moorish Spain. It was the original Toledo. Spain was one of the few nations where Islam has been in retreat for centuries, but that would also change.

Yusef Gamal was very happy at least that none of his fellow Palestinians could see him now seated on the flight to Toledo wearing a long, funereal black coat, black beaver hat and a wig fringed with stringy ringlets of hair called *paye*.

He was dressed as a Hasidic Jew. It was the perfect disguise, the Deaf Mullah had assured him by e-mail.

"They will be looking for a postal worker. Perhaps, if they detect our intentions, an Egyptian or Palestinian. Never a Hasidic Jew."

"I must be a Jew?" Yusef had e-mailed back.

"To escape, you must be a Jew. Allow your fearless Semitic nose to guide you to sanctuary."

"As you command, Holy One."

So Yusef sat quiet in the back of the plane with his ringlets shivering and shame in his hot eyes.

At least it was a short flight. That alone was consolation.

That and the fact that the kosher in-flight meal they had served him was technically *halal,* and so, could be eaten safely.

At the Toledo airport, Yusef was the last one off the plane and looked around for the True Believer who had been appointed to meet him.

The waiting area was crowded with passengers hugging their relatives in the most naked and unseemly fashion. The women did not wear veils, and their brazen lips were everywhere, like flowers dipped in poisonous blood.

Some held up signs. The Deaf Mullah had not said who was to meet him, but it was possible the messenger carried a sign also.

Scanning the crude cardboard signs, Yusef's eager eyes alighted on one that was held over the heads of two shamelessly kissing women. It read: Islamic Front For The National Association Of Letter Carriers.

Fortunately it was in Arabic, and so was not understandable to Western eyes.

"Here! I am here!" Yusef cried, pushing through the crowd.

A head poked up over the kissing female faces, and Yusef's eager expression turned to a glower. The face was darkly freckled, and the hair was very red.

"You!" Yusef spat, seeing that it was the Egyptian who was called Jihad Jones.

"I was right. It is true. You are a Jew. A Hasid, no less."

"It is a disguise ordained by the Deaf Mullah himself," Yusef said defensively.

"The Deaf Mullah did not instruct me to pick up a Jew, but a *mujahid*."

"I am that *mujahid*. Have you not heard of the wonderful carnage in Oklahoma City? I was the author of that carnage."

"I spit upon your carnage. My cousin Al Ladeen personally blew up several blocks in Manhattan where Jews such as you dwell, then drove his mail truck into the post office, obliterating the godless and himself in one mighty blow."

"I am no Jew. I have told you this. Why will you not listen?"

"Because the proof is standing before me, as black as a buzzard," Jihad Jones retorted hotly.

"The Deaf Mullah instructed you to take me to him. I insist that you do this at once."

Jihad Jones glowered, his face turning as scarlet as his disheveled hair. Yusef met his gaze with a contemptuous one of his own.

"Offspring of a Crusader!"

"Jew!"

"Idolworshiper!"

"Eater of pork!"

Finally Jihad Jones threw down his placard and said, "Very well. I will take you to the Deaf Mullah. But only because I know he will have you put to death."

"I am not afraid, because if I die a true Muslim, my allotment of seventy-two *houris* will be waiting for me in Paradise."

"We will see about that, too."

They drove south along a long, undulating highway. The area was very open, and there were barns. This was farm country.

"Where are we going?" asked Yusef Gamal.

"To the town of Greenburg."

"What is there?"

"The secret sanctuary of the Deaf Mullah. A place where no one would think of looking for him."

"The Deaf Mullah hides in a town with a Jewish name?"

"The name is Greenburg. With a *u*, not Greenberg with an *e*. It is not Jewish."

"It sounds Jewish."

"You should know, who look Jewish."

"I am not Jewish. I am a Semite, the same as you."

"I am an Egyptian."

"We are both brothers in Allah."

"Except that you secretly practice Jewishness."

"It is called Judaism."

"Hah! Your words are the very proof of my conviction."

"How do I know you are not secretly a Copt? You look like a Copt."

"If I am a Copt, you are a Jew for Jesus. This is worse than being a Hasid."

At that, Yusef shut his mouth, thinking, I am only getting myself in deeper with this idiot Egyptian camel driver.

Some thirty minutes into the journey, the broad highway lifted and swept into another highway.

And Yusef saw it, rearing up over the surrounding flatness like an alabaster vision. His eyes flew wide.

"Look, it is—"

"Yes."

"A mosque."

"Of course it is a mosque. Do you think the Deaf Mullah would dwell in a temple for Jews?"

"But it is so big. Why have I never heard of such a mosque here in Ohio?"

"Because it is more than a mosque," said Jihad Jones cryptically.

17

The flight to Oklahoma was routine except for the Japanese tourist in first class who, evidently impressed by the cut of Chiun's splendid traveling kimono, snapped a picture of the Master of Sinanju as he boarded.

In response, the Master of Sinanju snapped the Japanese tourist's shutter-pressing finger out of joint and relieved him of his camera, too. He returned it empty of film. When the Japanese complained, the overexposed roll somehow found its way into his throat, lodging there.

A stewardess, hearing the frightful choking sounds, rushed up and demanded, "What is it?"

"This man requires the Heimdall maneuver," sniffed Chiun. "He has stupidly swallowed something stupid."

"Oh, my God."

The stewardess fell on the man, grabbed him about the waist from behind and tried her mightiest to expel the foreign object from his throat. Every time she pulled back with her clasped hands, the tourist only strangled more loudly.

That was when Remo stepped on board. He took one look at the stewardess, apparently trying to break the back of a Japanese passenger, then the Master of Sinanju looking on with thin approval.

"*Now* what?" Remo demanded.

"This woman is attempting to preserve this Japanese's useless life," Chiun replied casually.

"What did you do to him?"

"He did it to himself."

Seeing that the stewardess wasn't exactly equal to the task, Remo loosened her fingers, spun the tourist around and clapped him on the middle of the back once very hard.

The roll of film shot out of his mouth like a plug of black plastic chewing tobacco, and rebounded from an overhead bin.

"He take a picture of you?" Remo asked Chiun as the tourist sank gasping into his first-class seat.

"This is unproven," sniffed Chiun, hurrying up the aisle.

The confused stewardess asked, "What happened?"

"I smacked him on the back," explained Remo.

"That's the old way. It's not supposed to work anymore."

"It worked for me."

"Oh," said the stewardess, who then noticed Remo's very thick wrists. "Are you a first-class passenger?"

"You wish," said Remo, who had had enough of amorous flight attendants of late.

The stewardess's shoulders collapsed, and her pretty face sagged like dough layered in pancake flour. Flakes of makeup were actually precipitated to the carpet, so profound was her change in expression.

"Maybe we can get you upgraded," she suggested.

"Not a chance. I always fly coach."

"What's wrong with first class?"

"If the plane goes down, first class always buys the farm."

She drew closer, preceded by a warm wave of frankincense, myrrh and overactive pheromones.

"If I buy the farm, will you miss me?"

"Aren't you in the wrong cabin?" asked Remo, dropping into the empty seat beside the Master of Sinanju.

"I am allowed in coach," she said huffily.

"Another stray?" asked Chiun after the stewardess had gone.

"Yeah," growled Remo. "What's wrong with stewardesses these days? They take to me like honeybees to nectar."

"They sense you are next in line to me."

"Then why don't they just skip over me and try to climb up *your* skirts?"

Chiun suppressed a distasteful pucker. "That is because when a Master achieves Reigning Master status, he learns to control his masculine lures without thinking."

Remo looked interested. "Teach me how."

"No."

"Why not?"

"We may yet need one of these bosomy cows to foal you a son."

"I'll pick my own brides, okay?"

"How vulgar. I do not understand how this nation can survive without the blessing of arranged marriages."

"Was your marriage arranged?"

"Of course."

"Who arranged it?"

"I did."

"Isn't that against the rules?"

"Possibly. But I was never caught."

"So? What's good enough for the Reigning Master should be good enough for the Apprentice Reigning Master."

"You will never be good enough until you unlearn your white ways," Chiun said, smoothing his plum-hued skirts on his lap.

The plane was delayed over an hour. The pilot came on the PA system and explained that the bombings in New York and Oklahoma City meant they were on a heightened FAA alert status and would be taking off "momentarily."

Then they did. An hour later.

SOMEWHERE OVER the Ohio Valley, the pilot came back on and drawled that their flight was diverted to Toledo because of a "minor problem."

"Great," growled Remo. "By the time we get there, Joe Camel will have blended in with the other dromedaries."

"We do not even know who we are looking for," Chiun complained, "other than a faceless camel."

From a pocket, Remo brought out a folded sheet of fax paper. It was the FBI file on Yusef Gamal. It included a Wanted poster, showing a blank face with a mailman's cap on it. A nose was sketched in—very prominent but somehow, at the same time, nondescript.

"Not much to go on," Remo muttered.

"I have seen this nose," Chiun murmured. "We are seeking a cattle Arab. A bedouin. I will recognize him when we meet, rest assured."

"How a guy with a name like Joe Camel got work in the post office beats me. You'd think someone would have gotten suspicious."

"I have read that these messengers are increasingly disgruntled, Remo. Why is this?"

"Search me. The way the country is going these days, killing your boss is a form of severance benefit."

On the ground in Toledo, they were put off the plane. Only then did it get out that a mail-bomb threat had been called against their flight.

A new plane was rolled up to the gate while the old one sat on a side runway being searched by ATF agents wearing blue bomb-disposal bunny suits.

While they were waiting to board, a flight from Oklahoma City landed. Remo noticed it and said, "You know, if I were Joe Camel, I'd be on the first flight out of town."

"You are correct, Remo. Let us quietly observe those who emerge from the aircraft. Perhaps our keen eyes will detect the one we seek."

At first it seemed like an ordinary crowd of people. Finally the last man stepped off the jetway. He wore the severe black of a Hasidic Jew.

"Well, I guess Camel wasn't on that flight," said Remo.

"None of those were cattle Arabs," Chiun agreed.

As they watched the crowd disperse, a high voice floated above the airport murmur.

Remo tracked the commotion with his ears, his eye falling almost automatically on two men walking out of the airport gesturing animatedly and arguing at the top of their lungs. One was the Hasidic Jew, and the other was a red-haired man who had been waiting in the crowd.

"Listen, Remo," Chiun said quietly.

"To what? I can't understand a word."

"That man is speaking Arabic."

"Yeah? What's he saying?"

"He is calling the other man a Jew."

"The guy in black?"

"The Hasid, yes. The other is reviling him for being a Jew."

"Well, he is, isn't he?"

"Yes, but the way the man is speaking, it is a curse, not a compliment."

"That redheaded guy doesn't look Arabic to me."

"He is not. He is an Egyptian, tainted by Crusader blood."

"Well, he can't be our man. He didn't get off the Oklahoma plane."

Chiun's eyes narrowed. Then the pair disappeared out the door.

Their new flight was called, and they were soon back aboard. With a sinking feeling, Remo noticed that the first-class stewardess from the last flight was now a coach stewardess on this one.

"I have a message from the Japanese tourist in first class," she purred, speaking to Remo and Chiun at once.

"I do not wish to hear it," said Chiun.

Addressing Remo, she said, "To you, he said, *Domo arrigato.*"

"That means 'thank you,'" translated Chiun.

"And to you he said..." She lowered her voice, whispering a single word.

"What! He said that! To me!"

"Take it easy, Chiun. Simmer down. What'd he say?"

"It is an insult."

"Fine. You were insulted. Take it easy. I'd like to get to Oklahoma City without being held up on murder charges."

"Yes, but only because the needs of the Emperor demand it, do I endure such abuse."

Halfway to Oklahoma City, Remo turned to the Master of Sinanju and asked, "So, fess up. What'd he say?"

Chiun made a distasteful face.

"It is a very grave insult Japanese fling at one another. I am astonished that *jokabare* would have the temerity to cast it at me."

"Okay, so what's it mean?"

"'Your honorable self.'"

Remo blinked. "That sounds like a compliment to me."

"It is not. It is very sarcastic and insulting, coming as it does from Japanese lips."

Remo shrugged. "If you say so."

"You do not understand the Japanese mind, Remo. They live out their lives in terrible frustration because they know they can never be Korean. It grates upon them."

"Must be hard," Remo said dryly.

Chiun nodded. "On the way out, I will get him back."

"Listen, it was bad enough you jammed his film down his throat. Just leave it alone."

"I will call him an even worse name," Chiun confided.

"Like what?"

Chiun rattled off a mouthful of Japanese Remo couldn't sort out into consonants or vowels.

"What's that mean?"

"'Your mother's belly button pokes out.'"

"Your mother is an outie?"

"It is a very bad thing to say to a Japanese."

Remo swallowed his emerging smile. "It's your neck. If you want to stick it out like that, go ahead. Let's hope he doesn't go postal."

"I do not understand this going postal. This disgruntledness. Why is this, Remo?"

"Maybe if we finally get to the Oklahoma City post office, we'll both know."

THE OKLAHOMA CITY post office still bore a few scars from the 1995 explosion of the Alfred P. Murrah building only a few blocks away, Remo saw as the cab dropped them off. At the same time, another cab dropped off a petite blond woman clutching an oversize shoulder bag. She hurried into the building, looking as if witches were chasing her.

"Behold, Remo—a postal worker."

"How can you tell?"

"Observe the frightened cast of the face, the nervous, erratic gestures. This one is clearly on the verge of posting someone or something."

"You mean going postal, and I think she's just in a hurry, Little Father."

As they were going in, the blond woman suddenly came spilling out. She did not look happy.

One heel caught on a step, and she went pitching forward. Remo caught her. And caught a clear look at her delicate-featured face.

"Don't I know you?" Remo asked, setting her on her feet.

She shook her blond shag, and every hair fell back into place as if individually trained.

"No. You never saw me before," she said distractedly. She avoided their eyes guiltily.

Remo looked closely. "I know that voice."

"I'm not from around here."

"I, too, recognize the voice," said Chiun, stroking his beard thoughtfully.

They studied her thin face, her sassy blond shag and red lips. Her nose was perfect, her complexion almost golden. She had the bluest eyes Remo had ever seen.

"You can let go now," she told Remo, pulling away.

A pouty lilt in her voice struck Remo's ear.

"Tamayo Tanaka!" he exploded.

"Who?" the woman said.

"Cut the crap," snapped Remo. "I know that voice."

"Yes," added Chiun. "You are Tamayo Tanaka, and you have turned white."

"Shh. Okay, okay. You got me. I'm on undercover assignment."

"In Oklahoma City? You're a Boston reporter."

"The station sent me to New York City to cover the bombings there, and I made the connection with the courtroom shooting, so I came here. I'm the only reporter covering both angles of the story."

"What is wrong with your eyes?" Chiun asked.

"Nothing."

"They are round. Tamayo Tanaka possesses Japanese eyes."

"Oh, that. Don't tell anyone. But this is my undercover disguise. I dab this gel at the corners of my eyes, and when it dries it stretches them so they look round. But we'll let that be our little secret, okay?"

"You are mad," Chiun retorted. "You are not a Japanese who has turned white! You are a white that has turned Japanese! Why would anyone in their right mind seek to appear so?"

Tamayo Tanaka suddenly wore the look of a trapped animal. Her blue eyes looked in both directions as if seeking the safest escape route.

"I categorically deny being white," she said. "I'm not ashamed of being white—if I was, you understand, which I'm not—but I'm Japanese. Really."

"You're white," Remo insisted.

"And yellow haired," added Chiun.

"Dye," Tamayo said stubbornly as her face reddened.

"I see no roots," said Chiun.

"Okay, okay. Since this isn't my market, what's the difference? My maternal grandmother was one-eighth Japanese. I have a little Japanese blood in me. Enough to get a job in broadcast journalism. I was going nowhere as a blonde."

"Tell that to Diane Sawyer," grunted Remo.

"She made it before Asian anchors became *de rigueur,*" Tamayo spat.

"Looks like it's not working for you today."

"The postmaster is stonewalling. No one is allowed in or out until coffee break is over. Have you ever heard of a post office being shut down for a coffee break? It's a cover-up."

"What about the mail?" asked Remo.

"Get real. Have you ever sent a videotape overnight with these people? You'll be lucky to see it within four days. And those three-day priority mail packages? Five to seven days minimum. Unless it's across town, then add an extra weekend. They don't even *try* to move mail across town on deadline."

"Come on, Little Father. Let's look into this."

"Take this in?" Tamayo asked, hefting her shoulder bag. "My undercover camera's inside. Oh, and my concealed mike. Turn around while I unhook my audio bra rig."

"Forget it," said Remo, brushing past her.

There was a uniformed security guard at the door, and he took up a position blocking the lobby, hand on holstered side arm. He might have been guarding Fort Knox from his cold expression.

"We're on break," the guard said flatly.

"You're not," Remo responded.

"I'm on duty."

"How would you like to be on break?" asked Remo.

"I must ask you to turn around and wait until the doors open again," the guard said stonily.

"They're open. See," said Remo, whose hands blurred toward the guard's gun belt, took hold and spun him around. The gun belt broke at its weakest link—the buckle—and the guard went spinning down the steps to land in a sprawl.

Remo shut the door in his face. Tamayo's face, too. She dropped to one knee and, ripping open her blouse like Clark Kent turning into Superman, said, "Look directly at my cleavage and tell me why this facility is on lock down."

GIRDING HIS PLUMMY SKIRTS, the Master of Sinanju put on a stern face and said, "We must prepare ourselves to enter the domain of the disgruntled."

"I don't think we're going to have any problem," said Remo.

They pushed open the inner doors to the service area and were surprised at the color. The walls were all a very bright pink.

"Someone should talk to the painter," Remo grunted, looking around. "Looks like Zsa Zsa Gabor's bedroom."

The teller windows were empty. But from the back, the aroma of fresh-brewed coffee wafted, and they heard a low, musical humming floating out.

"Sounds like a coffee commercial filming back there," said Remo. Looking around, he spotted the door that said Manager.

"Let's see the guy in charge."

The manager was working the telephone when they barged in. He looked up like a schoolboy who had been surprised picking his nose.

"Who are you?" he demanded.

"Postal inspector," said Remo.

"In a T-shirt?"

"Undercover. This is my partner, who's in deep cover."

Chiun bowed, saying, "The Japanese display my picture in all of their postal offices."

The manager sat back down. "The PG send you?"

"Could be," said Remo, who had no idea who the PG was.

"I think I've got everything under control here. They're on emergency sanity-maintainance coffee break now."

"They sounded pretty happy about it."

"Were they . . . singing?"

"Sounded like humming to me."

"My God. It works. I've got to see this."

They followed the postal manager to the back room, where canvas mail sacks were stretched on old metal frames, mail sat in pink pigeonholes and the entire sorting staff of the Oklahoma city post office lounged about drinking coffee and singing Barry Manilow songs.

"They always this chipper?" asked Remo.

"It's the Prozac in the coffee," the manager confided. "It kicked in like an adrenaline rush."

"You spiked their coffee?"

"I did not. This is USPS-issue coffee rations, laid in for psychological contingencies on orders from the PG himself." He lowered his voice. "Never thought I'd have to deploy it, though."

"What's it doing to them?"

"Prozac raises the serotonin levels."

"What's serotonin?" asked Remo.

"Some kind of soothing chemical produced in the brain, as I hear it. I'm exempt from drinking the stuff. Someone's gotta keep a clear head."

Evidently they were overheard, because one of the postal workers started to improvise a little ditty.

"Serotonin,
"Serotonin,
"Dormez-vous,
"Dormez-vous?"

The others joined in.

"Sonnez les matines!
"Sonnez les matines!
"Mailman mood.
"Mailman mood."

As they launched into their second chorus, Remo pulled out the blank FBI picture of Yusef Gamal and said, "We need you to fill in the blanks on this guy."

"You got the hat right. In fact, it's perfect."

"Thanks," Remo said dryly. "What about the face?"

"Joe only worked here about a year, all told. I don't remember the color of his eyes. Not sure about his hair. He had a pretty ordinary mouth, too."

"In other words, *nada.*"

"Well, he did have what you'd call a pronounced beak. Not like this one here, though."

"Like a falcon or an eagle?" squeaked Chiun.

"More like a camel, actually. It wasn't sharp. It was more bulbous."

From a sleeve of his kimono, the Master of Sinanju extracted a folded sheet of paper, unfolded it delicately and held it up to the postal manager's eyes.

"Such as this?" he asked.

"You know, I never noticed the resemblance before, but that's a right good one. Except for skin color. He was pretty white."

"What's this?" asked Remo, stepping around. Chiun directed the fluttering sheet of colored paper toward him. It was a cigarette ad, Remo saw. He blinked. Then blinked again.

"He looked like Joe Camel?" Remo blurted.

"Yes. More or less."

"What do you mean, more or less?"

"More the nose, less everything else."

"You had a postal worker named Joe Camel who looked like the cigarette character Joe Camel, and when the FBI asked you and your people to describe him all you came up with was a cap?"

"The PG asked us to cooperate as narrowly as possible."

"Let me ask you something. Did this Joe Camel look Middle Eastern or talk with an accent?"

"Sure, he talked funny. He was from New Jersey. They all talk funny out that way."

"But did he look Middle Eastern?"

"No, he looked Jewish. But so do a lot of folks from Jersey."

"Spoken like an Okie from Muskogee," said Remo. "What happens when they find Camel?"

"Not my concern. They always find these canceled stamps with a gun in their mouths. My job is to keep the others from going berserk."

Remo eyed the still-singing postal workers. They were doing a barbershop-quartet rendition of "Please, Mr. Postman" that got so hopelessly mangled in the third verse they gave up and picked up "Take a Letter, Maria" in midchorus.

"Hardly any chance of that now," Remo commented.

"Thank God."

"Getting the mail out will be interesting," added Remo, watching a mail sorter dive in a canvas-sided mail cart and start snoring "The Serotonin Song."

"Mail? We can always deliver the mail somewhere down the road. Preserving service cohesion is the priority today."

"Where does Gamal live?" Remo asked the postal manager.

"Over in Moore. You can't miss the place. FBI has it staked out like an anthill."

"Thanks," said Remo, walking out to the strains of "Message from Michael" as paper airplanes made from undelivered mail crisscrossed the air.

OUTSIDE they were followed by Tamayo Tanaka, who demanded, "What did you find out?"

"Prozac is good for the nerves," grunted Remo.

"I take Zoloft," Tamayo said. "It's great. Not only do I wake up humming, but I have daily bowel movements."

"Good for you."

"Begone, rice-for-brains. We are busy," said Chiun.

"We could share information."

"What makes you think we have information?"

"You guys are up to something. I can smell intrigue a mile away. Let's pool our facts."

"You first," said Chiun.

"Postal workers go nuts in two states. It's the beginning of the psychological disintegration of the whole postal system."

"What makes you say that?"

"I'm a psycho-journalist. Dual major. Psychology and communications, with a minor in cultural anthropology."

"Sounds like a career strategy," Remo said.

Tamayo yanked a green-covered book from her big bag. "This is your basic psychiatric-case-study book. Tells everything you need to know about any kind of psychotic and how to diagnose him. With this, I was able to discover the deepest, darkest secrets of the postal service.''

They looked at her.

"It's just *riddled* with psychotics,'' hissed Tamayo.

"Where do you get that?'' demanded Remo.

"From this book. According to this, psychotics are drawn to regimented and highly structured environments. Like the police, the military and the post office.''

"Yeah?''

"These guys all look, act and behave normally. Until you hit their specific area of paranoia. Then they go off. We psych majors call them land-mine personalities because they suffer from explosive personality disorder. Say an ordinary postal worker is on his rounds and he keeps stepping in dog pooh. It can happen once in a blue moon, and he'd be okay. But when it happens every week over three months, then, say, every two weeks, and then one day he steps in two different dog turds. Snap! Just like that, he suffers a psychotic break. Completely decompensates. Grabs up his trusty shotgun and blows away all his co-workers.''

"Why not shoot dogs?'' Remo wondered aloud.

"Because he's a postal worker, and once they go off, all rationality flies out the window. Don't you watch the news?''

"Sounds farfetched,'' said Remo, looking around for a pay phone.

"Did you know that Son of Sam was a postal worker?''

"I think I heard that.''

"And that creepy fat guy on *'Seinfeld,'* he's a postal worker, too.''

"That isn't reality."

"And Son of Sam was? The man took his orders from a dog that wasn't even his. Think of it. The way they run the postal service these days, they're practically breeding Son of Sams. If America doesn't get a grip on the mail system, we could all be massacred. Is that a story or what?"

"It's a load of crap."

"Yes," said Chiun, "it is bullock manure. You are speaking idiocy. None of these things explain what has happened."

"Then you explain it," retorted Tamayo.

"Muhammadans have—"

"Don't say it, Chiun—" Remo warned.

"—infiltrated the post office."

"Muhammadans? What are they?"

"For us to know and you to find out," said Remo, pulling the Master of Sinanju away.

Down the street, Remo found a pay phone. "Did you have to spill the beans?" he complained.

Chiun composed his expression. "They are true beans. Why should I not spill them?"

"We don't want her to cause a nationwide panic by going on the air with that story."

"Why would Muhammadans cause more panic than gruntless mailmen?"

"Actually it might cause less," Remo admitted. "But we don't want to blow our investigation."

Dialing Folcroft, Remo got Smith on the line. "Smitty, you'll never believe this. The local post office is feeding its employees Prozac to calm them down. They got the walls painted pink, too. And we know how *that* works."

"What about Joe Camel?" asked Smith.

"Can your computers take that blank face and superimpose another? Kinda morph them into a human face?"

"Yes."

"Good. Take one of those Joe Camel cigarette ads, paste the camel's face into the blank spot, then try to make him look as human as you can."

The line was dead for possibly fifteen seconds.

"That is not funny," Smith said tartly.

"And I am not joking. We showed the blank FBI poster to the local postal manager, and all he could remember was that the guy had a nose like a camel. That was when Chiun whipped out a magazine, and the manager said—I swear to God—'That's him.' Hey, Chiun, where'd you get that ad anyway?"

"From a magazine on the airplane."

"Are you telling me that Yusef Gamal looks like the Joe Camel of the cigarette advertisements?" Smith asked.

"At least close enough to give us something to work with. Try what I said and give it to the FBI. How's it going on your end?"

"I have alerted FBI branch offices to the identities and whereabouts of the other conspirators on the Gates of Paradise bulletin board. The roundup has begun."

"How'd you find them so quick?"

"Their Gates of Paradise user names turn out to be the names by which they are operating in this country."

"Yeah . . . ?"

"Most of them are listed in their local phone directories," added Smith.

Remo grunted. "Sounds like the World Trade Center screwups all over again."

"We cannot underestimate these people," Smith warned.

"Think picking them up will be as simple as that?"

"We can only hope."

Just then a single beep came over the line.

"Hold the line, please," said Smith, his voice turning tense. Remo recognized the sound of Smith's computer issuing a warning bulletin.

Smith's tone was urgent when it came back. "Remo, it appears that we have something. A SWAT team has cornered one of the suspect terrorists near the South Postal Annex in Boston. The man is up on the roof of South Station and will not come down. He is heavily armed."

"Can't they just pick him off?"

"That is what I am afraid of. I do not want him picked off before he can talk. We need to know who controls this terror group. You and Chiun fly to Boston."

"Let's hope we'll be on time," Remo said.

"His name is Mohamet Ali."

"No kidding. What do we do with him after we're done squeezing out information?"

"If the roundup goes well, his usefulness will be over once he talks," Smith said coldly.

18

The mosque was a pristine vision of white stone capped by an alabaster dome. Two lofty minarets lifted to the heathen, unclean sky of Greenburg, Ohio. Mosaic tiles trimmed its supreme beauty.

All this, Yusef Gamal saw as the Egyptian who was tainted with Crusader blood and might or might not be a secret Copt drove him up the winding access road.

The road was immaculate. All was immaculate. There was only one strange thing.

The mosque appeared empty of all life. No gardeners tended the green grounds. No light showed anywhere, though it was growing dusky. It might have been deserted.

And there was something else, which Yusef could not put his finger on. It was there, but it was hidden. It was palpable, but it was also ineffable.

"What is this place called?"

"Al-Bahlawan Mosque," he was told.

"A good name."

"An Islamic name," the red Egyptian agreed as the car rolled to a stop and it was time to get out.

"Why have I not heard of this mosque?"

"You will be told this."

"This is the greatest, most magnificent mosque in all of Christendom," Yusef marveled. "I have never seen its equal outside of the Holy Land."

"It is not a place of worship," Jihad Jones snapped.

"Is it not a mosque? Does it not possess magnificent minarets pointing the way to Paradise?"

"Yes, yes."

"Then why is Allah not worshiped within? Tell me this."

"I need tell you nothing, Jew. Except that Allah is served in other fashions by this mosque."

And because he never again wanted to be called a Jew by a man he suspected of being a Copt, Yusef Gamal ceased his questions. He was becoming very thin-skinned about this Jewish question. Also his side-lock-festooned wig itched, and he desired to remove the entire despised costume.

Inside, there was more magnificence. Arabesques. High ceilings. The clean smell Yusef always associated with the mosques of his homeland. Except here the smell was somehow...dead.

After they had removed their shoes and performed the ritual washing, they were greeted by Sargon, the Persian aide to the Deaf Mullah.

"As-salamu'alaykum."

"Peace be upon you," they returned in respectful Arabic.

"You are expected, for you have done well."

Yusef turned on the Egyptian, Jihad Jones. "See? I have done well. I am not to be killed."

"My cousin's carnage was better than your carnage," the other sneered. "And my carnage will exceed his."

"My carnage is not yet complete. You will see. The Deaf Mullah has further work for me."

"He has further work for *both* of you," said Sargon the Persian.

"If I am to meet the Deaf Mullah, I must rid myself of these offensive garments," Yusef protested.

"Proper attire awaits both of you," said Sargon.

Yusef did not know what this meant. Jihad Jones looked down at his own Western clothes and looked vaguely embarrassed.

"What is wrong with my attire?" he wondered aloud.

"It is unsuitable for the work that lies ahead of you."

"He means you dress like a Cross-worshiper," Yusef sneered.

"I spit upon you and your lies!"

But to himself, Yusef only smiled. He had gotten under the Egyptian's thick red skin.

IN A CHAMBER that looked as antiseptic as a hospital operating room, they were given strange garments of one piece. They were green, and the Western-style fly zipped up from crotch to collar.

"See?" said Yusef, pointing proudly. "This is an Arab's fly. For my tool is an Arab's tool."

"My fly is also large," Jihad Jones protested.

"It is not the same as having a large tool. Obviously your fly is only a disguise to convince unbelievers you are not Egyptian."

And so angered did Jihad Jones become that he whipped out his tool to prove the lie to Yusef's words. Yusef met his thrust with a matching one of his own.

"I win," said the Egyptian.

"Only because you have coaxed its girth by rubbing," Yusef accused.

"This is its natural size."

"And you are a natural liar!"

Sargon barked, "Enough! Zip your flies and your mouths both. The Deaf Mullah awaits."

In silence, they donned black boots and were given green checkered *kaffiyehs* to wear around their necks.

Yusef looked his *kaffiyeh* over, very pleased with its length. It would be large enough to conceal his offensive-to-Muslims nose. This was good. Perhaps now he would obtain respect from this penis-envying Egyptian.

They were taken to a room where the air was cool and the light was weak. It was guarded within and without by burly Afghan warriors who held AK-47 rifles, while curved scimitars were thrust into the sashes of their native costumes. They stood like fierce statues whose eyes were black points of malevolence.

"*Mujahideen* from the Afghan organization called Taliban," Sargon explained.

Yusef nodded. "Taliban" meant "Seekers of the Light." Such men as these had broken the back of the Russian Bear.

The Deaf Mullah sat in the chevron-shaped niche behind a partition of wavery green glass the color of the Red Sea in fall.

At their approach, he lifted his ear trumpet and placed it against his right ear, a pale, wavering shadow.

"*As-salamu'alaykum,* my *shuhada,*" the Deaf One intoned.

Yusef Gamal and Jihad Jones knelt on the rugs that were placed before the Deaf Mullah for that purpose, their hearts quickening. They had been called *shu-hada,* a title bequeathed only on martyrs en route to Paradise.

"You have done Allah's good work," the Deaf Mullah added.

"Thank you, *Amir al-mu'minin,*" they said in unison, using the preferred honorific meaning "Commander of the Faithful."

"But there is work yet to be done."

"I am ready," said Jihad Jones.

"I am more ready than this dog," Yusef spat.

"We will have peace in this place of peace while we talk of the destruction of this corrupt and infidel nation."

Yusef composed himself, resting his hands on his knees. Jihad Jones did the same, but Yusef saw with ill-concealed satisfaction that his posture was poor.

"Today we have restored the fear of Allah into the heart of the godless nation. This is good. Yet it is but the beginning."

They nodded. These were true words. The Deaf Mullah continued.

"Greater than the fear of jihad is the shadow of what the West calls the Islamic bomb. Long have they feared it. Great is their dread of it. But until this hour, there has been no such thing. It is only a jinni of smoke invoked to frighten the Western mind."

Yusef and Jihad Jones exchanged startled glances.

"Yes, I see it in your faces. It is too good, too wonderful to fall truly upon your believing ears. But it is true. While the Western intelligence organs chase Germans and Poles and Russian scientists, seeking to interdict the forbidden knowledge that will bless Islam with the might to enforce its will through peace and terror, we have in this place, in the heartland of the infidel nation, developed a true Islamic bomb.''

The silence hung in the cool air a long moment.

"For months it has brooded in a secret silence, only awaiting what some call a delivery system. This, too, has been created."

"A delivery system, Holy One?" asked Jihad Jones.

"A missile. The greatest missile in the history of the world."

"It is gigantic?" Yusef queried.

"Long as the tallest minaret. As formidable as—"

"As my Egyptian tool," said Jihad Jones boastfully.

"I will wager it more properly resembles my tool," Yusef insisted.

"You will soon judge for yourself," intoned the Deaf Mullah from behind the green-as-water glass screen. "For you have been chosen as pilot-martyrs."

And in the cool silence of the al-Bahlawan Mosque, Yusef Gamal and Jihad Jones exchanged pleased expressions.

They were going to die.

It was what they had lived for.

19

Ibrahim Suleiman, known to the Chicago post office as Ibrahim Lincoln, awoke to the four-times-repeated cry *"Allahu Akbar"* coming from his always-running personal computer.

Rising from his bed in his nightshirt, he scratched his beard as he padded barefoot in answer to the summons to the dawn prayer. It was afternoon, but since he worked the night shift he was allowed to say the dawn prayer in place of the afternoon prayer and so on all through the day.

The prayer rug faced Mecca. He knelt upon it for many thoughtful minutes.

His prayer done, he sat himself before the terminal whose screen was as green as the walls of his home. He loved green. Not only was it the color of Islam, but it was the perfect antidote to the pink walls of his place of work, which quelled the Islamic fervor in his heart.

Accessing the Gates of Paradise bulletin board, he found he had mail. It was from the Deaf Mullah. Ibrahim's heart skipped a beat.

For the message was tagged The Ordained Hour.

Calling up the message, he read it with avid eyes.

My *shahid,* the day you are fated to enter Paradise has come. Execute the task as instructed.

Make no mistakes, for you are blessed by Allah and guaranteed entry into Paradise for your holy sacrifice, which as a True Believer you know to be no sacrifice at all.

Il-Ya Islam!

Clapping his hands with joy, Ibrahim Lincoln shut down his system for the last time and went to the basement of his home.

There, the great plastic drums were ready. He began filling them with the ammonia-and-fertilizer mixture to create the powerful bombs that would catapult him into the arms of his allotment of seventy-two *houris*. The mixture required constant thickening, but Ibrahim had foreseen that.

Going to the corner, he pulled out a dirty canvas mail bag by its ropelike drawstring and dragged it to the cluster of containers.

Opening it, he lifted the bag with some difficulty, but once he had it in place at the plastic lip, was rewarded by a cascade of old junk mail.

It was ironic, Ibrahim thought, that the very mail he had been entrusted to deliver would intermingle with the witch's brew destined to destroy the post office from where it originated.

It was a very simple operation. The Chicago post office had been built over the eight lanes of the Congress Parkway. It would not even be necessary to crash the mail van into the building itself. Only to stop it at the point on the expressway directly beneath.

The resulting explosion was calculated to lift the grim ten-story building off its support columns and send the broken fragments raining down upon eight lanes of rush-hour traffic.

Raining down upon Ibrahim Lincoln, too, but this was necessary to prevent the spread of what the Deaf Mullah decried as Westoxification. And the blood of the infidel was lawful. For it was written in the Koran that Allah does not love the unbeliever, and further, that idolatry is worse than carnage.

It would be terrible, yes, but making widows and orphans was necessary in order to establish a pure Islamic theocracy upon the ashes of the United States. Besides, Ibrahim Lincoln would be spared the terrible sights and sounds of the dead and maimed because the explosion would catapult him into the waiting arms of the eternal virgins promised to him.

He hoped at least one of them had an oral fixation. Neither of his wives would do this for him, never mind spitting afterward.

Ibrahim Lincoln was contemplating his posthumous sex life when feet pounded down the stairs. The door was thrown open and he was thrown to the floor by a thick wave of men.

One knelt on his back while others pointed guns at him.

"Ibrahim Lincoln?"

"Yes, that is I."

"You are under arrest for the crime of sedition and waging a terroristic campaign against the United States."

"Does this carry the death penalty?" he asked unhappily.

"You bet it does."

"It is not as good as victory, but it is better than nothing," he said as they cuffed him and dragged him to his feet.

20

"I am to be martyred?" Yusef Gamal exclaimed.

"You are both to be martyred," the Deaf Mullah explained in his sweet-as-raisin-tea Persian voice. He was a dappled shadow behind the green glass partition.

The last echoes of his words reverberated in the great al-Bahlawan Mosque in Greenburg, Ohio, before a new sound stirred the dead air.

"I will go first," said Jihad Jones.

"No, I will."

The Deaf Mullah raised a quelling hand. "You will both go together through the true gates of Paradise."

Jihad Jones flared like a struck match. "With this Jew? Never!"

"I would sooner lose half my allotment of *houris*," spat Yusef.

"Allah has willed that you do this, and you will," intoned the Deaf Mullah.

"If Allah wills it, then I will do it," swore Yusef.

Jihad Jones made his face resolute. "Yes. If Allah wills that I have to die in the company of a Jew, then it cannot be avoided. My only solace is that the gates of Paradise will shut behind me and pinch cruelly the Hebrew nose that thinks it will follow me."

"This is an Arabian nose. You wish you possessed a nose as mighty as mine."

"I would rather have a mighty tool than a mighty nose. The *houris* will not supplicate themselves before a mere nose."

"Even with only my nostrils, I could pleasure a thousand times a thousand *houri*," Yusef hissed. "You could not do it if Allah himself blessed your limp Egyptian tool."

"Do not invoke Allah in such a disrespectful manner," the Deaf Mullah snapped. "It is improper."

Yusef subsided.

"You will both be trained to pilot the Fist of Allah, which is the name we have given to the missile that will punish the city we failed to punish before," the Deaf Mullah told them.

"I am ready," said Yusef.

"As am I," swore Jihad Jones.

"You are neither trained nor ready to pilot the Fist of Allah," returned the Deaf Mullah. "Only to die."

"That is what I meant," said Yusef.

"That is what I said, in truth," Jihad Jones added.

"Be patient. Martyrdom will both be yours. But first we must make demands upon the infidel nation."

"Let us demand they exile the Jews, starting with this fool," Jihad Jones suggested fiercely, digging a green elbow into Yusef's unprotected side.

"Better that we demand the unbelievers refer to us as Muslims, not Moslems. I rankle every time this is done. We Muslims are not cruel. We only seek to convert the godless and crush all who resist Islam."

The Deaf Mullah shook his ear trumpet angrily. "Silence! We will first make a demand of the American President."

"He is stubborn."

"But also very weak. And vacillating."

"We will make a demand to show that we have demands. Either they will meet this demand or they will not. If they do not, we will launch the Fist of Allah at the heart of their power."

"And if they do?" Yusef wondered aloud.

"Then we will make another demand, and if they fail to meet this demand, the Fist of Allah will come hurtling into their deepest heart."

"And if they meet this second demand?" asked Yusef.

"Then we will make demand upon demand until we finally demand the impossible," the Deaf Mullah said. "In the end, the Fist of Allah will strike because that is why it exists. To strike. And punish."

"Where is the Fist of Allah?" asked Yusef.

"In a secret place not far from here. You will see it when you have completed your training as pilot-martyrs."

"I live to die!" shouted Yusef.

"I will not be content to die once, but many times for the glory of Islam!" Jihad Jones howled.

"You will die at the appointed hour. First you will train."

His brow furrowing with worry, Yusef raised his hand.

"Will we have to take a test this time?"

The Deaf Mullah shook his bearded head. "No written examination."

"Good. I do not like written examinations."

"There will be no examinations. They are not required by Allah in this thrice-blessed enterprise."

Yusef raised his hand again. "Is cheating allowed?"

"Not in this enterprise."

"Oh," said Yusef Gamal, who hoped he could get by without cheating. He very much wanted to die. For he could not endure the thought of his allotment of *houris* pining away in Paradise without him, unkissed and uncaressed.

21

The flight back to Boston left the gate on schedule, lifted off on schedule and made excellent time to Logan airport.

Over Pennsylvania, the aircraft started its descent, and Remo heard the pilot promise an early arrival.

"We're going to crash," Remo told the Master of Sinanju.

"Why do you say this?" asked Chiun, quickly checking the aluminum wing outside his window for signs of structural weakness.

"On-time performance never happens anymore. God is trying to make our last hours on earth very special."

"Then why does He thrust stewardesses in your face at every turn?"

"He's thinking of the old Remo. In the old days, I never turned down an available stewardess."

"This was before the boon of Sinanju, of course."

"Yeah. Back when I was a cop, stewardesses hardly ever looked twice."

"And now you have them in abundance when you do not wish them. Is life not unfair?"

"Life is very unfair," agreed Remo.

"Therefore, we will not crash," said Chiun, settling the matter.

Over Rhode Island, Tamayo Tanaka came out of first class and hurried to a rear rest room, carrying a makeup case. She pointedly ignored them.

"I can't believe that's the same woman on Channel 4," Remo remarked.

"I cannot believe any white woman would lower herself the way that one does."

"When did white people slip beneath Japanese on the Korean evolutionary scale?"

The Master of Sinanju lifted his jade-capped index finger. "Since I was reduced to wearing this ornament."

Tamayo hogged the rest room for nearly half an hour, and when she came back up the aisle she was dabbing some shiny, slick stuff at the corners of her eyes, which were now as slanted as almonds. Her skin tone was now a dusky ivory, her lips very red.

"Don't look now, but Tamayo just turned Japanese."

"The brazen hussy. Look at her flaunt her false Japaneseness."

"Takes all kinds."

The 727 landed approximately twenty-two minutes early. Deplaning, Remo said, "I'll bet Smith pulled some strings with the FAA to get us here this fast."

There was no sign of Tamayo Tanaka in the airport waiting area. Downstairs the cabstand was backed up, so the Master of Sinanju simply went to the head of the line and stepped into the back of the next taxi to go.

Shrugging, Remo followed.

"Hey! You can't do that!" a familiar voice complained.

And to their dismay, Tamayo Tanaka hopped in with them. "Two can play this game," she said.

"You people all together?" the cabbie demanded through the cloudy Plexiglas partition.

"Yes," said Tamayo.

"No!" snapped Chiun.

"Maybe," said Remo, who alone understood that time was of the essence. "We're going to the main post office."

"South Postal Annex? Where that nut is holding the FBI off?"

"That's where I'm going, too," said Tamayo.

That was enough for the cabbie. He shot out from the curb.

In traffic, Tamayo pulled a cell phone from her purse and called her station.

"I'm almost to the Sumner Tunnel. Be at South Station in ten minutes. What's the latest?"

Remo and Chiun listened in.

"They've still got him treed on top of South Station, Tammy," a voice said.

"Tammy?" said Remo.

"Shh," Tamayo hissed, turning toward the car window. "Is he saying anything?"

"Only that he's disgruntled."

"Maybe I can talk him down."

"If you can, you're better than the FBI Violent Postal Worker Task Force."

"See you in ten," said Tamayo, clicking off.

"Violent Postal Worker Task Force?" said Remo as Tamayo shoved her cell phone into her purse.

"It's new."

"It's an idea whose time has come, I guess," said Remo.

"Are you two going to tell me who you're with?"

"Fraudulent Japanese Squad," sniffed Chiun. "We are new, too."

"There's no law against coaxing a person's recessive genes to the surface."

"There should be," said Chiun. "Christmas cake."

"Christmas cake?" Remo said.

"It is what one calls a Japanese woman who is not married by a certain age, Remo. A very deep insult, which is lost upon this imposter."

"I don't know why you're being so peppery," Tamayo said. "You and my maternal grandmother could be related."

Chiun made a shocked O with his papyrus lips. "Remo, I have been insulted."

"Inadvertently," said Remo.

"Stop this vehicle and deposit this tart-tongued witch."

"No time."

"Then I am getting out," Chiun snapped, grasping the door handle and opening the door a crack.

Reaching over, Remo pulled it shut again. "For Christ's sake, we're almost there."

And then they were there. Because of the crowds, the cab had to drop them off at Atlantic Avenue near the tall aluminum washboard that was the Federal Reserve Building.

It was dusk now. State-police helicopters crisscrossed the sky. Searchlights made hot circles in the ornate sandstone facade of Boston's South Station at the intersection of Atlantic and Summer Street. As they got out, one light fell upon the big green copperfaced clock, which showed exactly 8:22, and then moved up to the resting stone eagle at the roof comb.

A huddled figure in blue and gray withdrew from the light, slipping behind one outstretched stone wing.

"Looks like our man," said Remo.

Chiun nodded. "It will not be a simple thing to capture him living."

"Not with all these witnesses. Let's check in with Smith."

Remo was about to start off when the cabbie demanded his fare.

"Here's our share," said Remo, handing over a twenty.

"I'll need the other one's share, too."

Remo looked around. "Where'd she go?"

"Took off."

"How about that, Chiun? Tammy stiffed us for cab fare."

"We will have our revenge on her and all of her blood," Chiun vowed.

"Not over a twenty," said Remo, handing over another bill.

At a pay phone, Remo checked in with Harold Smith. "Smitty, he's still up on the train-station roof."

"I know. I am monitoring the situation."

"It looks like a parade route here. And that's not counting the FBI, police and media. Any suggestions?"

"According to early reports, the terrorist escaped through the rear exit of the South Postal Annex to the train terminal. From there, he was pursued to the roof."

"Ever hear of the FBI Violent Postal Worker Task Force?"

"Are you making this up?"

"I hear they're trying to talk him down."

"They will fail. They are dealing with a hardened terrorist, not a disgruntled postal worker."

"We go in with all these TV cameras, and we'll be all over the evening news."

"Try the rear route."

"Why not?" said Remo, hanging up.

Skirting Summer Street, they slipped to the South Postal Annex, which was still open but deserted except for a solitary mail clerk. Bypassing the lobby, they walked to the rear of the building. A short path took them to the Amtrak platforms at the rear of South Station.

They scrutinized the blank back end of South Station. Except for a few police officers preoccupied with listening to their shoulder radios, the field was clear.

"Looks like we're in luck," Remo said. "I see a couple of blind spots we can climb."

Chiun looked at his jade nail protector and made a face.

"Can you climb with that thing on?" asked Remo.

"Of course," Chiun said, his voice unconvincing.

"Maybe you should stick it in your pocket so you don't lose it."

"I have no pocket."

"Let's go, then."

Moving to a place where the rude sandstone came all the way to the ground, they started their ascent.

Remo went first. Laying his hands against the rough-textured blocks, he made his palms into shallow suction cups. Then, moving one hand up, he got a toehold. The toe pushed him along. And his other hand suctioned a higher spot on the facade. After that, he was a silent spider moving vertically.

Chiun, following, used his fingernails to gain purchase, assisted by the toes of his sandals. He quickly came even with Remo. Then, in a flutter of plum-colored skirts, he pulled ahead.

"This isn't a race," hissed Remo, noticing that the Master of Sinanju had crooked the nail protector against his palm to keep it safe.

"Then you will not mind losing," Chiun retorted.

They gained the coping at the same time, slithered over and crouched down so they wouldn't be spotted by the rattling helicopters overhead.

A pair of local news helicopters orbited at a much wider periphery, obviously under orders not to venture into sniper range.

Across the roof, a mailman hunkered down behind the spread-winged sandstone eagle, an Uzi cradled in one hand.

"Stay away!" he shouted at the crowd below. "I am disgruntled. I am feeling very disgruntled today. There is no telling what I am capable of in my present state of disgruntledness."

Chiun whispered, "Did you hear that, Remo? He is disgruntled."

"He's going to be a lot worse after we're done with him," Remo growled, starting forward.

They moved like two shadows, avoiding the searchlights of the hovering police choppers, pausing, resuming, backtracking until they were almost on their quarry.

MOHAMET ALI could not believe his evil luck.

He had been sorting mail in his hideous pink cubicle when the two Westerners with bad ties and stone faces came and announced their intentions.

"Mr. Mohamet Ali?" asked one.

"Yes. That is I."

"FBI. We need to speak to you."

Mohamet Ali froze inside. Outwardly he kept his composure. After all, these were not Muslims, but dull Westerners. It would be easy to outwit such stone-headed ones.

"I am speaking to you," he said.

"You'll have to accompany us to headquarters."

"I am very busy here. Can this not wait until I am finished for the day? The mail must go through. Do you not know this?"

"Now," said the senior of the two FBI agents.

"I must get permission from my supervisor. They are very strict about such things here."

"It's been cleared. Let's go, Mr. Ali."

They were taking no nonsense. So, containing his nervousness, Mohamet Ali shrugged and said, "If I must go with you, I must go with you—although I do not not why."

"We'll talk about it downtown."

On the way to the front exit, they walked on either side of him. They did not handcuff him. That was a mistake. For as they approached the exit, Mohamet Ali took his USPS-issue pepper spray from his pocket and turned on the man behind him.

One squirt, and the infidel's godless eyes were stung blind.

The other FBI unbeliever spun in time to accept the bitter taste of defeat in his face, as well.

Mohamet Ali left them shouting and cursing their unjust God as he returned to his work area, took up his Uzi from his locker and ran out the back door—right into the train platform as people were boarding.

His machine pistol was not noticed at first. But his blue sweater with the blue eagle of the USPS was immediately recognized.

The first people he encountered shrank back. A woman screamed. Someone yelled, "Look out, another one's gone postal!"

That was enough to start a panic.

Mohamet Ali found himself caught in a frantic boil of people, all running in different directions, including unwittingly at him.

Like a man who faces a herd of charging elephants, Mohamet Ali lifted his Uzi and triggered a stuttering skyward burst.

"Back! Back away, I tell you!"

That changed the direction of the human herd. People leaped into the empty train track bed and hunkered down.

Mohamet Ali fled into the great concourse of South Station—right into the approaching police officers.

"Stay back!" he cried. "I am disgruntled. I am very disgruntled!"

The police came to a halt, hands on service pistols.

One made calming gestures with his empty hands. "Stay cool, buddy. We won't hurt you. Just lay down your weapon. Okay?"

"I am feeling very disgruntled today. I will not lay down my weapon for any of you."

All shrank from his fearsome words.

"Look, we don't want this to get any worse than it already is."

"Then let me pass. The mail must go through. You cannot impede me, for there are laws against such things. Have you never heard of the crime of interfering with the mail? It is federal. A federal crime—which is the worst of all.''

''Gone nuts for sure,'' one of the policemen muttered.

''Let's talk about this. My name's Bob. What's yours?''

''Mohamet Ali.''

One of the policemen thought this was humorous, and to be taken seriously meant survival if not escape, so, Mohamet Ali set the Uzi to single shot and shot him dead.

The surviving police took him very seriously after that. They tried to kill him, in fact.

Mohamet Ali threw himself behind the big glass newsstand. Firing wildly over his shoulder, he made his way to a door.

The police wanted to shoot him but did not want to shoot other people. So their shots were infrequent and futile.

Mohamet Ali ran upstairs, downstairs and everywhere he ran, he found that there were U.S. police agents blocking his path of escape. From their expressions, they were very frightened of him.

Somehow he found his way to the roof of South Station, where he could command all approaches.

HOURS LATER, with night falling, Mohamet Ali still commanded his destiny—but escape was out of the question. The intersection below was filled to overflowing with infidels of all kinds.

His only hope lay in rescue. If not, then he would martyr himself in some spectacular way designed to bring great credit to the Warriors of Allah, which was the name of his jihad cell.

The trouble was, he could think of no suitable fashion to enter the gates of Paradise, and he possessed but one clip of bullets, now half-spent.

Meanwhile the criminal FBI down below kept trying to talk him down while news reporters shouted exhortations and entreaties from a distance.

"What do you want, Mr. Ali?"

"I wish to escape, fool. Is that not obvious?"

"Why do you want to escape? What do you want to escape from? Is it the pressure?"

"Yes, yes. The pressure of fools such as you."

"Talk to me about the pressure, Mohamet. What is it that's made you unhappy. Can you articulate it?"

"No, I cannot. It is unspeakable!"

"Nothing is so bad it can't be talked about. Come on, fella. Let it all come spilling out. You'll feel better."

Mohamet Ali considered these words. And angling the Uzi around the great decorative stone eagle, shot the fool dead.

After that, they did not try to talk him down. They pulled back and attempted to wait him out.

Infidels began calling for him to jump to his doom. It was a thought. But because infidels desired it, he would refuse their enticing entreaties.

At the hour when Mohamet Ali realized his best option was to suck on the erupting barrel of his own Uzi, his weapon was forcibly extracted from his hands.

Ali was stuck in his crouch, trying to keep his legs from going numb. He heard no approaching footsteps, felt no shadow, but his Uzi jumped from his hands.

Ali's gaze followed his weapon, and he saw a tall man with the shadow-hollowed eyes that made him look like a death's-head.

"Are you crazy!" he hissed. "I am a crazed mailman! Such a one as I am is very, very dangerous."

"Cut the crap. You're only a terrorist. Time to cough up."

And the Westerner gave the captured Uzi a squeeze. The gun actually complained as it twisted up. Then it fell to the roof, clearly maimed by the experience.

"That which you just did was impossible," Mohamet muttered.

"That which I am about to do will hurt very deeply."

"I fear no pain, not even death."

A different voice said, "You will learn fear, then, Muhammadan."

And Ali felt pain such as he had never known. The source seemed to be in the vicinity of his ear. It was very acute, as if the ear were being ripped away with exceeding slowness.

Ali screamed. And screamed some more.

The pain subsided to a dull achiness, and his tearing eyes sought out the source.

An Asian man. A little mummy of a man, impossibly old.

"Who are you, *mummia?*"

"Your doom," intoned the mummy whose eyes glowed in the waxing moonlight. He had the lobe of Mohamet's right ear pinned between his thumb and some sinister green implement of torture capping his forefinger.

"I will tell you nothing," Mohamet said bravely.

"You will divulge the name of him who commands you."

"Never!"

Then the sharp green torture tool pinched more deeply, and the pain returned. Not only to his ear, but to his shoulder and the back of his neck. It was like electricity. Ali understood that Westerners believed the human body to be electric. He had never accepted this heresy until now. Now his entire body felt like a jerking puppet of sparks and short circuits. Very painful ones.

Ali attempted to beseech Allah to help him withstand the wicked agony. But Allah did not hear him. He heard the words coming from his own mouth as if from far away.

"The Deaf Mullah! I serve the Deaf Mullah!"

"Nice try. The Deaf Mullah's in the federal pen. Better coax him harder, Chiun."

The pain became exquisite.

"The Deaf Mullah! By Allah, it is the Deaf Mullah who commands me!"

"Better let me try, Chiun. I think you're off your game."

"I am not. This man cannot resist me."

"He's telling lies."

"No, I swear by the Prophet's beard. No lies. I am a servant of the Deaf Mullah."

Then the hard steel fingers dug into his shoulder. Where the other dispensed electric pain, this one gave bone-breaking agony.

"The Deaf Mullah, by all that is holy! The Deaf Mullah! How can I say it that you will believe me?" Mohamet blubbered painfully.

Then, abruptly all varieties of pain went away.

The two withdrew, hovering some feet away in the dark. Ali could hear their urgent whisperings.

"He's telling the truth," said the tall Westerner with the death's-head face.

"I told you this, but you did not believe me," squeaked the ancient mummy.

"Maybe the Deaf Mullah's getting messages out of the pen."

"This is possible."

Then they returned, two grim moon shadows.

"What's the game plan?" asked the Westerner.

"To visit terror, shed infidel blood and create other anti-Western mischiefs," Mohamet grudgingly admitted. "So that the infidel nation collapses, and the pure flame of Islam flowers in the scorched soil of idolatry. It is really for your own good, for you are truly Muslims under your infidel skins."

"What was your part supposed to be?"

"When I was told, I was to blow things up."

"What things?"

"Whatever things I was told."

"What were you told?"

"I was not told! What manner of terrorist would I be if I fell into enemy hands and told of my missions?"

"A valuable one," said the mummy Asian.

That sunk in.

"Then I am not valuable?" asked Mohamet.

"Not to us," said the Westerner.

"You are going to kill me?"

"Nope. You're going to commit suicide."

"I wish to die. I admit this. Paradise calls to me. But I have no intention of committing suicide unless in doing so I can take infidels with me. That is not my mission. I am a suicide mailman, not a fool.''

''Maybe you're both.''

''I do not see how.''

Then the Westerner picked him up bodily and tossed him over the spread-winged eagle.

Mohamet Ali saw the pavement come rushing up to meet him, and his last conscious thought before his head pulped against hard Western concrete was, *I am too young to die.*

REMO AND CHIUN LEFT the roof by the back way and melted into the surging crowds.

''This may be easier than we thought,'' Remo was saying. ''We know where the Deaf Mullah is. All we have to do is take him out.''

''Smith's missions are never simple,'' Chiun said.

''This one will be.''

''You wish.''

They were moving back to the heart of the commotion at the corner of Atlantic Avenue and Summer Street. As the police pushed back the crowd to clear the way, an ambulance came scooting up Atlantic.

''What is the hurry?'' asked Chiun. ''He is dead.''

''I think they want to scoop him up so the cameras can't telecast every drop of blood.''

''What kind of cretins enjoy the sight of blood?''

''People who don't have to deal with it every day like you and me,'' Remo growled.

Chiun nodded, his hazel eyes roving. Abruptly they narrowed. A hiss escaped his papery lips.

Remo spotted Tamayo Tanaka almost as quickly. She was standing before a mobile microwave TV van, a Channel 4 microphone floating before her sensual red lips.

Her crisp words floated to their ears, thanks to their ability to filter out unwanted sounds and focus on the important.

"...unimpeachable information that the United States Postal Service has been infiltrated by Muslim terrorists bent on global domination, wholesale rapine and pillage and deeds even more unwholesome."

She touched her earphone connection to listen to the on-air anchor.

"Yes, Muslim terrorists. Not militia, as reported elsewhere. Nor a breakaway faction of the postal union."

Remo said to Chiun, "Nice going, Little Father. She's starting a panic."

"It is not my fault," Chiun said stiffly.

Over at the remote truck, Tamayo Tanaka said, "Back to you, Janice," and flipped her mike to a sound man, who had to tackle it so it didn't break on hard pavement.

She was touching up her makeup when Remo and Chiun suddenly appeared on either side of her.

"I thought you needed at least three sources to go on the air with something like that?" Remo demanded.

Tamayo didn't even look up from her compact mirror. "Well, you're two of them."

"Not on the record."

"And I'm the third," she added. "My numbers are good, which translates as automatic credibility."

"What if we're all wrong?" demanded Remo.

"Then a weekend anchor gives a fifteen-second retraction, and all the important careers go on. Are my eyes on straight?"

"One is drooping," Chiun said.

"Which one?"

"Figure it out," said Remo. "By the way, you owe us a twenty for the cab ride."

"It was my cab. You hijacked it. Be thankful I didn't kick you out."

"You know, you remind me of Cheeta Ching."

Tamayo grinned broadly. "She's my hero. I'm going to be the next her."

"The last her was pretty hard to take."

"Fly to any city in the country, and you'll find at least one Asian anchor, all competing to take Cheeta Ching's place in the constellation that is network news. And I just took a major step up the golden ladder."

She pressed her lips together, thought them too red and reached over to take the sound man by the sleeve of his white shirt. The sound man was busy coiling up the mike line and didn't notice he'd been hijacked until Tamayo delicately dabbed her mouth with his sleeve.

"Just right," she said, returning the arm. "Too red, and I look like a Ginza hooker on the make."

"Go with the feeling," said Remo. "Come on, Little Father."

From South Station, it was a straight subway run to Quincy, so they filtered through the emergency-services people and grabbed a Red Line train.

From the North Quincy T stop, it was a short walk home to Castle Sinanju, a converted church.

Remo used the kitchen telephone to report to Harold Smith. "Good news and bad news," said Remo. "Which do you want first?"

"The bad," said Smith.

"No surprise there. A local TV nitwit named Tamayo Tanaka just went public that Muslim terrorists have infiltrated the postal service."

Smith's lemony voice was now sounding startled. "What is the source of her information?"

"I think Chiun can explain that," said Remo, holding the phone down for the Master of Sinanju's convenience.

The Master of Sinanju grabbed the receiver in both hands and squeaked, "It is an impenetrable mystery without explanation. Do not attempt to fathom it lest you succumb to madness."

Remo took the phone back and said, "She got it out of him."

"She has no other sources for this?"

"No, but that doesn't seem to faze her much."

Smith vented a sigh like a creaking barn door. "What is the good news?" he asked.

"The terrorist gave up the name of his mastermind."

"Yes?"

"Ever hear of the Deaf Mullah?"

"He is in prison."

"So is John Gotti. And I hear he can still get things done with a phone call."

"This is very useful," said Smith. "If we isolate the Deaf Mullah from outside contact, we can hobble this conspiracy overnight."

"How's the roundup going?"

"The FBI has in custody seven of the principal suspects."

"That's a good dent. Anything we can do on this end?"

"Stand by. I am working on the composite sketch of Joe Camel."

"This is one terrorist I'd like to see in the flesh," Remo grunted.

"This may yet happen," said Smith, terminating the call.

Replacing the receiver, Remo said, "What say we catch up with the events of the day?"

"Only if we watch the proper Woo," Chiun said thinly.

"After Tamayo Tanaka," said Remo, "I'll take any Woo I can get."

22

In his private quarters in the al-Bahlawan Mosque in the upper reaches of Ohiostan, the Deaf Mullah sat before his computer terminal, his ear trumpet resting on the carpet beside him, his loyal Afghan guards arrayed outside, with their Russian rifles and their sharp scimitars.

Here was the perfect method of communications with his network of *mujahideen*. Especially for one to whom the entire world of sound rang and rang. Tinnitus, the Red Cresent doctors had called it. The result of the premature explosion of a bomb meant for the godless modern pharaoh of Egypt. Lies. It was the voice of Allah, believed the Deaf Mullah, to whom the incessant hardship was a spur to press forward his mission on earth.

The nightly contacts were coming in now, from Chicagostan, from Washingtonstan, from Los Angelestan—all major cities where his *mujahideen* could wreak great, Allah-blessed terror and destruction.

And it had only begun.

The message from Al Islam in Philadelphiastan was simple: "I await the call to arms."

"Patience," typed the Deaf Mullah. "Patience."

"When will I die with the dignity I deserve?" asked Patrick O'Shaughnessy O'Mecca in Washingtonstan.

"When Allah wills the time is correct," returned the Deaf Mullah.

There was no contact from Ibrahim Lincoln in Chicagostan, who was to have martyred himself by now. But he was often late, working the night shift as he did. Nor did Mohamet Ali in Bostonstan sign on at the ordained hour.

Time passed as the Deaf Mullah sat before his personal computer. It dragged.

At length, the computer dinged and the electronic muezzin called him to prayer.

Shifting to his prayer rug, he faced Mecca and indulged in contemplation and the evening prayer.

When he was done, the beard of the Deaf Mullah bristled at the absence of contact from many of his messengers.

After such a day of triumph, where were they? he thought bitterly. Were they men—or women afraid of what had been unleashed in Allah's name?

A message popped onto the screen from Abd Alhazred. It was tagged, Difficulties.

Punching it up, the Deaf Mullah read with dark, eager eyes.

"Mohamet in Boston martyred himself," the message began.

"How can that be?" the Deaf Mullah typed back. "It was not yet ordained."

"The criminal FBI found him out, and to avoid capture he martyred himself. It is on all the newses."

"The only news that matters comes from Allah, on whom all blessings are meet," typed the Deaf Mullah furiously.

"Are we discovered?"

"How could that be?" returned the Deaf Mullah.

"I see no word from many of our brethren."

"They are late. But they will post at the appointed hour, *inshallah.*"

But the hours passed, and there was no word from the missing. This was grave, the Deaf Mullah thought. This was very grave.

He considered. It was approaching the hour that the first demand was to be made. This demand had yet to be decided upon.

Perhaps the demand would be freedom for the missing, if they had fallen into godless hands.

No, that would indicate weakness, as well as show that the small group of martyrs were important in and of themselves. Better the infidel nation believe they had captured but a small number of a great many.

Then what demand would be made? What was worthy in the eyes of Allah?

The Deaf Mullah stared into the growing green screen of his Gates of Paradise network with its electronic minarets, praying to Allah to provide guidance.

It must be something that would be easy for the infidel to accede to. A political victory, not a military one. One that would show the Islamic world it was possible to foil the Great Satan, America.

As if in answer, a message popped onto the screen from Sid el-Cid, truly Siddiq el-Siddiq, and the heading was The Hypocrite Ghula Has Come!

A thin smile split the frizzled beard of the Deaf Mullah. Yes, this was the victory required.

Leaning into his keyboard, he began typing the demand that with the touch of a button would be automatically faxed to the FBI in Washingtonstan, as well as to all major news organs.

By midnight it would be the topic of "Nightmir-ror."

And this was only the end of the first day of the war against the infidel nation.

23

The fax rolled out of a machine in the Pennsylvania Avenue headquarters of the Federal Bureau of Investigation in Washington, D.C., and sat unnoticed in the tray of a plain paper Sharp faxphone as the director of the FBI tried to figure out what the hell was going on in his district offices.

"Who gave the order to arrest that subject in Boston?" he demanded of the agent in charge of the Boston branch of the FBI.

"Sir, we received a transmission this evening to pick up the subject, Mohamet Ali."

"The *boxer?*"

"This Mohamet Ali is spelled differently, sir."

"Who authorized that pickup order?"

"An ASAC named Smith, out of your office."

"First name?" asked the director, thinking assistant special agents in charge were as numerous as VPs at IBM.

"I'm looking at the transmittal order now, and there's no first name. Just a squiggle."

"What kind of a squiggle? Is it an initial? Can you make out an initial?"

"No, it's just a—squiggle."

"Can you make out any letter? Does the squiggle end on a recognizable letter?"

"Not that I can recognize."

"We have a dead postal worker on our hands, the major media outlets want to know why this man was picked up, I'm hearing from other branches that we have better than a half-dozen postal workers in custody and no one can tell me why."

"You should ask this Smith, sir."

"Which Smith? Do you have an idea how many Smiths there are down here?"

"We have a few here in Boston, too."

"All press releases and other public statements must be cleared through my office. Is that understood?"

"Yes, Mr. Director."

The director of the FBI hung up the telephone and asked himself how this was possible. At the CIA, rogue elements pulled this kind of shit all the time. Not at the Bureau. It just wasn't done.

Fortunately only the Boston incident had made news and only because the arresting agents had bungled the job. Whatever it was.

The intercom buzzed.

"St. Louis office for you, Director."

"Put him through."

"This is St. Louis Bureau Chief McBain, Mr. Director. Am I to understand we are to hold this suspect indefinitely?"

"I'm not telling you to do that," the director snapped.

"Do we release him?"

"No, don't do that, either. That was an off-the-record suggestion, by the way."

"I don't understand. What was the purpose of picking up this individual?"

"As soon as I have that nailed down, you'll receive further instructions," the director growled.

"I have orders to pick up and hold a USPS employee named Sal Adin for interrogation. What I need to know is who is to interrogate this subject and on what matter?"

"He's a postal worker, isn't he?"

"A letter carrier."

"We have mailmen going postal all across the country," the director bit out. "That's reason enough for now. Just keep the bastard on ice until I have further instructions for you."

"Yes, Mr. Director."

The director of the FBI slammed down the phone, wondering if the head of the Bureau of Alcohol, Tobacco and Firearms had anything to do with this PR disaster.

A moment later, he forgot all about ATF.

"This just came in," said his secretary, dropping a sheet of paper on his desk. "It looks important."

The director picked up the sheet and scanned it briefly. It had been a long day, so he didn't really take in the sense of the text at first, just the disconnected words themselves.

He had to read it a second time before the cobwebs melted from his fatigued brain.

"Oh, my God!" he said.

DR. HAROLD W. SMITH had computer taps on all levels of official Washington. If a fax came into the FBI, CIA, NSA or any of a number of official U.S. agencies, the transmission was intercepted and a duplicate fax was created in Smith's vast CURE data base.

Smith had his graphics program up and running and was meticulously filling in the blank areas of the FBI Joe Camel Wanted poster with an ad for Camel cigarettes. At first the brown cartoon face looked ridiculous. Then Smith ordered the automatic morphing program to anthropomorphize the image.

The nose receded, the eyes became humanlike and other features fluidly reconfigured what had been an exaggerated cartoon into a passable representation of a human being with a very pronounced, camel-like nose.

Since the transformation ended up as a line-drawn sketch, there was no need to concern himself with the niceties of hair and eye color. Once he had the image developed, Smith transmitted it to FBI field offices all over the country.

That task had been completed when the automatic program that captured incoming faxes began beeping. All at once.

Smith knew without checking what it meant.

Someone was simultaneously sending an important fax to official Washington.

Punching up the FBI faxfile intercept, Smith brought the text to his desktop screen:

The Islamic Front for the American Postal Worker's Union today decrees the following demandment upon the Infidel Nation:

That the apostate Abeer Ghula be barred forever from bringing her counter-Islamic poison to the shores of the Great Satan, otherwise America.

If the hypocrite Ghula steps onto American soil, she will be destroyed and a second wave of terror will be inflicted upon the Infidel Nation.

The first wave of terror you have experienced on this the dawning day of our glory.

Fail not to heed this warning, for there shall be no other. The Messengers of Muhammad are everywhere, their faces secret, their targets unknown and undiscoverable by you. We can strike anywhere and everywhere, and now that the Great Satan knows this, he cannot risk further action.

Il-Ya Islam!

Smith frowned. This was strange. He had expected a demand. And he knew what the demand had to be. The only demand that made sense.

If, as Remo and Chiun had determined in Boston, the terror group took their orders from and worked on behalf of the Deaf Mullah, the only logical first demand would be freedom for the Deaf Mullah.

If not that, then surely they would have sought the freedom of their recently captured terror agents.

Perhaps, thought Smith, they hadn't realized they had lost so many agents. It was conceivable.

But this demand was insignificant. A mere test of American political will.

For whether or not Abeer Ghula came to America or not was not worth arguing about, since among Muslim religious fanatics, she was the most fanatical of all. And the least likely to accomplish her grandiose goals to revive the guttering flame of Islam.

24

Abeer Ghula was the most hated woman in the Muslim world.

She was not hated for her alien faith, because she herself was a Muslim. She was not hated because she was a self-avowed feminist and refused the veil. Nor was she hated because she had undergone two abortions, kept two husbands in simultaneous ignorance and slept with three women of different faiths—activities all expressly forbidden by the Koran.

Although all of these transgressions had caused the thirty-three-year-old former University of Cairo political-history instructor to be chastised and shunned by good Muslims everywhere, the transgression that caused mullahs and sheikhs and other men of faith to issue a religious edict called a *fatwa,* calling for her immediate and unceremonious hanging, was her attempt to revise the Koran to bring it into the '90s.

It was bad enough, this talk of the '90s. For Islam recognized not the '90s but another calendar. It was sufficient insult that Abeer Ghula went through the Koran and randomly changed the proper nouns to their opposite, so that Muhammad became a female and his wives alternately male and female. These could be forgiven as the act of a madwoman, not a heretic and *murtad*—a renegade.

No, the crime of crimes was that in her *Women's Revised Koran,* Abeer Ghula insisted through empirical reasoning that enraged Westerners and Muslims alike that Allah is a woman.

When the sixteen computer-generated copies of her revised Koran were confiscated and destroyed, Abeer Ghula went into hiding and wrote "Allah Is a Woman."

A copy went out on the Internet and was published in Great Britain, and from there it radiated out like a broadcast of poisonous dandelion seeds.

That was when the Grand Ayatollah in Iran issued his *fatwa.*

Abeer Ghula issued one of her own. She told the world that the Grand Ayatollah in Iran could eat her pubic hair and swallow it dry.

The Grand Ayatollah issued a codical to the *fatwa*—hitherto unheard of in Islam—that while being hanged from the neck, the atheist Abeer Ghula must be stoned and clubbed naked.

Abeer Ghula transmitted a public entreaty to Um Allaha—her name for Allah—that the Grand Ayatollah's penis fall off the next time he took a squat.

Islamic radicals throughout Egypt hunted in vain for Abeer Ghula. Her face was plastered on walls, placards and transmitted through all available communications links. Rewards were offered for her head. Would-be martyrs were promised instant and unquestioned access to Paradise if they were to perish in the act of snuffing out the apostate Ghula. The beleaguered Egyptian government, sensitized to the issue, posted her face at all airports and border crossings in hopes of preventing her from leaving the country. They had no stomach to prosecute her or hand her over to an Islamic court. But they knew if she made it to a Western country, she would stir up the Islamic world as no one had since Salman Rushdie.

On the day Abeer Ghula walked into the Cairo airport, ticket to New York City via Paris in hand, no one looked twice at her. No one recognized her golden eyes, which women of her desert tribe possessed, or the thick eyebrows decried by men of faith as a certain sign of Satanic influence.

That was because her supple body swayed under the all-concealing black shroud of a *chador,* and contrary to all oaths she had professed in the past, Abeer Ghula had taken to the veil.

With the tasteful sunglasses, it was the perfect disguise.

No one questioned her or her ticket. Nor asked to see her identification. For no one prevented persons from leaving their home countries much these days. Only entering other lands.

And so she slipped out of Egypt unhindered.

THE CUSTOMS AGENT in New York City saw the tall, veiled apparition as she swayed toward his counter. He saw many veiled women pass through his post lately. It seemed that the Middle East was leaking citizens like a sieve these days.

This woman was unusual because she came unaccompanied. Most veiled Muslim women traveled with husbands or male family members.

"Passport," he ordered.

The woman took hold of her black garment and with a flourish, whipped it up.

It settled on Customs Agent Dan Dimmock's head like a collapsing parachute. He dragged it off his head, sputtering, "What the hell?"

The woman who stood before him now still had on her veil. That was all. Not even a stitch of underwear. Her body was a smoldering, dusky flame dotted by black brushfires.

"I am Abeer Ghula and I have come to America to spread the word of Um Allaha, creator of us all in her infinite wisdom and mercy."

"Um—?"

"Formerly known to you as Allah."

"I don't know anyone by that name."

"You are a Cross-worshiper?"

"Never heard it put that way before."

"Abandon your dead god Issa on his rude cross of misery. Um Allaha sends her kisses of love and mercy through me, her true prophet."

"I'll give you a second chance," said Agent Dimmock, amazed at the dark vividness of her jutting nipples. "Put this on and show me your passport, and I won't have you arrested."

"Neither the mullahs nor pharaoh could arrest me. What makes you think you can accomplish this impossible task?"

"Because if you don't have a visa, you're an illegal alien and subject to deportation," Dimmock said patiently.

"Arrest me. See if I care that you do this," Abeer Ghula spat.

"You *want* to be arrested?"

She set her black-nailed hands on her dusky, lyre-like hips defiantly. "It does not matter. I have succeeded in entering America, where I am free to proselytize in the name of Um Allaha.''

"Look, for the last time, do you have a visa or not?"

The woman spun in place, her arms outflung, firm breasts lifting to rubbery bullets as if in reply.

"Do you see a visa?"

"No," Dimmock admitted as an interested crowd gathered. "I guess I have no choice but to detain you for attempting to enter the U.S. illegally."

Abruptly the woman hopped up on the counter and spread her long legs.

"I come to America with my visa firmly clutched in my womanhood. Dare you pluck it out, godless unbeliever?"

"I believe in God," said Dimmock, trying to find a safe place to rest his eyes.

"Do you believe in Um Allaha, Mother of Mothers?"

"Not enough to stick my fingers where they don't belong," said Agent Dimmock as he signaled for INS backup.

THEY MARCHED Abeer Ghula to a detention cell, where the problem of the visa was discussed vigorously.

"She says it's in there," Dimmock told his supervisor.

"Get a matron," his supervisor said.

"We're not sure if we can legally go in, the matron or not."

"She won't cough it up—so to speak?"

"Refused. Dares us to fish around for it."

"What did she say her name was?"

"I didn't catch it. Last name Goola or something like that."

"Goola. Goola. Hold on. Let me call up the watch list of undesirables."

The watch list was checked on a terminal, and the supervisor asked, "First name 'Abeer' by any chance?"

"Yeah, that was it."

"Woman's a flake. Fundamentalist in Egypt want to hang her ass from the highest date palm."

"I'd pay to see that. She's a royal pain in the Allah."

"Let's kick this tarbaby upstairs."

"How far upstairs?"

"Far enough we don't have to mess with it."

The sticky matter of the Muslim heretic Abeer Ghula was kicked up to the head of the Immigration and Naturalization Service, then to the attorney general, who told INS, "I'd like to bring the executive branch into this."

"Fine," said INS, knowing there was no chance of getting a decision on political problems out of that permanent bottleneck.

The INS head was astonished less than an hour later when the attorney general's gravelly woman's voice came back and said, "Release her. We're granting emergency political-prisoner status."

"The President told you to say that?" the INS head sputtered.

"No. The First Lady. I went to the very top."

When she was first informed that she had been granted special-sexual-refugee-immigrant-victim status, Abeer Ghula had one question: "Does the press know of this?"

ABEER GHULA GAVE her first press conference in the nude, with the black *chador* wound around her waist for decorative purposes at the New York headquarters of the National Organization for Women, with a full-court press contingent in attendance.

"Cast down your male gods, your false prophets and your brazen phallic idols. I call upon all American women to embrace Um Allaha, the Mother of Us All, and compel their menfolk to take up the veil and kneel at her gold-painted toes."

A reporter asked, "Are you renouncing Allah?"

"No. I spit in his false face. There is no Allah. He is only a stern stone mask the imams and mullahs cower behind because they are too old to hide behind the skirts of their mother's *chador.*"

"What about the *fatwa?*"

"Up here with the *fatwa,*" said Abeer Ghula, pointing to her naked buttocks.

"Aren't you afraid?" a reporter from *People* asked.

"I am in America now. What can the mullahs do to me now that I enjoy the protection of the Second Commandment?"

"That's 'Thou shalt not take the Lord's name in vain.'"

"No, the other thing."

"That's the right to bear arms. You probably mean the First Amendment of the Constitution."

"I intend to wallow in all amendments as I prosecute my religious freedoms upon all Americans of every faith."

"Have you heard about the Muslim attacks in New York City?"

"I hear about them all the time. I left them behind in Cairo. Such male thunderings are behind me now."

"A jihad group calling itself the Messengers of Muhammad has infiltrated the post office. They're wreaking havoc everywhere."

Abeer Ghula didn't skip a beat. "I demand protection, then. If I am killed, a terrible blow will be struck against freedom of worship, not only here but in other countries where women are repressed by masculine oppression."

"This group has called for you to be sent back to Cairo in irons."

"They cannot compel me to go," Abeer sneered.

"They've made the demand on the White House."

"The Very First Lady has cast the iron shadow of her womanly protection over my mission."

"What happens if she's voted out of office next month?"

"They would not dare!" Abeer flared, gold eyes flashing.

"Happens almost every four years like clockwork," a reporter said dryly.

And before the eyes of the assembled press, Abeer Ghula paled from her shiny forehead to her ebony toenails.

Without another word, she unwound her *chador* and dropped it over her body, covering her face with her trembling hands.

"I am not afraid," she quavered.

25

By 9:00 p.m. the postmaster general thought the worst was over.

There had been no more explosions up in Manhattan. The Oklahoma City situation had died down. They were still looking for the assailant, but no one was reporting his capture, and with luck the SOB would hold out until the New York story had blown over.

Best of all, the President had not called back. He would be easy to wait out. The man was at the end of his term of office, and he still hadn't filled some empty cabinet posts.

Post offices over the nation were on emergency sanity-maintenance programs. That would bring the mail stream to a near-halt for at least a week, but these days people expected sluggish mail delivery. After all, what did the American public expect for a lousy thirty-two-cent stamp? Personalized service?

The postmaster general was filling his briefcase with rolls of stamps intended as Christmas presents for immediate relatives when his executive secretary buzzed him.

"Boston postmaster on the line."

"Find out what it's about."

The secretary was not long. "A postal worker committed suicide."

"What's with these nervous nellies? I have a huge operation to run. Employees self-destruct every damn week."

"He's saying the man died fleeing FBI custody."

"Find out if he's the shooter from Oklahoma City."

The secretary was back in ten seconds this time. "He doesn't believe so, but he's really anxious to talk to you."

"Take a message. I've had a long day."

Shoveling the last sheets of mint Elvis stamps into his briefcase, the postmaster general of the United States got up and walked past his secretary as she was trying to record the message from the Boston postmaster on a yellow legal pad.

He was almost out the door when the secretary hung up, tore off the top sheet and turned in her seat.

"You might want to read this."

Growling, the postmaster general said, "Read it to me."

"'Local TV station here is reporting that the USPS has been infiltrated by a Muslim terrorist group for the purpose of waging a campaign of terror on entire populace. No further details.'"

The postmaster general froze with his hand on the brass doorknob. His sweat turned cold in his palm.

"Get Boston back on the line. Right away," he barked, whirling back into his office, his long face almost matching his tie in length.

The Boston postmaster was trying to explain himself when the postmaster general cut him off. "You just let the FBI walk off with an employee?"

"They *were* the FBI."

"A branch of the Justice Department. USPS is part of the executive branch. Do I have to tell you what that means, Boston? We report to the President directly. We don't go through that ball-busting arsonist over at Justice."

"It seems un-American to stonewall the FBI."

"If it was good enough for Dick Nixon, it's good enough for me." Calming down, the postmaster general asked, "Did they say why they wanted him?"

"No. Only that one agent was with something called the Violent Postal Worker Task Force and the other was Counterterrorism."

"Violent Postal Worker—"

"Yes. I never heard of it, have you?"

"No, but I guarantee you by the time I'm done, it will be abolished. Is Justice crazy? They can't tar the service with that kind of bureaucratic slander."

"After today I wouldn't be so confident, sir," said Boston dispiritedly. "The man who jumped is on file as Mohamet Ali."

"And you didn't report him?"

"For what? Being a Muslim? We don't disqualify on the basis of religion. He's a citizen and he passed all tests."

"You get back to business, or I'll bust you down to mail sorter. Is that understood?"

"Yes, sir," said Boston.

The postmaster general was in the middle of dictating a firm denial of the Muslim-infiltration rumor when Ned Doppler called.

"Damon, this is Ned," said the crisp voice of the host of "Nightmirror."

"Ned, how are you?" the postmaster general said broadly. He had been a guest on "Nightmirror" over the years. Every time they raised the price of a stamp, as a matter of fact. Took the sting out of it whenever he hearkened back to the halcyon days of the Pony Express and two mail deliveries a day.

"Tonight's topic is the Manhattan bombings, and we'd like to give you the opportunity to present your side of the story."

"I don't have a side. None of those had anything to do with the service."

"We've booked Boston reporter Tamayo Tanaka, who broke the story of the Muslim infiltration of your organization."

"You can't go on the air with that wild rumor! There's no substantiation for any of it!"

"She broadcast it, it's news. Do you want to rebut or not?"

"I do not. It would be irresponsible to give credence to this crap. Do you want to terrify the American public? Do you want to sink the service? Do you, Ned? Do you?"

"No," returned Ned Doppler, cool and crisp as a celery stalk, "but you might be interested to know that highly placed sources at Justice are telling us they are in the middle of a roundup of elements of this jihad group, and a terrorist organization has taken responsibility and promises more strikes if Abeer Ghula isn't deported by tomorrow."

"Who's Abeer Ghula?"

"Imagine a cross between Salman Rushdie and Martha Stewart."

"Is that possible?"

"Why don't you be at the studio at eleven sharp and see? She's a guest, too."

"It doesn't sound like I have a damn choice, do I?" the postmaster general demanded.

Ned Doppler's chuckle was as dry as bone chips settling in a stopped blender. "The making of news is kinda like the manufacture of sausage. Watching the process doesn't make the product go down any better."

Stonefaced, the postmaster general of the United States replaced the receiver and tripped his intercom. "Contact all major city branches. Find out what you can about an FBI roundup of postal employees."

"Yes, sir."

Then the postmaster general sat back in his handsome red leather chair and felt as though he was shriveling inside.

Ten minutes ago, he'd thought the long day was over. Now he understood the night was just getting started.

26

Tamayo Tanaka could hardly contain herself.

She was going to be on network TV. Better than that. On "Nightmirror." Even better than that. On "Nightmirror" during a genuine national crisis. Which meant both Letterman and Leno would be left trailing in the dust of the overnights. Her dust.

It was all she had ever dreamed of.

Which is why Tamayo Tanaka wanted to be extra, extra certain she had her face on perfectly.

It was not easy obliterating her corn-fed white-bread looks every morning. There was the long, slinky black wig, the brown-tinted contacts and the pale golden pancake makeup. But hardest of all was keeping her eyes straight. The damn Mongoloid eye-fold had to be exactly right in both eyes, or she looked cross-eyed or Chinese or worse, like a female Two-Face from that *Batman* movie.

As the cab raced from Dulles Airport to the Washington, D.C., studios of "Nightmirror," Tamayo fussed with her eyes. In the early days of her career, she'd used Scotch transparent tape to effect the transformation. That had been during her pre-broadcast career when she'd discovered that she could earn her way through college by acting in skin flicks.

"A lot of actresses start out this way," she was told by a producer who tried to pick her up in a University of Indiana disco.

"I'm not going into acting, but TV journalism."

"Gloria Steinem once posed for *Playboy*."

"Nice try. She was a Playboy bunny, and it was an undercover assignment. Doesn't count."

"Suit yourself," the producer said, finishing his drink. "I was thinking of casting that cute little Jap trick in the corner anyway."

Tammy Terrill's blue gaze went to the smoky corner where a girl in a flame red slit dress was toying with a Bloody Mary as red as her lips.

"Her? I don't think she'd know how."

"Asian women are more supple anyway. I need a contortionist for this flick. She's gotta be able to blow the male lead while twisted into a pretzel shape."

"Not my department. I'm strictly missionary. Face-to-face, turn over and go to sleep. I have to be up in the morning for the rest of my professional life."

"Too bad," said the producer. "Pays five grand for three days' work—if you can call it work."

Tammy blinked. Five grand was her tuition for a whole quarter. And she was hauling a double major.

She caught herself muttering, "Never work. I do this and it ever gets out, I'm dead in broadcast journalism."

"We can make you look different," said the producer, sensing a chink in her armor.

"How different?" Tammy asked, stirring her C-breeze.

"Just like that almond-eyed fly-teaser over there."

The swizzle stick went spinning out of control. "You can make me *Japanese?*"

"Sure. Our makeup guy once made Roxanne Roeg-Elephante look halfway fuckable. He can work miracles."

"No one will recognize me?"

"Myrna Loy got her start playing Orientals, though not in skin flicks, that's for sure."

"Who?"

The producer beamed like a porcelain knicknack. "See? You just proved my point."

Over the next two years, Tammy Terrill made a half-dozen direct-to-video and pay-per-view films as Suzy Suzuki, including *Jade Crack, Dildo Fury* and her favorite, *Ben-wa Ballbuster,* where she got to lift a guy up by the scruff of his scrotum and drop him bodily into a car crusher—with a little help from the FX department.

No one at the University of Indiana ever caught on.

But when Tammy graduated, doors were slammed in her face everywhere she went.

"What's wrong with me?" she moaned at the end of six months of rejected résumés.

"Take a look around," her TV agent told her. "Deborah Norville's career just crashed, taking the whole perky-young-blonde trend with her."

"How could she? Didn't she know she was the Great Blonde Hope?"

"'Golden Lads and girls all must...' I think you know the rest. Anyway, the hottest thing going now are Asian anchorettes. That leaves you out."

"My maternal grandmother was one-eighth Asian," Tammy ventured.

"What was her last name?"

"Tanaka. They tossed her butt into an internment camp during WWI."

"That was WWII."

"I got the initials right, didn't I?"

"Listen, Tammy, how do you feel about a name change?"

"To what?"

"Tamayo Tanaka. It's legit. The name is in the family, just lying around unexploited. We update your résumé, put you down as Japanese-American and you have your second chance."

"With this hair and these baby blues?"

"Squint."

Tammy squinted. Her face became a cream puff with sapphires for eyes.

"Can you read a cue card like that?"

"I can't even tell if you have one nostril or two."

Her agent sighed. "Well, it was a long shot anyway. Even with a wig, you'd never pass."

"Yeah, that kind of stuff only worked for Myrna Loy."

The agent's glum expression got interested. "Myrna Loy? I remember her. Thirties actress who got her start playing Chinese types. After she drank that well dry, she came out as a Caucasian and had a whole new career."

Their eyes met, collided, ricocheted and locked together with a growing but nervous interest.

"You know, they can do amazing things with makeup these days," Tammy said.

"You'd have to lead a double life," the agent warned.

"I could go undercover as myself!"

"What if you got caught?"

"Then I'd be the story! I'd go through the roof."

"We could sell your story. Sultry Japanese reporter unmasked as corn-fed Iowa farm girl."

"I'm from Indiana," said Tammy.

"Plays just the same in Peoria. Let's give it a whirl. If it doesn't pan out, you're still Tammy Terrill."

"No, I'm going to be the next Cheeta Ching."

Four years and six local markets later, and she was on her way to a face-off with Ned Doppler on "Nightmirror."

"It's the American dream come true," she murmured, touching up her slim eyebrows. "It doesn't matter who you are, you can go anywhere you want in life if you just play by the rules of the moment."

"Eh?" asked the cabbie, who was some kind of Hindu.

"Someday your kind will get their turn," she said, snapping her compact closed.

Then they were at the studio, and it was time for Tamayo Tanaka's moment of truth. More or less.

A network page greeted her inside the studio, and she was taken to a soundproof booth where she was seated on a plain chair. A camera dollied up so close the glassy lens almost kissed the tip of her nose. The tally light wasn't on, so she relaxed and said, "When do I meet Ned?"

"You don't," she was told.

"Ever?"

"You'll be up on the screen with the others so it looks like he's talking to all of you at once," the busy technician explained.

"Where are the others?"

"The booths on either side."

"Shouldn't we be seated all together?"

The technician shook his head. "We did that in the early days. Had too many on-camera punch-outs and hair pulls. Just think of the camera as Ned's face and you'll do fine."

The technician shut the soundproof door before Tamayo thought to ask, "What others?" Didn't she own the story? Who else was there? And how important could they possibly be?

All at once, she could feel the flop-sweat oozing up through her pores, pushing aside her facial makeup. The network lights were a lot hotter than affiliate lights.

THE DIRECTOR OF THE FBI would have given his pension to avoid it all.

"Nightmirror" was no place for the mentally unnimble. He'd seen bureaucrats mousetrapped live and sweating by Ned Doppler more times than he could count. He did not want to be one of them.

But when "Nightmirror" called, even the director of the FBI had to answer. Especially with the nation lurching toward panic and needing answers.

The President of the United States had personally put it to him this way: "You go on."

"The Bureau's investigation is in its earliest stages," he protested. "We'd be at risk of tipping our hand."

"What do you have?"

"We're still sorting it all out, Mr. President. But the mail-truck bomber in New York has been identified from dental records as the suspect in the string of relay-box explosions. Guy named Al Ladeen."

"You go on. Otherwise, I'll have to. And I don't have any more answers than you do."

"Yes, sir," said the director of the FBI, realizing that he had been demoted to sacrificial lamb.

THE POSTMASTER GENERAL took his seat in the remote broadcast booth that was in reality not thirty feet from the set where Ned Doppler nightly deconstructed guests with a twinkle in his eye and a stiletto up his sleeve.

It was a problem. But it wasn't a big problem. All Doppler had was rumor and half-assed reportage.

Damon Post had the two mightiest tools in a bureaucrat's arsenal—the ability to stonewall, and utter and total deniability.

They should be more than enough to hold off the smug bastard for thirty minutes, minus commercials.

Then the strident "Nightmirror" fanfare began, and the red tally light eyed him warningly.

IN THE BELL-TOWER meditation room in their Quincy, Massachusetts, home, Remo Williams and the Master of Sinanju both reached for the clicker at the same time, Remo to switch from the overfed Bev Woo and Chiun to shut off the set for the evening.

"I want you see what they're saying on 'Nightmirror,'" Remo explained.

"It is your bedtime," Chiun argued.

"Smith said to stand by in case we have to fly out on short notice."

"Which is why you need your five hours of sleep."

"I'm not sleepy and I want to know what the latest is, the same as the rest of America."

"I cannot sleep with this machine yodeling, so I will watch with you."

"You just don't want me sneaking a peek at the nice Bev Woo."

"I would tolerate this so long as you do not seek out the false wiles of Tamayo Tanaka."

"Not a chance," said Remo as the "Nightmirror" fanfare started to blare and the cobalt blue computer animation went into its inevitable cycle.

Ned Doppler's puffy face came on.

"Tonight on 'Nightmirror'—Bomb scare. The terror in Manhattan. With me are the postmaster general of the U.S., Damon Post, Gunter Frisch, director of the FBI, and Tamayo Tanaka, the woman who may have broken the story of the bizarre link between a hitherto-unknown terror group and one of the oldest and most respected organs of our government, the United States Postal Service."

"Argh," said the Master of Sinanju, tearing at the cloudy puffs of hair over each ear.

"Let's hope our names don't come up," Remo said unhappily.

"First a recap of the day's events. At approximately 12:20 EST today, simultaneously in Oklahoma City and midtown Manhattan terror struck. The vehicle—men and equipment of your postal service. And tonight in Boston, a postal worker with the vaguely familiar name of Mohamet Ali leaped to his death before TV cameras and a crowd of witnesses. Are these events connected? What does it mean? Joining us in our Washington studio is the man heading the investigation, Gunter Frisch. Mr. Director, what can the FBI tell us?"

"Our investigation is at a sensitive stage, and I would rather not get into details, Ned."

"I understand," Doppler returned smoothly. "We don't want to jeopardize the investigation for ratings, not even for the public's right to know. But I must tell you there are wire-service reports that an FBI roundup of suspect postal workers is under way at this hour."

"I have ordered no such roundup," the director said quickly.

"So that means what? You're denying these reports?"

"My answer stands, Ned."

"Given that a reported eight or nine relay boxes literally blew up in New York City today, could we not assume that postal workers are being looked at?"

"We at FBI overlook no suspects in our efforts to get to the bottom of this matter. I would stress that nothing is being ruled in or out at this juncture."

"On that careful note, I would like to bring the postmaster general into this discussion," Ned Doppler said smoothly.

Damon Post came on the screen, replacing the FBI director.

"Mr. Post? No sense dancing around it. Has the postal service been compromised?"

"Absolutely, categorically not."

"Yet someone planted infernal devices in midtown relay boxes. Someone wearing a letter-carrier uniform burst into an Oklahoma City courtroom and literally massacred some twenty people. I don't have any more facts than you, but come on, it looks bad, doesn't it?"

"I know how it looks, Ned. But we lose master keys to theft from time to time. And letter-carrier uniforms can be purchased through the manufacturer without proof of employment in USPS."

"So you're saying . . . ?"

"Imposters, until proved otherwise. The mail system has not been compromised by militia, Muslims or any other group, as certain irresponsible reports have it."

"But you don't know that, do you?" Doppler prodded.

"I don't know my relay drivers aren't Martians, either. But I don't worry about the possibility."

"Yet in recent years, there have been, to put it charitably, certain violent incidents involving postal workers. Have there not been?"

"Stress is a big part of everyone's lives these days. I run a first-class operation, and in a first-class operation, people have to hustle. Some people just don't hustle well. They crack. We try to keep these things to a minimum."

"You do see a connection between these personnel failures and the events today?"

"None whatsoever."

"And the man who jumped to his death in Boston. What was he? Just another letter carrier who took a swan dive into hard concrete rather than face another irate customer? And not a Muslim terrorist? Tell me."

The postmaster general struggled with his glower. "There are no terrorists in the Boston office," he said tightly. "The American public is perfectly safe."

"Unless they walk past a relay box that just happens to blow up. Or have the bad luck to be standing under a falling postal employee," Ned Doppler suggested with an irritating lack of sarcasm.

"That's not fair, Ned, and you know it. You don't burn down the whole orchard because of a few wormy apples."

"The question of Muslim terrorists aside, what are you doing about the stress level among your people?" Doppler asked.

"We've instituted a broad-based five-year plan to ensure that psychological decompensation levels attrit at a predetermined rate until achieving parity or near-parity with comparable package-delivery companies."

"What's that mean in layman's language?"

"We're weeding out the problematic people."

"So you admit there are problematic workers?"

"There are problematic workers driving school buses and frying up Whoppers," Damon Post said tightly.

"Granted. But you're artfully dodging the issue at hand. Forgive me for putting too fine a point on it, but even if we accept as dubious the proposition there are no terrorists in the postal service, there are Muslims, aren't there?"

"I imagine so. We don't discriminate at USPS."

"Are you looking into the backgrounds of these people, just on the off chance that they, shall we say, studied in the Bekaa Valley?"

"We're migrating in that direction," the postmaster general admitted cautiously. "But I would like to assure the general public that all employees of the postal service are required by law to be U.S. citizens."

"Correct me if I'm wrong, but weren't U.S. citizens behind the Oklahoma City bomb blast last year?" Doppler countered.

"Yes. But they were military wackos."

"I'd like to call your attention to a fax our news department received in the last few hours, purportedly from a group calling itself the Messengers of

Muhammad. I won't read it all, but they hint strongly and unmistakably that the events of today were their work and they are preparing to strike again if Abeer Ghula is allowed to remain in this country.''

"Who's Abeer Ghula?" Remo wondered aloud.

The Master of Sinanju waved the question away.

"I wouldn't put much stock in an anonymous fax," the postmaster general countered brittlely. "Anyone can send a fax."

"And on that note, let me bring in the third person in this mystery, Tamayo Tanaka."

Tamayo Tanaka's sultry face replaced that of the postmaster general.

"It's great being here, Ned," she said.

"Thank you. I only wish the circumstances had been more pleasant."

"I'll take a network debut any way I can get it."

On the screen, Ned Doppler tightened his face and pressed on. "You broke the post-office-terrorist connection before the first faxes were received. What was your source?"

"I'm afraid I'll have to invoke my journalistic prerogatives on that one, Ned. But they are unimpeachable until events suggest otherwise."

Doppler cocked a skeptical eyebrow. "Sounds like you're hedging a little."

"No, I'm not hedging. Just being careful. I trust my sources. I just refuse to name them."

Remo turned to Chiun and said, "Looks like we get to keep our jobs."

"This was never in doubt."

"If she fingered us, we'd be history."

"No, Smith would only alter your plastic face once again."

Touching the tight skin over his high cheekbones, Remo said, "I don't think I have another plastic surgery in me."

"Let me ask you this," Ned Doppler was saying. "Does your information square with what the major news outlets have been getting?"

"I'm a psycho-journalist, Ned, and I can only tell you, based on my knowledge of the psychological profiles of postal workers who snap, that unless something serious is done, and soon, we could be facing a reign of terror that will make what we've seen today look like a third-grade pajama party."

"Is she crazy?" Remo exploded. "She's going to start a panic."

"Why do you say that?" Ned Doppler asked.

"Again I don't want to get into sources, but imagine the deadly combination of trained terrorists and crazed postal workers."

"Well, they have to be one but not the other. I mean, I've never heard of a trained psychotic."

"Ned, this is bigger and juicier than Watergate and O. J. Simpson combined."

An exasperated voice said, "Ned, can I get a word in here?"

The postmaster general's annoyed face popped onto the screen.

"I would like to add my input," the FBI director inserted off camera.

"One at a time. You first, Mr. Post."

"This is outrageous and irresponsible. None of these allegations are true."

"I second that," said the FBI director. "We do not want panic."

"Miss Tanaka?"

"I stand by my sources," Tamayo Tanaka said firmly.

"Is her left eye drooping?" Remo asked Chiun.

"No, her right eye is straightening."

"Looks like the hot lights are decompensating her makeup job."

"If she is unmasked for all the world to see, it will be her own fault, the brazen hussy."

"Shh. I want to hear this."

THE PRESIDENT of the United States didn't want to hear any more. He was watching his reelection plans disintegrating on network television as some New England anchorwoman he'd never even heard of calmly and almost maliciously predict that the American public was risking life and limb every time they mailed a postcard or checked their porch mailbox for bills. And the idiot FBI director and postmaster general were letting her get away with it.

When in the second segment, Ned Doppler got the postmaster general to concede that if the postal service were infiltrated by Muslim terrorists he couldn't take action until they actually committed a crime, the President excused himself from the First Bed and ran to the Lincoln Bedroom to call Harold Smith.

Smith answered on the second ring. "Yes, Mr. President?"

"I'm watching 'Nightmirror' and they're showing the headline for tomorrow's *New York Times*."

"I know," said Smith.

"It reads Postal Apocalypse."

"What if these threats are true?"

"You can deport Abeer Ghula. I believe you have grounds."

"Tell that to the First Nag. She signed on to this."

"It may be that Abeer Ghula could be useful to us."

"How?"

"She is an absolute magnet for the wrath of these people. She may draw them out. We still have a handful of suspects not yet in FBI hands."

"That reminds me. Last time I spoke with the FBI director, he didn't say anything about a roundup. And he's denying it now."

"He has nothing to do with it," Smith said crisply.

"Then who does?"

"I have pulled certain strings."

"You have people in the Bureau?"

"Moles, yes. Informants. But the roundup orders came from this office."

"I would like to know where this office is."

"This information is strictly on a need-to-know basis."

"Can you give me a little hint?" the President wheedled.

"No," Smith said flatly.

"I kinda imagine you in some windowless room on the thirteenth floor of a New York skyscraper that can be gotten into only by a secret door and a keyed elevator."

"You have been reading too many spy novels, Mr. President. I will have my people protect Abeer Ghula. This may buy us time."

"And if it doesn't?"

"One day at a time, Mr. President."

"That's easy for you to say. Nobody gets to reelect you."

"The continuity of this office over successive administrations is built into the charter," Smith said thinly.

"Is that a written charter?"

"No."

"Well, keep me informed."

"Of course," said Smith, who hung up the red telephone and immediately picked up the blue contact telephone with the old rotary dial, which Smith favored because he made fewer mistakes than with a push-button phone.

Remo answered. "What's the latest?"

"You and Chiun will proceed immediately to New York City and the Marriot Marquis Hotel, where you will protect Abeer Ghula from these terrorists."

"What good will that do?"

"She is the most likely target."

"Any sign of Joe Camel?"

"If we are fortunate, the FBI roundup has decimated their ranks, and Camel or one of the other survivors will surface in New York. It will be your job to handle that end."

"What about the Deaf Mullah?"

"I am reliably informed the Deaf Mullah is in solitary confinement and it is impossible for him to communicate with the outside world."

"I don't think that terrorist was lying."

"It is entirely reasonable that he was continuing the Deaf Mullah's mandate for jihad. Question more carefully the next terrorist you encounter."

"Will do."

The line went dead. In his Folcroft office, where he was working late, Harold Smith turned up the sound on the TV screen in time to hear Ned Doppler.

Abeer Ghula had been brought into the discussion. Her sharp, dusky face smoldered at the viewing public.

"I fear no terrorists, for I am under the protection of the Very First Lady and the National Organization of Women, two of the most potent political entities in all of America."

"Is there anything you can tell us about these Messengers of Muhammad?"

"Nothing. There is nothing to tell. Muhammad is a false prophet. I am the new prophet. With those who follow me, I will sweep across the face of America and then the world like an angry ocean, drowning those who do not believe as I do and carrying believers in Um Allaha to Paradise, where women will liberate the enslaved *houris* from the dead Muslim males who rape and enslave them cruelly."

An off-camera voice cut in. "I have something to say, Ned."

"I'm still with Miss Ghula, Miss Tanaka."

"But she doesn't know anything about the terrorists. I do."

"Just a second. Your turn will come."

"She has had her turn," Abeer Ghula spat. "I am speaking now."

"This is my story," Tamayo Tanaka said petulantly.

"And this is my show," countered Ned Doppler. "And according to the little voice in my earpiece, we have to take a break."

The camera captured Doppler's fleshy jack-o'-lantern face.

"I'll be back after this."

"THAT MEANS the show's over," said Remo as they cut to a commercial.

"He said he would be back," Chiun argued.

"He always says that to trick people into watching the last three commercials."

"But he was not done."

"Doesn't matter. He's done."

"We will watch to be certain," said Chiun, confiscating the remote control.

After the commercial break, Ned Doppler's face reappeared. "That's all we have time for tonight. Good of you all to come on 'Nightmirror.'"

Amid the unhappy murmurs from the FBI director and the postmaster general, Tamayo Tanaka's miserable voice said, "Thank you for hosting my network debut."

"Told you so," said Remo, hitting the remote's Off button.

AT FOLCROFT, Harold Smith blinked. Was Tamayo Tanaka's left eye deformed? It looked positively swollen next to the slim, dark almond that was her right.

27

Abeer Ghula woke up in a luxury suite of the Marriot Marquis Hotel in the heart of Manhattan's theater district and kicked the sleeping woman in the bed beside her.

"Get me breakfast."

The woman—Abeer could not recall her name—awoke with a start. She looked about, saw her clothes on the floor and her NOW button on the end table with her watch and slowly remembered who she was and how she had gotten here.

"What did you say?" she asked sleepily.

"I said, 'Get me breakfast, wench.'"

"I'm not your wench."

"You were given to me by NOW to serve my every need. I have had you in bed, and now I would like breakfast in bed."

"I'm strictly security. Call room service."

"You call them."

"I'm not your slave!"

"Yes, you are. You were given to me."

A pungent personal characterization and an oversize pillow came flying in Abeer Ghula's sharp-nosed face.

Whipping it away, she reached over and smacked her erstwhile bed partner in the face.

"That's for your insolence, woman."

The woman grabbed her stung cheek. "I—I thought you loved me."

"I did love you. Last night. Now I am hungry. I love food. You will bring me all I ask, or I will find another who worships my womanly wisdom."

Her lower lip quivering, the woman whimpered, "What do you want?"

"For breakfast, pork. All kinds of pork. Pork is forbidden by Allah, but Um Allaha has decreed it *halam* not *haram*. I will have pork and endless cups of black Turkish coffee. And if you give me these things before my stomach growls, I may allow you to lavish your caresses upon the perfection that is my back. For it aches."

Meekly the white woman left the bed.

"And for lunch, I would like a man," Abeer Ghula called after her.

The woman started. "A *man!*"

"I like men—when I am not in the mood for women. I had two husbands until they discovered each other."

"I can't love a woman who loves men!"

"You will love who I tell you to, or Allaha will turn her scornful back upon you," said Abeer Ghula, turning her own scornful back on the angry, hurt face of the white woman whose name was unimportant because she was only the first white woman Abeer Ghula intended to despoil on the path Um Allaha had chosen for her.

The door slammed angrily, and when the woman from NOW did not return, Abeer Ghula called room service herself.

"I would like pork for breakfast and Turkish coffee."

"Will that be all?"

"Yes. Have it delivered by a blond-haired man with very broad shoulders. We do not have blond-haired men in my homeland. I would like to taste one. Blue eyes are my preference."

But the man who delivered the breakfast tray was neither blond nor blue eyed, and at first Abeer Ghula's eagle eyes flashed in her anger. Then she took another look at him.

"You are not what I asked for."

"I didn't exactly beg for this job, either," he said, wheeling the gleaming service cart to a stop and reaching into his pocket. He had deep-set dark eyes and wrists as thick around as bedposts.

"Remo Clear. FBI."

"I do not understand," said Abeer Ghula, sitting up in bed so that the royal blue covers fell from one dark-nippled breast.

"I'm your bodyguard until further notice."

"Do your duties include pleasing me?"

"Within reason."

"Excellent," said Abeer Ghula, who let the lustrous black cloud of her disheveled hair fall back into the pillows. She whipped the bed clothes away and said, "Pleasure me, my dark infidel."

"Thought you wanted breakfast," said Remo Clear, lifting the trays. He recoiled from the hot, pungent smells.

"What is this stuff?"

"What does it look like?"

"Sausage links, sausage patties, bacon and pork chops smothered in apple sauce. I thought Muslims were forbidden pork."

"Old, outdated Muslims. I am of the new wave of Muslims who will dominate the universe. And I have selected you to be my first male infidel conquest."

"This place smells like you've already worn out that track."

"You are very insolent for a mere Western male. Have you not read that you are soon to be extinct?"

"I'm not the one eating my way to an early coronary."

"I am merely going through a pork phase. Would you like to pork me? Is that not the Western slang?"

"Am I going to have to satisfy you in order to get you off my back?"

"Yes. And I am willing to let you get on my back," said Abeer Ghula, turning over on her back.

"If I don't have a choice," sighed the FBI agent.

Remo Williams had been briefed that Abeer Ghula was going to be a problem and decided the sooner he got the obligatory sex out of the way, the better.

"Put it anywhere you wish to start," she said casually. "I will allow this. After you have climaxed, I will tell you where to put it so that I receive the maximum enjoyment."

"I know exactly where to put it," growled Remo as he ignored the long, arching back and tensed buttocks that were laid out before him and found Abeer Ghula's left wrist. Turning it over, he began tapping.

"What are you doing?" she asked doubtfully.

"Foreplay."

"You are tapping my wrist as if you are bored and you are calling it foreplay?"

"Wait for it," said Remo in a bored tone.

In the middle of this, a knock came at the door.

"Who is it?" asked Remo.

A squeaky voice asked, "You do not recognize my knock? Allow me in."

"Can you wait?"

"Why should I wait?" demanded the Master of Sinanju.

"Because Abeer and I are having sex."

"If you impregnate her, see that it is a boy."

"I don't think she has the stamina to get that far."

"I will never have your child," Abeer Ghula spat into the pillow. "I want your hard maleness, not your seed. I spit your foul-tasting seed back in your unblessed face."

"Let's get past the foreplay before we break out in a cold sweat over the rest," said Remo.

"If I were to become pregnant by you, I would abort the baby."

"No surprise there."

"I would abort the baby and send the dead thing to you in a box to show my contempt for your seed, which had the temerity to grow within my belly."

"Forget my seed. Concentrate on my finger."

"It is in the wrong place. You should be using it to plumb my warm, liquid depths."

"Here it comes," said Remo, varying the rhythm and concentrating on the sensitive nerve in Abeer Ghula's left wrist, very near to her pulse. Remo was tapping in time with the pulse, which was accelerating. That was his cue to switch to a dissynchronous tapping, as the Master of Sinanju had taught him so long ago. It was step one in the thirty-seven steps to bringing a woman to sexual fulfillment. Remo once got a woman to step two before she turned to contented but untouchable jelly.

Six taps in, Abeer Ghula gave a low animal moan and arched her back so sharply the gully over her spine filled with a sudden musky moisture.

"What are you—?"

"Almost finished," said Remo as Abeer's buttocks clenched as if touched by an electric prod and her cloudy black hair began shaking back and forth and back and forth sharply, in the involuntary torment of her approaching ecstasy.

"What is happening?" she screamed.

"It usually helps to take a mouthful of pillow and bite down hard," Remo suggested casually.

"Uhh," said Abeer Ghula, her face contorting in a pure orgasmic rictus.

Then, thrusting her face into the pillow, she vented her sexual pleasure as her body writhed and twisted in the exquisite sexual release caused by the monotonously tapping finger.

A final gasp, and she collapsed as if her bones had melted under her relaxing muscles and skin.

Remo lifted her face from the pillow and turned her head to one side so she wouldn't suffocate by accident and went to the door to let the Master of Sinanju in.

"You are done?" asked Chiun, his wrinkled face tight. He wore stealth black, with thin, deep red piping that would disappear under night conditions.

"Covered her up and everything."

Chiun walked over to the bed and peered at the sleepy face. "Her lips are tight."

"She's a little high-strung."

Chiun regarded Remo with stern disappointment. "I taught you the proper first steps to pleasuring a woman. If you did it correctly, her lips would be parted, her mouth open and her breathing just so. Instead, I see thin lips that are not parted."

"Sue me for malpractice. At least you won't have to hear about how she's going to sweep across America like a flood."

Changing the subject, Chiun said, "I have checked this floor and those above and below."

"Any mailmen?"

"None."

"Good. Because if the Messengers of Muhammad send their guys after her, they're probably going to be wearing letter-carrier blue."

Abruptly Chiun began sniffing the air. "That smell . . ."

"Pork. It was supposed to be breakfast."

"Dispose of it. For the stink of burned pig offends me above all other meat smells."

Because it offended Remo Williams's nostrils, too, he did as the Master of Sinanju bid. Neither of them ate meat except for duck and fish. Down the toilet went the breakfast fixings.

"What happens when she wakes up?" Remo asked, surveying the now-snoring Abeer Ghula.

"You will please her opposite wrist."

"Not me. I did my duty. You take the next trick."

Chiun made a distasteful face. "Let us hope the Messengers of Muhammad strike before then."

28

Patrick O'Shaughnessy O'Mecca was whistling "Peace Train" as he stepped off the Greyhound bus at the Port Authority Terminal. He had been told to take the bus instead of flying, because while buses crashed as readily as aircraft, one could survive a bus accident. Few survived a falling airplane.

Patrick O'Shaughnessy O'Mecca, born Farouk Shazzam, took this as a sign that the Messengers of Muhammad were soon to target American aircraft. He had no knowledge that of the original band of messengers, he was one of the few survivors. For he did not watch "Nightmirror" or any of that Western filth.

So when the e-mail summons to go to New York City came, he did not think it strange. New York City had been targeted the day before. No doubt those True Believers who executed the New York operation were now lying on arabesqued couches, being fanned by *houris* beyond compare, happily deceased.

Now it was Farouk's turn.

He had been told to take his uniform leather bag and other equipment with him but not to wear it.

As he left the busy Port Authority terminal, he could understand why.

The police bomb squad was X-raying a blue collection box just outside the terminal. He himself had to walk around the yellow police tape that cordoned off the area.

Farther down Ninth Avenue, they had a wheeled robot circling an olive-drab relay box. The robot looked like a mechanical dog on wheels, but he understood how such devices worked. This one was sniffing for explosives. If any were found, it would be made to shoot a charge into the box while the bomb squad stood off at a safe distance behind steel body bunkers and other armor.

But there was no bomb in the relay box. Farouk knew this. He had been advised that as long as he was on his holy mission of murder, New York would not explode in whole or part.

It was a wonderful feeling, to be told that New York City was safe only as long as Farouk Shazzam had work to do in it.

Going to the Marriot Marquis Hotel near Times Square, he was confronted at the entrance door by an FBI agent who demanded his hotel-room confirmation number. In the lobby, an ugly woman in black leather and a red beret emblazoned with the letters NOW demanded the same information.

This accomplished, he checked in as Patrick O'Shaughnessy O'Mecca and was given a key. No one questioned him further, for he was neither dressed as a postal worker nor did he look Middle Eastern, although he was a Hashemite born in Jordan. His dark Moorish good looks struck many as quintessentially Black Irish.

The glass capsule elevator took him to the sixteenth floor. When he got off, the corridor was very ordinary, but when he left the area of the elevator bank it became very strange.

The hotel, he saw, was built about a great concrete cathedral-like atrium. The entire center was hollow. It seemed foolish to Farouk, especially with real-estate prices as they were, but many things were strange in the land of the infidel.

The rooms all faced outward, along the square concrete walkway. A low, fern-tipped concrete wall prevented one from tumbling over into the cavernous space through which thin light spilled down from great skylights.

Farouk found his room number and entered with a magnetic pass-card.

Unpacking his bag, he removed his letter-carrier uniforms, leather pouch, ear protectors and Uzi with spare clips. His red prayer rug he unrolled on the plain hotel carpet so that it faced Mecca.

Kneeling, he bowed his head and began to pray.

Into his mind came his favorite verse from the Koran: "No man knows the land in which he will die."

It was a favorite Koranic saying. And very poignant on this day, on which he was fated to die in the supreme act of annihilating the heretic Abeer Ghula.

Assuming, of course, that the call came.

At exactly noon, the room telephone began shivering.

"Yes. Hello?" he said in his unaccented English.

A sweet voice said only, "It is the ordained hour."

"I understand."

The line went dead. Nothing more needed to be said. The Deaf Mullah had spoken. His pronouncements were absolute.

Reciting one final prayer—the afternoon prayer—Farouk donned the uncouth blue gray uniform with the eagle's head on blouse and shoulder patch, added the blue cap and, after checking the action of his Uzi, stowed it into the leather pouch, which he then shouldered. It was filled with junk mail he had neglected to deliver on his Washington route. These useless things concealed the Uzi.

Clapping the ear protectors over his head, he stepped out and took the elevator down to the tenth floor, where it was said that Abeer Ghula dwelt in imagined safety, but in truth cowered in terror.

The difficulty lay in that it wasn't said which room the hypocrite cowered.

This was easily discovered, Farouk thought. Starting with the first numbered room, he knocked on all doors and, when someone answered, he handed them a piece of gaudy junk mail addressed to Occupant.

Many were surprised by him. Some shrank from his smiling face. And why should he not smile? This was his last day on the unhappy earth.

At the room numbered 1013, his knock was answered by a querulous "Who is it?"

"I have mail."

"Leave it."

"I must give this to you personally, for otherwise it will not be considered delivered by the mighty postmaster general."

"For whom have you mail?"

"I must look. One moment," said Farouk, feigning ignorance. "Ah, yes, here it is. I have a special-delivery letter for Abeer Ghula. Is there an Abeer Ghula at this address?"

"I will look."

"Thank you," said Farouk, smiling broadly. They were checking. No doubt they were being careful.

When the door opened, it did so without warning. And a thick-wristed hand snapped out, took hold of his throat and withdrew with amazing speed.

Farouk could feel his shoe soles actually burn and smoke so swiftly was he carried inside.

His back was slammed against a wall, and the air exploded from his stunned lungs.

At which point Farouk clawed for his well-hidden Uzi. Digging into the jumbled mail, he ignored the paper cuts and found the butt of the submachine gun. His fingers wrapped around it.

Then other unfamiliar fingers wrapped around his fingers. They squeezed. And the pain traveling up Farouk's right arm turned to crimson when it reached his eyeballs.

He screamed. The words were inarticulate. If they were even words.

The crushing hand withdrew, and Farouk whipped out his burning hand.

His eyes cleared of the red pain, and he stood stunned, looking at his gun hand.

It was not bleeding. This was very surprising. He associated the red haze before his eyes with the color of blood. His blood. But the hand was not bleeding. It was very black, actually. The fingers were bent in strange ways—as was the much more sturdy Uzi submachine gun.

Farouk was not absorbing the fact that his fingers and the Uzi were an inextricable lump of broken and fused matter when the face of his assailant loomed up in his line of sight.

It was a cold face, very pale and Western.

"Messengers of Muhammad?" he asked.

"I do not say yes and I do not say no," he said.

"That is a yes," a squeaky voice piped up.

And nearby, Farouk saw a little Asian, wrinkled features like a wise old monkey's, dressed for a funeral.

"My name is Patrick O'Shaughnessy O'Mecca," he said.

"He is a Moor," said the Asian.

"Truthfully I am Black Irish."

"His eyes do not smile," the Asian said.

"Before we punch out your lights," the other said, "who do you work for?"

"The postal service, of course. Do you not recognize my proud and honorable uniform?"

A hard hand backed by a thick wrist wrapped itself around the Uzi again and gave a forceful squeeze.

This time Farouk's eyeballs exploded into pinwheels of colored light. The pain clutched at his stomach, and though he screamed, no words issued forth. It was that painful.

"Here we go again. Who sent you here to erase Abeer Ghula?"

"The Deaf One."

"The Deaf Mullah?"

"Yes, yes," he gasped. "None other."

"The Deaf Mullah's in solitary."

"The Deaf Mullah is wiser than infidels. He walks free, breathing clean air and eating *halal* food, which is denied him by his supposed captors."

"I'm going to say this one last time. Who gave you the order to come here?"

"The Deaf Mullah."

"You see him?"

"In the holy flesh."

"Where and when?"

"Many months ago, in the storefront mosque in Jersey City. Although he sat behind a bulletproof screen to protect him from those who would do violence against him, it was unmistakably he. I swear by the Holy Beard."

The death's-headed one turned to the Asian. "How's he sound to you?"

"He is telling the truth. You can hear it in his pounding heart."

"I am telling the truth. Now I must kill and die."

"No killing, but you get to die."

"I cannot die until I kill the heretic."

"She's sleeping and doesn't want to be killed right now," said the Westerner in a serious voice, although his words were foolish in meaning.

"Then I will refuse to martyr myself."

"That's what they all say," said the white infidel.

And the irresistible vise of a hand on the Uzi-and-mangled-hand combination led him out into the rectangular corridor and to the low edge of the retaining wall.

"What are you going to do?" asked Farouk.

"Nothing. You're going to commit suicide."

"Gladly. If you tie Abeer Ghula's feet to my own."

"Out of rope today," said the man, peering down. "Not here," he muttered.

"Good. I am not ready to die just yet."

But Farouk's relief was short-lived. He was walked around the corner to another point of vantage.

The infidel leaned over. "This looks good."

"Why is this spot good and not the other?" Farouk wondered aloud.

"Because there's a restaurant down there, and I didn't want to drop you in somebody's Caesar salad."

"I do not mind taking infidels with me when I go to my welcome death."

"But I do."

And though the infidel with the thick wrists was on the lean side and showed insufficient muscle for the task, Patrick O'Shaughnessy O'Mecca, a.k.a. Farouk Shazzam, found himself lifted bodily and dangled over yawning space.

"There is still time for you to relent and embrace Allah," Farouk offered hopefully.

"Have him give me a call," said the infidel, letting go.

It was not so terrible. The force of gravity simply took hold of Farouk's stomach, and he fell, pulling the rest of him with it. He enjoyed the acceleration, the lightheadedness and the wild thrill that comes from free-falling at over one hundred miles per hour without a bungee cord.

When he struck the parquet floor, he became an instant bag of blood, brains and loose bone that lay flatter than it seemed possible for a fully grown human being to lie.

But he died with a smile of joyous expectation on his shattered face.

REMO SHUT THE DOOR to the screams wafting up and told the Master of Sinanju, "That should give the FBI guys reason to tighten their security."

"They are not perfect," said Chiun, who was watching the local Korean-language channel on TV.

"They let one get through."

On the bed, Abeer Ghula stirred. She twisted one way and then the other like a cat, the royal blue bed clothes slipping off her supple, dusky form.

One arm flopped over the edge of the mattress, and as she began a subvocal murmuring that promised full wakefulness, Remo indicated the exposed underside of her wrist and said to the Master of Sinanju, "Your turn."

Chiun refused to drag his hazel eyes from the screen. "I will wait. It may yet be possible that the Messengers of Muhammad will succeed in their task and I will be spared the ignominy."

"Fat chance."

"Another five minutes will do no harm."

DR. HAROLD W. SMITH snapped up the receiver as soon as it rang. It was the blue contact phone.

"Yes, Remo?"

"M.O.M. just tried again."

"Did you interrogate the assassin?"

"I wouldn't dignify him with that word," Remo said dryly. "But yeah. He was dressed up like a mailman. Somehow he got through the FBI security ring. Or maybe the NOW bruisers."

"Go ahead."

"He swore on Allah's beard it's the Deaf Mullah."

"Allah is not known to wear a beard. You mean the Prophet."

"He swore, he spoke the truth as he saw it, and as a lesson to the FBI, we disposed of him after we were done. Expect to hear about another postal suicide before long."

"They will not give up this easily," warned Smith.

"Just look into the Deaf Mullah thing. Something's not right here."

"My thinking exactly."·

"If these people served the Deaf Mullah, wouldn't they be calling for his release rather than screw around with the Middle Eastern version of Bella Abzug?"

"There is something very wrong here, I agree. I will get back to you."

"Can't be soon enough," said Remo.

A rippling ululation like a grieving woman at a Lebanese funeral came across the wire.

"What is that sound?" asked Smith.

"Oh, that's just Abeer Ghula going into paroxysms of ecstasy."

"Who is—?"

"It's Chiun's turn."

"You are joking, of course."

Then a squeaky voice rang out. "Remo! Come look. See the lips? They are relaxed. See how the mouth is parted? That is how a woman is pleasured."

"What is going on down there?" Harold Smith demanded.

"We're just keeping Abeer out of trouble our way," explained Remo.

"Do nothing to her that cannot be explained to the First Lady."

"I think the First Lady knows about this kind of stuff by now," said Remo, hanging up.

SMITH USED the untappable blue contact telephone to reach the warden of a Missouri federal prison.

"This is Assistant Special Agent Smith, FBI Washington."

"Go ahead."

"We are calling to confirm the security of Prisoner 96669."

"How many times do I have to tell you people? He's in administrative detention. That's solitary to you."

"Can you assure me he has no contact with the outside world?"

"That's why they call it solitary. He's in a bare cell, with no loose items except a fireproof blanket and a paper prison uniform. He gets one hour a day to shower and exercise under armed guard."

"How does his counsel communicate with him?"

"He doesn't. The lawyers stopped coming around about six months ago."

"Do you know the status of his appeal?"

"Dropped."

"Dropped?" Smith asked sharply.

"Dropped cold."

"Doesn't that strike you as unusual?"

"Yeah. We assume his people are waiting for the day they can ransom him out through hostage taking or terror threats and are saving their money for blasting caps."

"I concur with that assumption," Smith said tightly.

"If I'm told to release him by a federal authority, I will. Until then, he's just Prisoner 96669 and a son of a bitch besides."

"You should consider doubling his guards."

"I can guarantee you they won't be busting him out."

"A simple precaution may save you embarrassment, if not serious career consequences."

"I'll take it under advisement," said the warden just before he hung up.

29

In the al-Bahlawan Mosque in the flat state of Ohio-stan, the Deaf Mullah read the news that a postal worker had jumped to his death in the Marriot Marquis Hotel in Manhattan.

Farouk Shazzam of the Moorish-Irish face had failed. That meant he had been murdered by U.S. secret agents, his mission unfulfilled. That further meant that the Messengers of Muhammad lacked another willing martyr.

And Abeer Ghula lived.

He considered this at length. To send another messenger? Or not? They were intended to be used in this way, but with so many in FBI hands, they were now precious. And the two at hand, Yusef and Jihad Jones, were critical to the next phase.

Tapping a chime, he sat back and listened to the incessant ringing that troubled his waking hours and whispered of the vengeful god he served.

Sargon appeared.

"Farouk is no more, but the hypocrite lives," the Deaf Mullah intoned.

"Her hours are numbered," Sargon replied.

"As are yours."

"I hear and obey."

And without another word, Sargon, trusted Sargon the Infallible, left the room never to return.

For it was his duty to prepare the Fist of Allah for launch.

Facing the electronic green minarets of his terminal, the Deaf Mullah began composing the communiqué that would signal to the godless the nearness of Allah's holy wrath.

ON THE OHIO TURNPIKE, Yusef Gamal watched the miles speed by as Jihad Jones drove the practice missile eastward.

"When will it be my turn to drive the practice missile?" he complained.

"When it is," the Egyptian spat.

"Why do you always take this tone with me?"

"Because you annoy me always."

"I am hungry," Yusef said suddenly.

"I, too, am hungry," Jihad admitted.

"There was a seafood restaurant two miles back. Since I may die at any hour, I am in the mood for seafood."

"I myself am in the mood for shrimp."

"I do not eat shellfish," Yusef muttered. "I belong to the Hanafi school. Shellfish is impermissible."

"I am a follower of the Shafeii school. Shellfish is *halal* with us. We eat it up and say, *Alhamdulillah.*"

"That is your school," said Yusef as Jihad wrestled the big silver bus off the turnpike exit.

After a silence, Jihad said, "The Jews are forbidden to eat shellfish, too."

"I am not responsible for this," Yusef said unhappily, wondering when this son of a Crusader would cease hectoring him.

"I am just pointing out a known fact. Jews do not eat shellfish. You do not eat shellfish. There may possibly be a connection. I do not know. I cannot say. I am just saying it."

"Say it to yourself," said Yusef. "I am wondering something else."

"And what is this you are wondering?"

"Why if we are to pilot a missile called the Fist of Allah into Paradise, Sargon is making us practice by driving a mere bus. A bus rides on wheels. A missile streaks through the air like an arrow."

"There is a good reason, never fear."

"I know there is a good reason. What I am wondering is what this reason is."

"I am wondering this same thing, too," Jihad Jones said as he pulled into the seafood restaurant in exotic Ohiostan.

Yusef took the cell phone with him because Sargon the Persian had insisted he carry it at all times in case they were to be summoned.

After they entered the restaurant, a convoy of official FBI cars and Light Armored Vehicles raced along the Ohio Turnpike in the direction of the Al-Bahlawan Mosque.

But neither man saw this.

30

Tamayo Tanaka wasn't going to take it lying down.

She was supposed to be the story. Now Abeer Ghula was the story. If Tamayo Tanaka wasn't going to be the story, then she had to get next to the story.

And that meant getting next to Abeer Ghula, distasteful as it was.

Not that it was going to be easy.

Everyone wanted to get next to Abeer Ghula. Especially after it was reported an attempt had been made on her life. The First Lady herself had denounced the attempt and thrown the awesome weight of her political power behind Abeer Ghula. That made it the lead story of the day. And Tamayo Tanaka had to own that story.

So she called her news director up in Boston from her Washington hotel.

"Check it out, Tammy. Still got your hidden camera?"

"It's my pillow at night, you know that."

"After last night, your face will be recognizable all over Manhattan."

"Don't worry. I'll wear a fright wig and dark glasses."

"Try to blend in with the other Asian reporters.

There must be a tidal wave of them down there by now."

"Got it covered," said Tamayo Tanaka, blow-drying her pert blond coif. No one was going to recognize her in her undercover disguise. No one at all.

Except maybe her mother.

THEY WERE TAKING OUT the body when the Yellow Checker cab dropped Tamayo off at the corner of Broadway and West Forty-fifth Street ninety minutes later. A sheet shrouded the gunman, but as they bumped him into the back of the waiting ambulance, an arm flopped out. Literally flopped. It was as thin and boneless as a noodle. But it was covered in fabric that, while stained burgundy, showed clean patches of USPS blue gray.

With her hidden camera, Tamayo Tanaka captured it all.

Then, breezing past the stony-faced FBI agents once she gave them her hotel confirmation number, she took a glass elevator to the upstairs reception area.

It was a joke. The FBI had the place guarded against mailmen and famous-faced journalists, but it was still a public building and one of the best hotels in the city.

No one could stop a guest from checking in.

"I want a room as far above Abeer Ghula's as possible," she told the reception clerk, "unless she's on a lower floor, in which case give me one beneath her in case I have to evacuate for a bomb threat. I don't trust these glass elevators. They make me nervous."

"Will the third floor do?"

"It'll do perfectly," Tamayo Tanaka said, suppressing a grin. That narrowed the floors down.

At her room door, the bellboy accepted a twenty-dollar bill in return for revealing the floor where Abeer Ghula was holed up.

"I don't know the room number," he said.

"Not necessary," Tamayo said. "I don't suppose I could talk you out of that uniform?"

"I'm not allowed to fraternize with the guests."

"Bend a rule for a blonde with a problem."

"Man, this never happens to me," the bellboy said, shucking off his uniform tunic and stripping down his fly.

"Change in the bathroom and toss your duds out as you go," Tamayo told him.

The bellboy shrugged. "It's your party."

When he was done, the bellboy was chagrined to see the blonde was buttoning his tunic over her pink silk bra.

"Is this a TV kind of deal?" he asked.

"I'm not on TV."

"I mean transvestite TV. Because if it is, I'll wear whatever I have to if it makes you horny—I mean happy."

Zipping up her fly, Tamayo threw open the room door.

"Where are you going?" the bellboy called after her.

"I'll be back as soon as I can. Sit tight."

"What do I do with this hard-on?"

"Soak it in something."

"Wait!"

But the door slammed in his face and his unhappy "Oh, shit."

On the tenth floor, Tamayo Tanaka walked as if she were wrapped in a starched straitjacket. That was how it felt, but if it worked she was back in the game.

And nothing was going to knock her out of the game again.

YASSIR NOSSAIR HAD a problem.

It was not a little problem. It was a very big problem.

Hiring the aircraft to fly over Manhattan was not the problem. This was easily done for the right amount of money. Many journalists were hiring aircraft, so it was not unusual to do this.

The problem was crashing the aircraft into the hotel room of the hypocrite Abeer Ghula.

It had been leaked, the floor. Counting up from the first floor was easy. Yassir Nossair used his Zeiss field glasses. He had the floor pinpointed exactly.

It was the correct side of the hotel. The correct room would have been better, but this was impossible. Obtaining the correct side ensured success. Once the aircraft smashed into the appropriate side of the hotel, the explosion would totally rip that wall of her building apart, ripping Abeer Ghula's heretical bones apart with them.

"Want to circle again?" asked the pilot.

"Yes, I am thinking."

Would it be the side facing Mecca? he ruminated. No, it would not be the side facing Mecca. Abeer Ghula was too contrary.

Perhaps it was the side opposite, facing away from Mecca. Would that not make sense?

At last, after careful thought because he possessed only one plane and one life, Yassir Nossair decided it would be the side opposite Mecca.

"It is time," he announced.

"You're done?" the pilot asked.

"Nearly so. I must ask you now to fly closer to the hotel."

"How close?"

"Point it at the hotel and fly toward it."

"Sure."

The Piper Cherokee banked and came in on a level line.

"Lower, slightly," said Yassir Nossair, looking through the windscreen with his field glasses. Quickly he counted up.

"Yes, remain on this level."

"Aren't you going to take a picture?"

"Yes, yes. How stupid of me."

And from the gym bag at his feet, Yassir Nossair took up a 9 mm pistol and placed it against the pilot's unsuspecting temple.

He fired once. The pilot's eyes were dragged from their sockets to smear like burst grapes against the suddenly-shattered side window.

Yassir Nossair took the control wheel from him and held the plane steady as he shouted, "*Allah Akbar!* God is Great!"

THERE WERE approximately ten doors on each of the four sides of the tenth floor of the Marriot Marquis. The sun was high in the sky now, and the autumn light streaming down through the skylights made eerie golden shafts in the cathedral interior.

Tamayo walked the wide, rectangular corridors as softly as possible, so that she could catch any sound that came from behind the doors.

At each door where she heard a noise, she knelt beneath the glass eye of the peephole and laid an ear to the panel.

She heard TVs, afternoon lovemaking, but nothing that suggested Abeer Ghula's strident voice.

At one door, she heard a TV set tuned to CNN, a network she loathed because their anchors might as well be working in a factory as a broadcast studio for all the publicity their careers got. Not one of them had ever been asked to appear on Leno, never mind Letterman.

About to rise, she heard a squeaky voice say, "See who is lurking at the door, Remo."

The voice sounded familiar, but before Tamayo could think it through, the door swung inward and she spilled inside, yelping like a cat with a trampled tail.

Her big bag was taken from her, and a hand reached down and grabbed her by the collar. She was hoisted up as if weightless.

When her face came level with her molester, she recognized the deep-set eyes and high cheekbones, not to mention the T-shirt and chinos.

"What are you doing here?" asked the man she knew only as Remo.

"None of your business," Tamayo retorted.

"That's not the answer I want to hear."

"Look, give me ten minutes with Abeer Ghula, a worldwide exclusive, and I won't tell anybody she's in this room."

"No deal."

"Fine. But think of the inconvenience when I go on the air with this."

"You're not going on the air with anything."

And Tamayo Tanaka found herself being led over to a queen-size bed where a raven-haired woman lay under the royal blue covers.

"Is she dead?" she gasped, seeing her story take a dark turn into a brief, third-segment obituary.

"Just sleeping one off."

"Muslims don't drink alcohol."

"That's not what she's sleeping off," said the voice of the hand that squeezed her neck.

Tamayo Tanaka didn't remember pitching face-first into the bedding. Only waking up later, with the foul garlic and olive stench of Abeer Ghula's breath in her face.

"Mmm," Abeer murmured.

"I'm Tamayo Tanaka and I'm wired for sound. Can I get a quote?"

"Mmm."

"Psst! Remember me? Tammy? From 'Nightmirror?'"

Abeer Ghula opened one golden eye. It fell on Tamayo's face, flicked up to her hair and came to rest on her eager blue eyes.

"Are you my blue-eyed blonde?"

"If I can get a quote, I'll be your little pink poodle."

Abeer Ghula smiled dreamily. "I have never fellated a blond man," she said. "Did you know *fellatio* is an Arabic word?"

"I'm not a—"

"I will tell you whatever you wish if you allow me to taste your blond infidel hardness."

"Sure," said Tamayo, making her voice husky. "But we have to do it under the covers in the dark."

"Yes, it will be very exciting this way."

"Close them. Are you ready?"

"Put it in my mouth, and I will suck it dry."

IN THE OTHER ROOM, Remo Williams said, "Sounds like a certain someone's awake."

"Both are awake," said Chiun on the floor, where he could watch TV in comfort.

"What are they saying?"

"The false Japanese wench is trying to coax words from the harlot."

"Let her. She's not going anywhere."

"And the other is promising to suck it dry."

"Suck what dry?"

Chiun shrugged. "Who can say when a false prophet awakens beside a blond-haired Japanese?"

"I'd better look into this."

"Do not forget. It is your turn to please the female Ghula. And see that her smile is correct this time."

"Maybe I'll just show Tammy how to do it and save us both a week of boredom."

Remo stepped into the bedroom and saw a double lump under the bed covers. It was a very active lump, with distinctive sucking sounds coming from it.

He was hesitating between breaking it up or letting the orgasms fall where they may when a flash of silver caught his eye.

A light plane was circling outside the window. It lined up nose-first on the hotel. Approaching, it dropped until it was level with his window.

Remo's eyes had been trained to see in darkness, under difficult light conditions and as far away as the human lens mechanisms allowed for optimum sight.

He saw that there were two men in the cockpit. Then the passenger placed a pistol to the pilot's head and shot him through the temple.

That was all Remo needed to see.

Racing to the bed, he yelled, "Make for the door, Little Father! Incoming!"

"Incoming what?" asked Chiun.

"No time! Run for it!"

Tucking a squirming bundle tucked under his arm, Remo got out of the room fast on the heels of the Master of Sinanju's skirts as Chiun flashed out the door.

Remo pulled the door shut, thinking it might not help but who knew.

The splintering of glass came as they mounted the low retainer wall, flipped over it and, using one hand for leverage, swung downward and in, landing on the floor below.

From there, they ran to the opposite side of the floor.

The explosion shook the building like a milk shake. Up above, a skylight cracked. Down came shards of glass. The second boom was lighter, but it made the door to their room cartwheel out and tumble past them in a hot breath of air to land far below.

The rest of it was mostly fire and crackling.

When it sounded safe to get up off the floor, Remo whipped the blanket off the prone forms of Tamayo Tanaka and Abeer Ghula.

Eyes closed, Abeer was energetically sucking on Tamayo Tanaka's thumb.

"Just another minute, okay?" Tamayo whispered. "We're almost done here."

31

Dr. Harold W. Smith was assuring the President that all was well with Abeer Ghula when the blue contact telephone rang.

"I assure you, Mr. President, the woman is being protected by the best."

"Do you know what my wife will do to me if that woman is killed? It'll be worse than if I'm not re-elected and she's out of office."

"Your wife holds no public office."

"Tell her that. Right now she's plotting my new Southern strategy."

"The South appears lost to your party."

"Tell my wife. She thinks she can flip the South like a hamburger if only someone will hand her a big enough spatula."

"Excuse me," said Harold Smith. "I must get this other line."

Scooping up the blue contact telephone, Smith placed the red receiver to his gray chest.

"Yes?"

"Smitty, they tried again," Remo said unhappily.

"They failed, of course."

"Yeah, but there's a Piper Cherokee or something burning in Abeer's old suite, and she's sucking on the thumb of that dip-shit reporter I told you about."

"Say again?"

"Forget it. We can't stay here if they're going to drop aircraft on us. We need a new locality."

"Hold the line."

"Sure." Over the line, Smith heard Remo ask the Master of Sinanju, "Are they done yet?"

"I do not know. The blond one's thumb is bleeding, and the other is sucking it harder now."

"Leave them alone. They obviously know what they're doing."

"What is going on there?" Smith demanded hoarsely.

"You don't want to know."

"I have the President on the dedicated line. Wait, please."

Swapping receivers, Smith told the President, "I am back."

"What's wrong?"

"What do you mean?"

"I could hear your heartbeat. It went into overdrive."

Smith cleared his throat uncomfortably. "There was another attempt on Abeer Ghula's life, but she is safe. I am going to have to move her to a safer location."

"Whatever you do, don't send her to Washington. The last thing I need is terrorists attacking the capital. The pundits are already calling me the President who let the postal system lurch into chaos. The damn Speaker of the House is right now talking up legislation to abolish the postal service."

"I will be back to you."

"If it's bad news, keep it to yourself as long as possible. After the reelection would do just fine."

Hanging up on the White House, Harold Smith resumed speaking with Remo Williams.

Remo said, "Did he really tell you to keep a lid on the bad news?"

"He did."

"He's sure running scared."

"Not our problem, Remo. I want you to move Abeer Ghula to the World Trade Center."

"Why there?"

"Since the 1993 bombing, it has become the hardest, safest structure in all of Manhattan. They would not dare to attack her there."

"You ask me, they'd dare to attack her in the Vatican."

"I stand corrected. They will be unable to breach the World Trade Center security. Move her immediately. I will arrange for an FBI counterstrike force to meet you."

"On our way. What about the dip-shit?"

"Leave her behind. Of course."

"Prying her thumb out of Ghula's mouth may be more work than just pretending they're Siamese lesbians and treating them as a set."

"Leave her," Smith said coldly.

Terminating the call, Remo spoke to the Master of Sinanju. "Smitty says we gotta take Abeer to a safer location, but to leave the dip behind."

"What about the dip's thumb?"

"Won't it come out?"

"I refuse to attempt such a thing. Besides, it is your turn."

"Does this count toward pleasuring Abeer?"

Chiun gave the question barely a second's thought. "Yes. Definitely."

"Sounds like a fair trade to me," said Remo, grinning.

"I will guard the approach and thus spare my aged eyes the terrible sight of what it is you must do."

As Chiun padded away, Remo dropped to one knee beside the two preoccupied women. Abeer was completely oblivious to everything except Tamayo Tanaka's thumb, while Tamayo was biting her lips to keep from crying out in her pain.

"Whatever this is, it's over," Remo said.

Tamayo said, "Shh. She thinks I'm a guy."

"She should open her eyes."

"Not until I get my quotes. I'm wired for sound."

"Where's the mike?"

"In my bra, where else?"

"Thanks," said Remo, squeezing Tamayo by the neck until her eyes rolled up in her head and she sank back into a soundless state of unconsciousness. Her blond head went *bonk* off the floor. Remo didn't attempt to cushion it, figuring she could use a hard knock on her skull.

As she fell, her hand tugged at Abeer Ghula's mouth. Abeer responded by flying into some kind of religious ecstasy and sucked all the harder.

Finally she released Tamayo's bloody thumb and sank back herself, sighing with a rush of contentment.

"All done?" asked Remo, standing over her.

"Yes. It was wonderful. The blond one's seed tasted just like blood."

"Glad you got your money's worth. We gotta go now."

And reaching down, Remo gathered her up, blue blanket and all.

"I will go nowhere without my blond infidel."

"Where we're going, all the blond infidels you could want will be waiting," Remo promised.

"I will accept my fate, then, if it includes blond infidels."

"You know AIDS is transmitted through the blood."

"I am the Prophetess of Allaha. She will protect me from AIDS."

"Spoken like a congenital thumb sucker," muttered Remo.

"I am very oral," said Abeer. "Especially with congenitals."

They took the elevator to the ground floor, where a bell captain, seeing a tall man and an elderly Asian attempting to abscond with a Marriot blanket, blocked their way.

"You can't remove that from the premises. Hotel property."

"We'll bring it back," Remo assured him.

"I am sorry, you cannot."

The Master of Sinanju stepped up and showed the bell captain the trivial nature of his complaint by dislocating his kneecap with an expert side-kick.

They left the angrily hopping bell captain behind and took the next cab in line.

"World Trade Center," Remo told the cabbie.

"Tower One or Two?"

"One. If it's not One, it's a short ride to Two."

The cab slithered into traffic.

AN FBI counterterrorist SWAT team in full battle gear was waiting when they pulled up before Tower One.

"Tower One it is," Remo said cheerily.

The FBI commander on the scene rushed up and said briskly, "Sorry. We'll have to search you."

"Search this first," said Remo, letting the blanket unroll and depositing Abeer Ghula at the man's black boots.

Abeer looked up, blinked and said, "Are you my blond infidel?"

"No."

"'Yes' will get better cooperation," Remo advised.

"I have a few white hairs coming in," the FBI commander allowed.

"Guaranteed to multiply by shift's end," said Remo. "Just show us where to go."

"This way."

Tucking Abeer Ghula under one arm, Remo allowed an FBI unit to form a moving wedge around them. They were escorted in.

Chiun trailed along, hands tucked into his kimono sleeves and hazel eyes scanning their surroundings, not wishing to defer to white customs.

"You know," Remo told the FBI commander after they made it into the lobby, "a better approach might have been incognito."

"Normally. But the Oval Office wants this done right."

"Right is subtle."

"Subtle is open to criticism. Up front and out in the open means no one can haul our butt before a congressional inquiry."

"Point taken," said Remo.

The elevator whisked them to an upper floor where they were led to a spacious room that had been hastily converted into an FBI command center.

"No bed?" asked Remo, eyeing the nest of communications equipment.

"We're working on it."

"She likes to sleep."

The room was packed with FBI agents, and Abeer Ghula walked among them, eyeing them sleepily and asking, "Are you my blond infidel?" over and over in a petulant voice.

Remo mouthed "Say no" whenever he could.

"Then where is my blond infidel?"

"Working on his roots. Haven't you had enough for one day?"

"I am insatiable for this one. For this one, I will willingly renounce all women, all other men. Even if his penis is short and stubby, it was as hard as bone and salty as the rich blood of my period, which I have tasted in the slavish mouths of my own lovers."

"Give him time to recover. You were very hard on him."

"All men will be slaves under Um Allaha."

"Don't quit your day job just yet," Remo said.

Turning to Chiun, he saw that the Master of Sinanju had his hands over his small, delicate ears.

Remo made a sign that indicated it was okay to listen.

"She is finished?" Chiun asked.

"For now."

"The harlot has a mouth like a sewer and the habits of certain lower animals I will not name for fear of offending them."

"Good move," said Remo, who then invited the FBI to leave the room.

The FBI commander shook his head stubbornly. "Can't. She's our responsibility."

"No. Guarding the building is your responsibility. Guarding her is ours."

"What agency are you with?"

"A secret one," said Chiun. "If its name so much as falls upon your ears, I must slay you on the spot."

The unit commander cracked half a smile, then suppressed it when he saw the serious expressions confronting him.

"I take my orders from Special Agent Smith. No one else."

"Smith your ramrod?" asked Remo.

"Yes."

"Let's call him."

"Sorry, I don't have the number."

"But I do," said Remo, picking up the phone and thumbing the 1 button. When he heard the first ring, he handed the phone to the commander, knowing Smith would pick up before the second ring.

"This is Commander Strong, on site at WTC."

Smith's voice was sharp. "How did you get this number?"

"Tell him Remo dialed it for you," Remo suggested.

"He says his name is Remo and he's ordering us out of the secure room. What do we do?"

"Obey him. Guard the building."

"Sir, I can't."

"That is a direct order," said ASAC Smith.

"Yes, sir."

Taking the receiver back, Remo held open the door as the FBI SWAT team trooped out, looking dejected and unappreciated.

"Remember, keep this floor clear. The last FBI team had really sloppy security habits."

Then Remo shut the door.

Abeer Ghula was huddled in a chair, the blue blanket slipping off her dusky shoulders, exposing portions of her anatomy neither Remo nor Chiun cared to contemplate at that particular time.

"I want my blond infidel," she muttered darkly.

"Your turn, Little Father," said Remo.

Hearing this, Abeer Ghula tucked her wrists protectively under her hairy armpits.

"I know what it is you desire," she spat. "But you cannot touch my precious new erogenous zones."

"I do not want them," Chiun sniffed.

"I want my blond infidel."

"It's going to be a while," Remo explained. "Would you rather sleep through the long wait?"

"I am very hungry."

"We'll order up. What do you want?"

"Blond infidel *au jus.*"

"Settle for steamed rice?"

ABEER GHULA WAS still whining an hour later when Harold Smith walked in unannounced.

Remo was moving toward the door, ready to take out the intruder when the sound of Smith's familiar heartbeat reached his sensitive ears and he pulled back.

"Nice going, Smitty. I almost took your head off."

"It is a good test of security," Smith returned.

Chiun bustled up, tight features breaking into a sunrise of pleased wrinkles. "Greetings, O Smith. What service may we render?"

"I am taking charge of this woman."

"You?"

"I need you both elsewhere."

"Great," said Remo.

Chiun bowed more deeply than Remo had ever seen him bow to anyone. Another foot, and he could almost kiss Smith's immaculately buffed Cordovans.

"Your munificence enriches our dreary toil. Speak the service, and it will be done with glad, adoring hands."

"I have traced the anonymous computer-server link to the Gates of Paradise."

"Yeah? Where?" asked Remo.

"A mosque in Toledo, Ohio."

"There's a mosque in Toledo?"

"One of the largest in the nation. But it's supposedly not in use."

"Why not?"

"It was built with its orientation slightly askew, and does not face Mecca."

"So why don't you just have it raided?"

"It is still a mosque. A raid would be politically embarrassing for the President and the nation, and would only inflame these people."

"And sending us in won't?"

"If what I suspect is true, you may find the Deaf Mullah there. He is overdue for a heart attack."

Chiun bowed again, a sly smile upon his face. "Spoken like a true Caesar."

"Think you can handle her?" Remo asked, jerking a thumb back in Abeer Ghula's direction.

Smith checked the knot of his Dartmouth tie uneasily. "Of course."

"If she gets cranky, slip her a pacifier. She likes those."

Smith's blank, lemony expression followed them out of room.

After they were gone, Harold Smith faced the woman called Abeer Ghula.

"You are not my blond infidel," she said petulantly.

"I am FBI Agent Smith."

"You are too stringy for my tastes. But if I am sufficiently bored, I may allow you to pleasure me in unexpected ways."

"I am married," Smith said uncomfortably.

"I am not afraid of the ménage à trois. Are you?"

Harold Smith swallowed and tried to block the unwanted images from his mind. He felt as though he were being scrutinized by a hungry bird of prey.

32

The director of the FBI was dictating a memo explicitly denying the existence of a Violent Postal Worker Task Force when his secretary informed him that an urgent call was coming out of Toledo.

The director looked surprised. He was unaware of a Toledo office. "I'll take it."

The voice on the line was tense. "This is SAC Rush. Toledo. We've secured the mosque."

"Mosque?"

"The al-Bahlawan Mosque. No one can go in or come out."

"What mosque? What are you talking about?"

"Operation Sound Surround."

"I authorized no such damn mission! Where are you? What mosque? What is this about?"

"Orders came out of your office, by telex."

The FBI director groaned. "Don't tell me. An assistant special agent named Smith."

"That's right. Smith."

The director leaned into the phone. "You wouldn't have a first name, would you?"

"One moment." When the SAC's voice came back on the line, it was to the accompaniment of a rustle of paper. "It's just a squiggle. I can't even make out the first initial."

"Brief me from the top," the director said resign-edly.

"We've secured all approaches to the suspected HQ of the Messengers of Muhammad."

"And it's a mosque, you say?"

"Biggest one I've ever seen. Got two tall minarets that look like rockets ready for launching."

"Do nothing."

"Our orders were to hold secure until instructed otherwise."

"We can't have another Waco here. That's job one."

"We all understand that, sir. This *is* Ohio."

"Just hold on, I'll be back to you."

Hanging up, the FBI director called the President of the United States.

"Sir, I have good news and, I'm afraid, bad news, as well."

"Go ahead," the hoarse voice of the Chief Executive said.

"The Bureau may have found the headquarters of the Messengers of Muhammad jihad group."

"Where is it? Iran? Iraq? Libya?"

"Toledo, Ohio. There's a mosque out there as big as a circus tent, and we believe the conspirators are bunkered inside."

"Is that the good news or the bad?" the President wondered aloud.

"We have the place surrounded."

"Is ATF there?"

"They aren't in the loop."

"At all costs, keep them out," the President said savagely. "And whatever you do, don't do a damn thing. I'll get back with you," he added, his voice sounding as if the lining of his throat was coming up through his clenched teeth.

THE PRESIDENT of the United States called Harold Smith, and it took an entire three rings before Smith's exasperated voice said, "Yes, Mr. President?"

"Do you know anything about a mosque being surrounded by the FBI?"

"It was my doing."

"Do you have any idea how this will play in the media?"

"Not if we contain the situation before the Messengers of Muhammad strike again."

"But a mosque. It's a house of worship. If anything goes wrong, the entire Muslim world will be inflamed like one gigantic, angry boil. We're just getting the Israelis and the Palestinians to simmer down."

"We have to think of U.S. security first, Mr. President," Harold Smith said stiffly. "These jihad groups operate under the command of religious leaders seeking religious goals, and to a significant degree are sheltered by U.S. laws protecting freedom of worship. That can only be dealt with through extraconstitutional means."

"What the hell do these people want?"

"To establish a global Islamic theocracy by converting the entire world to their faith by force of arms and terror."

"They're using our constitutional freedoms to take them away from us?" the President blurted out.

"It is for exactly such conscienceless predators that my organization was created."

In the background, a pouty voice said, "I want my blond infidel. I can taste his salty juices in the mouth of my face and my other mouth, which only he will be allowed to devour."

"Who was that?" the President asked.

"Abeer Ghula."

"You have her there with you?"

"No, in a secure room in the World Trade Center."

"Is this line secure?"

"It's a scrambled cellular patch-through from the dedicated line."

"Oh. I wondered why it took you three rings."

"Mr. President, I have just dispatched my people to the al-Bahlawan Mosque. If our intelligence is correct, we will find the mastermind behind this jihad group within."

"Then what?"

"My people will penetrate it and come out unseen. After a while, the FBI will be withdrawn. And the bodies of the conspirators will be discovered by the appropriate parties. Dead of natural causes."

"Sounds foolproof."

"Nothing is foolproof, Mr. President."

"They saved my presidential butt once. I trust them to close this out quietly and with absolute deniability."

"That is their function," said Harold Smith.

"Good. Gotta go. I got a grips-and-grins function in the Rose Garden, and it'll be the perfect opportunity to assure the voters we're working the problem to a successful wrap-up."

The line terminated, and Harold Smith went into the bathroom to check on the condition of Abeer Ghula, the most hated woman in the Muslim world.

He was relieved to find her hanging from the shower curtain just as he'd left her. Her gold eyes glared at him venomously.

"When you are agreeable to behaving properly, I will cut you down," Smith told her.

Smith stepped back just ahead of a naked kicking foot and decided the time was not yet right to untie her wrists.

THE PRESIDENT WAS in the Rose Garden when the fax was handed to him.

The portable presidential podium had been set up and he was standing before it waiting for the grinning ghouls—as he was calling the White House press corps this week—to settle down so he could begin.

The President glanced at the fax. It was from the FBI and read, "Purported communiqué received from M.O.M. via fax at 11:11 today. No verification."

The President figured "no verification" meant it was not important. He was here to reassure the nation, not pass on new threats, so he didn't read the text of the communiqué.

Clearing his throat, he began to speak. "I just want to say a few words to reassure Americans everywhere that the nation is secure, the post office functions as it should and the FBI is working diligently to get to the bottom of yesterday's terrible events."

There. Short, concise and guaranteed not to be misquoted or misconstrued by the press.

Then came the barrage of questions.

"Mr. President, is it true you have ordered a postal holiday—effectively shutting down the mail?"

"Absolutely not."

"Then why has mail delivery virtually ground to a halt?"

"No follow-up questions today," the presidential press secretary inserted. "You know the rules."

"Mr. President, some airlines are refusing to transport mail for fear of mail bombs. Will you order them to reverse their decisions in the national interest?"

"That's under advisement," said the President, who was hearing this for the first time.

The verbal tennis balls kept coming, and the President lobbed them back with ease and aplomb. This was going to look great on the evening news.

"Mr. President, word is coming out of Justice that the so-called Messengers of Muhammad have threatened to launch what they claim is a nuclear missile called the Fist of Allah at an unidentified target on U.S. soil. What can you tell us about this report?"

The President experienced a frozen moment in time.

Off to one side, his press secretary was surreptitiously pointing to the fax lying on the podium.

"Let me refresh my memory," the Chief Executive said quickly.

Scanning the unread text of the FBI fax, his eyes widened.

The reasonable demandment of the Messengers of Muhammad not having been met by the godless of America, we have no choice but to announce this day the existence of the dread Islamic bomb. This bomb had been installed in a missile unlike any the Western world has before seen. And the name of this missile is the Fist of Allah. It is to be launched on this day at a target unknown to the Infidel Nation, for the purpose of destroying it utterly, thereby showing the Western world that Islam is as powerful as the pagan science of the West.

Ma sha'Allah!

The President actually paled three shades of color on national television. Every viewer with good color balance saw it. They also heard the White House press corps lob question after question the President could not convincingly answer, and they saw that, too.

"I want all Americans to know that, while we cannot accept this threat at face value, neither do we dismiss it out of hand. That would be unwise. We have no hard intelligence confirming the existence of any so-called Islamic bomb. But I have ordered our early-warning missile-defense systems on the highest state of alert possible as a precaution."

Then the President stalked off to give the order, hoping he was in time to do exactly that.

HAROLD SMITH WAS HACKING through the original FBI reports of the arrest of the Deaf Mullah in the Abu al-Kalbin Mosque in Jersey City in the aftermath of the failed terror spree of three years ago when his computer alerted him of incoming mission-critical intelligence.

A fax intercept popped up at the touch of a key.

Smith read the Messengers of Muhammad warning of a nuclear missile called the Fist of Allah, and in one reading reached a firm conclusion.

There was no such missile, unless it was a war-surplus Scud. And for a short-range Scud missile to reach the continental U.S., it would have to be launched from either Canada or Mexico, neither prospect very likely.

As for the Islamic bomb, it was also doubtful.

M.O.M., most of its messengers of terror in FBI custody, was attempting to ratchet up the level of fear and anxiety among the American populace. Whether it worked or not depended upon how the media treated the story.

Smith went back to the FBI computer files, his gray face frowning. The Deaf Mullah was in federal prison, yet his followers were making no attempts to liberate him.

There had to be an explanation.

And Harold Smith was determined to find it.

33

The clerk at the car-rental agency in the Toledo airport proudly informed Remo Williams that his car was equipped with the latest satellite navigational system for his convenience.

"Just give me directions," said Remo.

"The Groundstar system will get you to your destination without fail or the rental is free," the clerk chirped.

"I like directions. They save me time and trouble and keep me from breaking things," said Remo, snapping in half with his thumb the pen he'd just used to sign the rental agreement. A squirt of ink speckled the clerk's white shirtfront.

Taking the hint, the clerk opened his mouth to offer clear directions when the Master of Sinanju piped up.

"I will be the navigator."

"You can't handle a navigational computer," Remo said quickly.

"A child could do it," the clerk insisted.

"You stay out of this," Remo snapped.

"I will navigate," Chiun repeated. "I have watched Smith work his oracle machine. It is very simple."

Remo rolled his eyes and hoped for the best.

TWENTY MINUTES LATER they were on the banks of the Maumee River, south of Lake Erie, and Remo was saying, "We're lost."

"We are not lost," said Chiun, tapping the computer screen with his jade nail protector. "See? This is the strange lake."

"Lake Erie is not green," said Remo. "And the state of Ohio is not blue."

"The color does not matter. This is Lake Erie, and this red spot is us. For it moves when we do."

"So where are we?" asked Remo with more patience than he felt.

"In a place called Havana."

"Havana, Cuba?"

"It only says 'Havana.'"

Remo looked at the screen. "That green 'lake' is the island of Cuba, Little Father. We are not anywhere near it."

"These machines do not lie."

"We'll ask at the next gas station," growled Remo.

"You would take the word of a smelly purveyor of chemicals to that of the Master of Sinanju?" Chiun asked indignantly.

"I'd like to wrap this up. According to the radio, militia crazies are trying to lynch letter carriers in Montana and Arizona. People are locking their doors when they see a mailman. They're grounding commercial flights everywhere because the mail goes by plane and nobody wants to lose a 747 to a letter bomb. Not to mention the fact that the mail has ground to a dead halt because postal employees everywhere are all singing 'The Serotonin Song.'"

"It is good when lowly messengers enjoy their toil."

On the Ohio Turnpike, a bus came barreling up on them at a high rate of speed, and Remo looked into his rearview mirror.

He did a double take. "Chiun. Look behind us."

Chiun turned in his seat. "I see an angry bus."

"Look at the guy inside," Remo suggested.

"I see a red-haired Egyptian."

"I mean the other guy. Tell me that isn't Joe Camel."

"That is not Joe Camel. But it is. Who could mistake that nose?"

"What the hell is he doing driving a bus out here?" asked Remo.

"He is trying to run us off the road, of course."

In a moment he nearly did.

The bus bore down like a silver juggernaut, horn blaring. Remo eased back on the gas, hoping to slow the bus down.

"He is not slowing. He is speeding up," warned Chiun.

Then the bus surged ahead, intent upon knocking them out of its path.

Remo cut to the shoulder of the road, bounced and came to a jolting stop. The rear tires spun in soft soil. Remo got out, cursing as the exhaust of the speeding bus filled the air.

Reaching under the rear bumper, Remo suddenly straightened. The car's rear end came out of the ditch, and Remo walked it over to hard asphalt, making it look easy. It was not a feat of strength so much as one of absolute physical harmony. Sinanju enabled one to harness one's mind and body so fully that any superhuman capability was within Remo's reach, no matter how extreme.

Getting behind the wheel, he heard the Master of Sinanju give the good news.

"We are back in Ohio. The computer has assured me of this. If we follow the yellow line, we will reach our destination."

"Count on us reaching our destination by following the big silver bus," growled Remo, throwing the car into gear.

MATT BROPHY, FBI SWAT tactical commander, was confident he had the al-Bahlawan Mosque secured against invasion or egress. His black-clad forces had mustered a ring of Light Armored Vehicles around the gleaming mosque, whose opalescent dome changed hue as the sun climbed the Ohio sky.

No one in their right mind would try to get into the mosque now. Not with it surrounded by heavily armed FBI agents.

To get in was to be trapped.

And those trapped inside were not coming out. Not that Brophy was calling for that. He wasn't calling for anything. He was standing pat, as instructed. The last place he wanted to land was before an angry Congress. Or in a locked room with the attorney general of the United States, who, it was said, could break a man's back with a hard, steely glare, not to mention bust his career all to pieces.

Prepared for any contingency from within, the last thing Brophy expected was a hurtling bus from without.

The bus came roaring up the Ohio Turnpike and then down onto Route 75. Then it screamed onto the mosque access road.

Brophy took one look, and his heart stopped beating.

"Incoming bus!" someone yelled.

"Anybody see any markings? Postal service...anything?" Brophy demanded.

No one did.

"How about explosives?"

"No," a countersniper called after consulting his scope.

"Could it be a bus bomb?" someone asked.

The thought alone was enough to freeze the blood.

And there was no time to think it through.

So, when the bus roared straight at them, Matt Brophy ordered the blocking FBI armored vehicles to pull apart which they did in the nick of time.

The bus roared through the impenetrable FBI cordon and lumbered up to a big portal. It went through the door, breaking it down like so much old cake frosting. One slim minaret listed alarmingly. The other only quivered.

The bus did not explode.

That was the good news.

The bad was that the cordon had been broken, and no one knew by whom or, more importantly, why.

There was nothing to do but wait for the next development and hope this was not the last day of their FBI careers.

THE SUMMONS CAME by cell phone.

It was Yusef Gamal's turn at the wheel of the practice missile. So Jihad Jones took the call.

"Yes, yes?" he said. "Yes, yes. Yes, yes!"

Then Jihad Jones hung up the cell phone.

"Yes?" Yusef said.

"It is Sargon. The criminal FBI has surrounded the mosque."

"Imbeciles! Have they learned nothing from Waco or Ruby Ridge? What are our instructions?"

"The Fist of Allah is to be launched immediately."

"But where is it?"

"We are told to return to the mosque with all speed and at all costs."

"Then it is the ordained hour for you and I, my brother."

"Do not call me your brother. I am not your brother."

"We are cousins, then."

"You are driving this practice missile now. Therefore, I will pilot the true Fist of Allah."

"That will be for Sargon to say," spat Yusef as he bore down on the gas and the big silver bus roared down the Ohio Turnpike.

It was a simple matter to reach the ring of FBI armor. The infidel made it easy for them. Then, because there was no time, Yusef threw the bus into the great portal as instructed.

The portal caved inward, despoiling the mosque. But this was the only way.

Inside they piled out, only to be met by the Afghan Taliban guards, who were pledged to protect the Deaf Mullah.

"Sargon awaits in the launch-preparation room," one thundered.

"Where is it?" asked Yusef.

"Two doors down. The green door. It is unlocked, *inshallah.*"

Jihad Jones saluted. "May Allah protect you brave ones."

They raced on.

"The Fist of Allah is here!" Yusef said excitedly. "And we never suspected."

"Obviously it is one of the minarets," Jihad said. "The left."

"No, the right. It is closer to Mecca."

"I favor the left minaret."

"And you may pilot it to foolishness if you wish while I pilot the true Fist of Allah into Paradise."

"The Deaf Mullah will decide this."

"He will decide nothing. It was ordained before the beginning of time."

"Then your prayers are but the yapping of the dogs that follow the caravan," Yusef growled.

The green door was thick but fell open at a touch. Inside there was gloom, and the sense of a great shape.

Jihad Jones lifted his voice. "Sargon, where are you?"

The Persian's voice said, "Wait. I am nearly done." It sounded as if it were coming from some vast, enclosed space—a cave or a chamber where giants might dwell.

"We are beneath the right minaret," Jihad whispered.

Yusef said nothing.

Then came a sound like that of a vast brazen portal clanging shut.

"Prepare yourselves for the sight that will freeze the blood of infidels the world over," proclaimed Sargon the Persian in a doomful voice.

The snapping of a light switch preceded a blinding burst of light and between that and the enormous shape that stood before them, Yusef and Jihad let out gasps of comingled awe and pride.

REMO PARKED the rental car on the green grass near where the Ohio Turnpike merged with Route 75.

Chiun got out first. His hazel eyes took in the austere beauty of the al-Bahlawan Mosque.

"It is Seljuq," he said.

"What?"

"The architecture. Seljuq dynasty. A good period for Arabic architecture. Later they went mad with mosaics and arabesques."

The bus had already disappeared into the portal, breaking it down and leaving a gaping hole.

"Guess we got our work cut out for us," said Remo.

"If a blundering bus can breach those *ninjas*, we can do the same."

"Those aren't ninjas, Little Father, but an FBI SWAT team."

"After today, they will learn the true meaning of *swat*."

"Just remember they're on our side, okay?"

They were moving closer. The FBI's attention was fixated on the mosque, and no one noticed them slipping up a grassy incline.

Remo noticed Chiun sniffing the air.

"I smell Afghans," said Chiun.

"They'll die just as easy as Arabs," growled Remo.

"No, harder. But only slightly."

They were very close now. Close enough that they had to part and move in separately so that they were less likely to be spotted.

Remo took a southerly approach, Chiun easterly.

Their techniques were similar. They found weak spots and exploited them. Remo slipped under the chassis of an LAV, and the Master of Sinanju made noises of distraction by breaking a twig with a sandaled foot. While FBI heads snapped one way, he flitted by the other with utter soundlessness.

They were neither seen nor smelled nor challenged as they reached the broken and gaping portal together.

"Okay, let's see how easy this will be," said Remo.

"How difficult can it be when our foe is himself deaf as a post?"

"Good point," said Remo, starting in first.

HAROLD SMITH WAS TRYING to assure the President that there was no such thing as the Fist of Allah and that an Islamic bomb, if it did exist, could not successfully be delivered against sovereign U.S. soil.

"How can you be sure?" the President demanded.

"Common sense. A low-technology jihad group such as the Messengers of Muhammad simply does not have access to the funding or tools to construct a working thermonuclear device. Their bombs to date have been crude but effective chemical bombs."

"I can't tell the nation this. Not without proof."

"You can point them in the direction of common sense."

"How are your people doing?"

"No report yet," said Smith.

"Keep me posted—ouch. Poor choice of words there."

"I will be back to you, Mr. President," said Smith, hanging up the handset of his attaché-case phone and returning to his screen.

The deep background report on the Deaf Mullah included his penchant for using doubles to fool arresting authorities in Egypt and elsewhere. But he had used it one time too many, it seemed.

When the FBI had surrounded the Abu al-Kalbin Mosque in Jersey City three years before, they were prepared for a decoy double to be deployed.

A man wearing the gray garments and red felt turban of the Deaf Mullah's particular religious school had in fact emerged and surrendered peacefully. He was being handcuffed when one arresting FBI agent noticed he wore a modern hearing aid. The agent was sharper than the others. He had read translations of several of the Deaf Mullah's sermons railing against Western science and technology.

Smith reasoned that the real Deaf Mullah wouldn't be caught dead wearing a hearing aid.

The double was detained on-site, and the siege continued. It was broken only when cooler heads prevailed and the Deaf Mullah's lawyers convinced their client that to die in an Islamic Waco would not be in the best interests of the world Islamic movement.

The Deaf Mullah, carved horn ear trumpet in hand, staggered out of the mosque to be cuffed and taken away for arraignment.

Smith paused. He searched for the name and legal deposition of the double. There was no further mention of him. Clearly he had not been charged.

"I wonder," he murmured.

THE AFGHAN GUARDS toted Kalashnikov rifles and great curved scimitars, Remo saw as he slipped into the al-Bahlawan Mosque.

They were standing before a shut green door.

"If we take them quietly," Remo whispered, "the FBI won't come storming in to muck everything up."

Chiun nodded.

One of the guards was looking right at Remo and didn't see him until Remo took hold of his skull and shook it violently, until the man's unseeing eyes rolled up in his head.

His companion noticed this out of the corner of his eye and lifted his great filigreed scimitar.

That was when the Master of Sinanju stepped up to him and took the man's wrists in his own irresistible hands.

The Afghan was big. He struggled for control of his scimitar. His struggle was in vain.

On wide-planted feet, but without exerting himself, Chiun angled the scimitar up and around so that the Afghan realized he was about to decapitate himself just before his guided hands abruptly changed direction and split his own face down the middle like a bony but ripe melon.

Both guards died standing up. Remo and Chiun moved on.

There were other Afghans farther down the corridor. Three this time.

Chiun caught their attention by raising his voice in an ancient Afghan insult. They snapped Kalashnikov rifles to bear, then, seeing Chiun's black silks and un-Western face, called a curiously hesitant challenge at him.

Chiun returned the challenge in kind.

Moving along a parallel corridor, Remo popped out behind them and batted the butt ends of their rifle stocks.

The Afghans watched their rifles go skittering and spinning down the corridor, and when they turned to face their unexpected foe, even as their hands streaked toward the jeweled scimitar hilts, a smooth white palm smacked their glowering faces to assorted jelly and pulp.

"So far so good," said Remo as the trio hit the ground with a dead thud.

Chiun moved ahead. "The Deaf Mullah is this way."

"If you say so," said Remo, glancing at the heavy green door. "But I'd say there's something important behind this door, too."

"It must wait."

THE SUDDEN LIGHT was piercing Yusef Gamal's clearing eyes as they came to rest on the grandeur of the Fist of Allah.

"It is magnificent," he breathed.

"It is colossal," said Jihad Jones.

It was a steely construct of slablike plates and angles, wide, tall and massive in its brutish lines. Every surface gleamed of chilled steel except a sheet of plate glass mounted high on a forward edge. It looked too heavy to move, never mind fly through the skies.

Then a thought struck them.

"Why does it rest upon great rolling wheels?"

"To carry it to its ultimate destination," explained Sargon the Persian.

"The launch pad?"

"No, to the target the Deaf Mullah most desires above all others."

"Abeer Ghula, of course," said Jihad Jones.

"No, more than that harlot."

"What could be more desirous of destruction than the hypocrite who insults the pure flame of Islam by her very existence?"

"A target whose destruction will bring the heart of Zionist-occupied America to a standstill and maim infidels without number," said Sargon the Persian in a flat, dead voice.

"What saddens your voice?" asked Jihad.

"I have just armed the Fist of Allah, therefore I am doomed."

"Doomed?"

"I have placed its atomic heart within the missile without proper protection."

"The warhead?"

Sargon shook his head. "It is in the back. You will drive from the front."

"What will be your part, Sargon?"

"I will recite the countdown, at which point you will drive over my doomed body, saving me from an agonizing, un-Islamic death and catapulting me to Paradise."

THERE WAS A HEARTBEAT on the other side of an ornate door, and Remo said, "Let's just bust in."

Chiun nodded.

Remo stepped back and lifted one foot. Kicking high, he sent the panel flying inward like a big wooden kite that skimmed along the floor to impale a far wall.

Two startled Afghan guards shrank from the unexpected commotion and wheeled, their Kalashnikov rifles dropping into line. Remo went for one, while Chiun took the other.

One got off a shot. Remo wove aside, avoiding the bullet by instinct more than conscious design, and broke the Afghan's spine by the indirect expedient of punching him in his stomach. When Remo's knuckles encountered hard bone, they withdrew. The Afghan folded in the middle like a pair of colorful pants, his bearded face slapping the tiled floor.

Chiun's Afghan was cocking his AK-47 when a flutter of sharp fingernails like a swarm of dragonflies became busy about his face. They retreated, leaving stunned eyes staring from the rags and tatters of what had been a moment before a bearded human visage.

The man pitched forward on his face—what remained of it.

At the far end of the great room under the mosque dome was a chevron-shaped niche whose blue walls were a riot of Arabic calligraphy.

Before it stood a plain green glass shield. Behind the shield a seated figure moved like something seen through cloudy water.

A hand lifted an ear trumpet to one side of his head.

"Bingo," said Remo.

They advanced.

A DETACHABLE LADDER of steel hung from the forward portion of the towering hulk that was the Fist of Allah.

"This is the nose cone," said Yusef Gamal, patting it proudly. Hollow, it rang like a great bell.

"The nose cone points to the sky," Jihad countered. "This points toward the east."

"Enter, both of you, quickly," said Sargon.

"I will go first," said Yusef.

"The pilot goes first," growled Jihad Jones.

"This does not matter. You must go now."

Yusef clambered up the ladder and entered through the stainless-steel hatch in the side of the multi-wheeled behemoth.

Inside were two bucket seats. He took the right one, where there was a steering wheel. Too late, he noticed a steering wheel before the left-hand seat. It was the type of steering wheel used on airplanes, a crescent rather than a circle, which reassured him.

Jihad Jones took the left seat. Both men wore their Islamic green pilot-martyr uniforms.

The door clanged shut, locking them in.

Then a voice came from the dashboard. It was Sargon.

"It is time to commence the countdown," he intoned.

"We are ready to die."

"I am more ready to die than you," said Yusef.

"There is a red button. At the word *sifr,* for 'zero', you will press it. That will be the launch."

"Should we not be pointing skyward?" asked Yusef.

"You are pointing east. When you press the red button, the great engines will start."

"More than one?"

"Many engines are needed to propel the Fist of Allah."

Yusef nodded. "Redundancy. It is a Western idea that is good."

"You are the redundant one, not I," spit Jihad Jones.

"When the engines are hot, you will press the floor pedal and go forward. Press it as hard as you can, for it will travel faster this way. Make the Fist of Allah travel as fast as possible."

"Yes," exclaimed Yusef. "Until it is airborne."

"No, until it achieves its destiny."

Yusef and Jihad exchanged questioning glances.

"Where is the brake?" Jihad wondered aloud. "I see no brake pedal."

"None is needed. For you are on a suicide mission with no turning back."

"Yes, yes, of course."

"When you reach your target, you will drive directly into it while the other turns the great crank that sits between you and will cause the Fist of Allah to explode in atomic hellfire."

"Yes. I see the crank. But who is the blessed pilot-martyr and who is the holy crank-turner?" asked Yusef.

"You will drive by turns, and the one who is not driving when you reach the target turns the crank. Is this understood?"

"Yes, it is understood. But what is the target? How do we get to it?"

"Take the Ohiostan Turnpike east. The path to Paradise is marked on the map you will find in the glove compartment."

"Yes, yes. I see the map. What then?"

"The map will show you which roads to follow."

Jihad and Yusef exchanged another look of confusion.

"We are to fly over certain roads," Yusef whispered. "It is a good system, for there is no navigation system to fail."

"Stand by," Sargon called out.

"This is it," Yusef said excitedly. "We are going to die."

"Only if you drive correctly during your turn at the wheel," said Jihad Jones.

And Yusef Gamal settled into his seat, winding his *kaffiyeh* around his face, thinking, *It is just my mis-*

fortune to spend my last living hours with this haughty snob of an Egyptian.

Then the countdown began.

"Ashra ... tisha ... tanany. ... sab'a ... sitta ..."

REMO WALKED UP to the bulletproof green partition and flicked a finger at it. The glass disintegrated into gritty pebbles like a windshield after a high-speed collision.

There sat a wizened-faced man with a frizzy iron gray beard and the signature red turban that had been a common TV sight only a few years before. He flinched, but otherwise showed no emotion.

"Looks like the Deaf Mullah to me," said Remo.

The ear trumpet angled in Remo's direction. "Eh?"

"Sounds like the Deaf Mullah, too."

Chiun snapped out a warning in Arabic.

The answer came back, spiteful and bitter.

"What's he saying?" asked Remo.

"That we are too late," Chiun relayed.

"Too late for what?"

"Too late to stop the launch of the Fist of Allah."

Remo frowned. "What's the Fist of Allah?"

Chiun put the question to the Deaf Mullah, and translated the answer, which was given freely.

"This Moslem says it is an atomic missile which will crush the infidel nation and break its heart," Chiun spit.

Remo lifted an eyebrow. "Thought it was 'Muslim.'"

"For this cruel shedder of innocent blood, I have used the correct pronunciation."

"He sound like he's telling the truth to you?"

"He does," said Chiun.

"Then we'd better strangle some facts out of him and get back to Smith. This sounds serious."

Before they could take the Deaf Mullah by his throat, the floor under their feet began to vibrate. It was a low vibration at first. Then it became a roar, and the roar swelled and swelled until the mosque shook and rattled, while on the floor the Deaf Mullah's face broke into a beatific grin as the great dome above their heads began to fracture and drop large chunks of white building material.

Amid the quaking and breaking, the Deaf Mullah threw back his head and his beard split in the peal of triumphant laughter rolling out from his clenched teeth like crazed thunder.

"It is the Fist of Allah!" he shrieked as Remo's hands lunged for his neck. "Destined to burn away all un-Islamic corruption. And you can do nothing to stop it now!"

34

FBI SWAT Tactical Commander Matt Brophy saw the side wall crack and bulge outward amid the shaking of the earth. "What's in there? What's doing that?" he screamed.

The answer came crashing out of the opposite side of the al-Bahlawan Mosque like a colossal rhinoceros.

It was as tall as a three-story building, as wide as a two-lane highway and ran lumbering out on eight wheels, each as tall as five men. The stubby-finned rear section ran on a giant, tanklike track system, giving it tremendous earth-chewing traction.

At first Brophy thought of the giant missile transports NASA used to move Atlas rockets. But there was no missile. It was only a carrier. Gigantic, plated and armored to the teeth.

"Open fire on that thing!" he ordered.

Sharpshooters opened up. Their bullets dinged and spanged off the angular plates without effect. Then the remorseless behemoth came lumbering at them.

There wasn't time to get the LAVs out of the path. So the men just scattered. It didn't matter. The giant monster of steel plate simply rolled over two LAVs, crushing them flat on exploding tires.

"What is that thing?" a sharpshooter howled, getting out of its way.

"I don't know. I better call this in."

"Call what in? What is it?"

"Damned if I know," Brophy muttered as they retreated to watch the steely monster lunge across the median strip to straddle the Ohio Turnpike. "But if that isn't the postal-service eagle on one side, I'll eat my pension."

THE WORD WENT from the director of the FBI to the President of the United States, who saw his political life melt down before his blinking eyes.

"What is it?" he croaked.

"Unknown. But it's big enough to hog most of the Ohio Turnpike. That makes it too big for the Bureau. I'd call in the Air Force, were I you."

"I'll get back to you. Do nothing."

"Nothing sounds very safe right now," the FBI director said. "Politically speaking."

The President reached out to Harold Smith.

SMITH WAS IN THE MIDDLE of one awful epiphany when the President handed him another.

"Mr. President, I believe I have solved the riddle of the Deaf Mullah," Smith said, his gray eyes glued to his briefcase computer system as Abeer Ghula grunted helplessly in the background.

"I don't care about him."

"You should. He is behind this campaign of terror. My analysis of the facts indicates he tricked the FBI into arresting him and immediately letting him go, thinking he was only a double. Then the true double was arrested in his place."

"Your analysis also says there was no such thing as the Fist of Allah," the President said bitterly.

"What do you mean?"

"While NORAD has been combing the skies, the Messengers of Muhammad have launched the damn thing on the ground."

"Sir?"

The President described the gigantic vehicle that had rolled out of the al-Bahlawan Mosque.

"Why do you think this is the Fist of Allah?" asked Harold Smith.

"Because FBI says there's a clenched fist painted on one side of the thing. And on the other is painted We Deliver For You. There's also the USPS eagle and one of those Islamic red-crescent symbols on the hood or nose or whatever it is."

"A wheeled missile?"

"They think it's a converted missile carrier."

"It cannot be nuclear."

"Do you want to bet the farm on it?" asked the President.

"No, I do not. My people are on-site. Let me get back to you on this."

Hanging up, Smith waited. If what the President said was true, it would be only a matter of minutes before Remo checked in.

It was thirty-nine seconds later, by Harold Smith's Timex.

"Smitty. Something big just blew out of the mosque."

"I know, Remo. The President just informed me. Can you describe it?"

"Imagine a cross between the mother of all tanks and one of those monster missile carriers."

"Do you see a missile?"

"No, it's armored up like crazy, though. And there are two guys driving it. One's Joe Camel."

Smith's voice turned low and incredulous. "Then it is the missile."

"What missile?" asked Remo.

"The M.O.M. have threatened to launch a nuclear missile called the Fist of Allah."

"If there's a missile inside that thing, I don't see how it can be fired. It looks like it's made out of welded surplus bank vaults."

"No, it *is* the missile."

"Huh?"

"A suicide-bomber ground missile," Smith said in a nail-chewing voice. "Riding below radar, too big to stop or interdict by ordinary means. A low-tech death-delivery system of destruction. No doubt the two men inside are the suicide drivers."

"So where's it headed?" asked Remo.

"Your guess is as good as mine. But you must stop it."

"It's too big to run off the road, but we'll give it a shot," Remo promised.

"Keep me informed."

REMO TORE ALONG the Ohio Turnpike in the wake of the Fist of Allah, saying, "It may be big but it sure isn't fast."

"We will stop the monster," Chiun said firmly.

Accelerating, Remo came up to the machine's rump, hung there pacing it while he said, "You can jump out and climb aboard, then I'll stop in front of it and do my thing."

"Stop in front of it. Then we will both step out with the serene dignity we deserve and do our awesome things."

"Suit yourself," said Remo, angling the wheel and nailing the accelerator to the floor.

YUSEF GAMAL SAW the speeding sedan race around on his side of the Fist of Allah and gave the wheel a jerk to the left.

Seeing this, Jihad Jones gave his wheel a jerk to the right.

"What are you doing?" Yusef complained. "I have the wheel."

"I am trying to keep us on our Allah-blessed trajectory."

"And I am trying to squash an infidel bug."

Too late. The sedan pulled up alongside him and got in front.

"You may squash him now," said Jihad Jones, relinquishing his wheel.

Up ahead, the car braked, slewing to a stop, blocking the way, its tires smoking. The doors opened, and two men popped out.

"Those infidels are crazy. They think they can stop the Fist of Allah's wrath?"

"Squash them like the godless bugs that they are!" Jihad Jones exploded.

REMO AND CHIUN TOOK UP a position before the Fist of Allah like two matadors facing the bull of bulls.

"When they get close, break away and grab your side of that thing while I grab mine," Remo suggested. "Then we'll nail the guys inside."

Chiun nodded. "Yes. This is a sound plan."

And it almost worked.

The monster of plated steel rumbled toward them, and Remo broke left while Chiun slipped off to the right in a flutter of ebony skirts.

There were enough projections on the angular and irregular surfaces of the Fist of Allah that grabbing a handy one was no problem.

Remo got ready. Lifting his feet off the speeding asphalt, he grabbed a jutting projection and started to climb.

Partway up, he knew something was wrong.

His vision started to cloud over, and his arms began to tingle. A numbness crept down his body like a slow-acting poison.

Fear touching his eyes, Remo looked up and saw the yellow disk with the three black triangles he knew from childhood fallout-shelter drills emblazoned on a sealed hatch.

This thing was as radioactive as Chernobyl, he thought just before his grip gave way.

YUSEF GAMAL MADE a point of crushing flat the car that had dared to block the path of righteousness, then settled down for the long drive east.

"You have the map?" he asked Jihad Jones.

"Yes. I am studying it now."

"Where do we go, then?"

"We follow this turnpike to Route 79 south, there. See?"

Yusef looked over. "Yes. I see. Then what?"

"Then we take the 80 to Wayne, New Jersey. Then south to Jersey City. From there, it is a short drive to our ordained target."

"What is our ordained target, O brother?"

"That is for me to know," Jihad crowed. "For I will be the favored one to drive the last holy mile to Paradise."

Yusef tried to mask his disappointment by bluff. "If you drive the last mile, I will have the honor of arming the Fist of Allah."

"You are welcome to the honor. For he who pilots the Fist of Allah into Paradise will be the first to claim his *houris*."

"My *houris* will not mind waiting a few mere moments longer, eager as they are."

"Attend to your driving, then. I must study my map."

After a while, Yusef said, "I do not think the Fist of Allah is going to take to the air, Jihad."

"Of course it will not," Jihad said, contempt in his voice.

"What manner of missile refuses to fly?"

Jihad was silent a long moment. At length, he said, "An Islamic missile, of course."

"Yes, you are undoubtedly correct. Only an Islamic missile is clever enough not to fly into heathen skies where it will be shot down before fulfilling its religious mission."

REMO LAY SHAKING on the ground until his body finished isolating and purging the foreign elements that had paralyzed it. Metallic sweat oozed from every pore, instantly soaking his thin clothes. He shook his head once violently, throwing off hot beads of radiation-poisoned perspiration.

Then he snap-rolled to his feet.

On the other side of the highway, the Master of Sinanju was climbing to his sandaled feet, his wrinkled face like a sweat-varnished raisin.

"The brute is televisionactive, Remo."

Remo shook a few final droplets of sweat from his forearms. "Radioactive. Yeah, I know. Radioactivity is like Kryptonite to us."

"I do not know that word. But look. Our vehicle was destroyed by that lumbering steel beast."

Remo's gaze fell where the jade nail protector pointed. The rental looked as if an asteroid had flattened the entire trunk.

"Let's see if the car phone still works," Remo said, rushing toward it.

AT THE WORLD TRADE CENTER, Harold Smith scooped up the briefcase satellite telephone handset when it rang.

"You have succeeded," he said.

"We wish," said Remo. "That damn thing is so radioactive we can't touch it."

"God blast it!" exploded Smith.

"But we will try again, O Emperor," squeaked Chiun in the background. "Never fear."

"Smitty, maybe you should just bomb the thing," suggested Remo.

"Impossible! It is a nuclear device—it will detonate."

"Well, the way it's barreling along, flattening everything in its path, it's a sure bet it's going to detonate somewhere someplace soon."

"There must be some way to stop it," said Smith. "If it is a crude form of guided missile, it must have a predetermined target."

"Well, right now it's following the Ohio Turnpike east."

"One moment."

Harold Smith brought up a map of the continental U.S. and created a red blip that signified the Fist of Allah.

He input its probable speed, trajectory and commanded his system to extrapolate likely targets of national significance, as well as times of impact.

The system was fast. It came up with the possibilities in less than a minute. The highways and interstates turned red as if flooding with arterial blood.

There were three probabilities.

Washington, D.C.

New York City.

Or a less important third option, possibly even in Ohio.

The dilemma for Harold Smith was to identify the target and interdict the threat before the first nuclear strike on U.S. soil threw the West into collision with the Muslim world.

The President of the United States ordered Air National Guard F-16 Flying Falcons of the 180th Bomber Group scrambled out of Toledo, Ohio.

The aircraft launched, formed up into a screaming V and flew low cover down the Ohio Turnpike and back, ready to strike if ordered.

Harold Smith told the President, "We cannot destroy it by conventional means. The risk of nuclear fallout is too great."

"Well, I can't just let it crash into any damn thing it wants to. This is worse than the mail crisis."

"This *is* the mail crisis," Smith reminded. "It has escalated."

The President's voice turned low and urgent. "I can't not take action, Smith. You know that."

"I need more time."

"How can I help?"

"I require instant updates on the Fist's progress."

"Last reports are it's skirting Lake Erie. You don't suppose it intends to vaporize the entire lake, do you?"

"That is impossible. I still cannot accept that they have a nuclear device on board."

"Your people said it was radioactive."

"Radioactive is not nuclear," said Smith.

The blue contact line light began blinking, and Smith excused himself.

"Remo, where are you?" he asked.

"About a mile behind the thing, or south of Dallas, Texas—depending on whether you want to believe my eyes or the satellite navigation system in this new rental car," Remo said wearily.

"You have a navigational computer in your car?"

"When it works."

"Remo, can you remove it and attach it to the Fist of Allah?"

"Can you tell me what to look for?"

"Yes."

"Gladly," said Remo.

"JIHAD, MY BROTHER," said Yusef Gamal as his control wheel turned before him and the crescent-emblazoned nose of the Fist of Allah ate white line.

"What is it now?" Jihad growled as he managed his wheel.

"I have to make water."

"Why did you not go before we left?"

"We were rushed. I did not think. There was no time."

"I refuse to stop the vehicle now that I am pilot-martyr. Besides, there is no brake, as you know."

"Then what do I do? I cannot enter the gates of Paradise with my trousers stained. My sweet *houris* would be shocked. I would make a terrible first impression on them."

"I do not care what you do," muttered Jihad Jones, wrestling the wheel.

"Then I will do what I must," said Yusef, unzipping his fly from the throat down.

As a spattery tinkle filled the cockpit of the Fist of Allah, Jihad Jones muttered, "You are worse than a Jew. When we are dead and in Paradise, do not speak to me."

"I will not."

"Then do not, weak-bladdered one."

"My Arab tool is still bigger than your Egyptian tool," Yusef boasted, zipping up again.

REMO STAYED ON THE TAIL of the Fist of Allah as it chewed up a long stretch of the Ohio Turnpike. The rear tracks spit gravel and gouged up pieces of asphalt.

Remo steered around them as F-16s crisscrossed overhead, low and menacing. A wind was coming down off Lake Erie, clean as fresh laundry.

"Okay, I'll pull up alongside, you toss the navigation thing. Just make sure it lands in one piece."

"I will not fail," Chiun promised.

"Because if you break it, it'll be no good and if it slides back off, it's useless."

"I am not a child," Chiun sniffed.

"Just don't blow it," said Remo, accelerating steadily.

It should have been easy. But they had been exposed to hard radiation, and their systems were hypersensitive to it now.

Remo felt a tingling in his fingertips as he held the wheel straight.

Coming up in the gargantuan rear deck that resembled the back end of an aircraft carrier, Remo cut around to the left and paced the gigantic vehicle. Its whirling tires dwarfed them.

Chiun had one pipe-stem arm out the window and held the instrument package that Remo had extracted from under the hood.

Chiun gave it a casual toss. It veered out and up to land with a clink in the V of an angled tailfin.

Breaking, Remo watched.

The package did not slide off. He picked up the cell phone and called Harold Smith.

"Package delivered, Smitty."

"I have the navigational signal," said Smith.

"That didn't take long."

"I acquired it while it was still in your possession."

"Okay, what do we do now?" asked Remo.

"I have arranged for an Army helicopter to pick you up."

"Where are we going?"

"You will remain with the Fist of Allah until you are needed."

"Gotcha."

HAROLD SMITH watched the red blip on his computer screen. The Fist of Allah was now crossing the Ohio-

Pennsylvania border. That meant ground zero was not in Ohio. That reduced the pool of target options.

The only question was where they would go when the Ohio Turnpike petered out.

"WHAT ARE YOU DOING?" Jihad Jones asked Yusef Gamal.

"I am consulting the map."

"I forbid this. I am custodian of the sacred map."

"You are pilot-martyr right now. The map therefore reverts to the martyr-navigator."

"I am navigator."

"When I have the wheel again, yes," said Yusef.

"I forbid you to look at the target. It is *haram*. Especially to a Jew such as yourself."

"I will agree not to look at the target if you stop calling me a Jew."

Jihad Jones was silent a long, fuming moment. "Very well," he snapped. "I will no longer denounce you as a Jew."

"Good."

"Gamal Mahour."

"You cannot call me Camel Nose, either."

"You did not stipulate this."

"I think we should take Route 6," said Yusef, changing the subject.

"The sacred map said to follow 80."

"The Six is also good."

"We will take Eighty."

"And I will take the wheel again soon, for it is almost my turn," said Yusef.

"Until then, keep your camel's nose out of the sacred map."

HAROLD SMITH SAW the red dot take Route 80 east, and automatically the tracking program displayed a new bar graph of optimum targets. Washington, D.C. was still possible. New York City, however, looked more likely.

Smith input additional data and asked the system to narrow down the working list.

The system responded with the same list. Mostly post offices along the route and significant military targets.

Smith frowned. The limitations of the computer were the same as in his Univac days. To discover the truth, human reasoning would have to be brought to bear.

IN THE HUEY HELICOPTER Remo watched the Fist of Allah roll along Route 80 and felt helpless. Pennsylvania State Police cars were following the giant machine at a discreet distance, roof lights pulsating.

"There's gotta be a way to stop that overgrown Tonka toy."

"I agree," said Chiun.

"But I can't think what that might be."

"In the days of the Mongol Khanates, a Master of Sinanju encountered such a conundrum."

"They had something like this back then?"

"No, but there were war elephants in those days."

"Yeah?"

Chiun nodded. "When Kublai Khan sought to conquer Annam, now called Vietnam, they were beaten by the hot, steamy air, which rotted their stout Mongol bows, and by armored Annamese war elephants, which rotted their courage. So a Master was hired. Boo, it was."

"How'd he deal with war elephants?"

"In the best way possible."

"I'm listening," Remo said.

And leaning over beneath the rattling main rotor, the Master of Sinanju whispered in Remo's ear.

"You're kidding!" Remo exploded.

HAROLD SMITH TRIED TO tell the Chief Executive there was a ninety-five percent probability that the Fist of Allah was targeted at New York City.

"Are you sure?"

"I said ninety-five," said Smith, wondering at the presidential educational level.

"What in New York City? Can they blow up the whole island?"

"Theoretically, yes. Practically speaking, I doubt it. There must be a specific target. One of practical or symbolic importance."

"In New York City, there have to be dozens. Wall Street. The UN. The Statue of Liberty. The Liberty Bell. No, that's Philadelphia, isn't it?"

Smith froze. His bone marrow suddenly turned to ice water.

"Mr. President, this is only an educated guess, but I believe I can postulate the likeliest ground-zero target."

"What is it?"

"The same target the Deaf Mullah originally attempted to demolish. A target through which airline traffic-control phone lines, television broadcast signals and other critical communications systems pass. By coincidence, the place where the Deaf Mullah's most hated enemy now resides."

The President started to ask the question when Harold Smith answered it for him.

"I am standing on ground zero."

IN THE MOSQUE in Greenburg, Ohio, FBI Tactical Commander Matt Brophy picked through the wreckage as his men cleared various chambers.

The mosque was a total disaster, and since that was probably going to be the ultimate state of everyone's careers, there was no point in standing on ceremony.

In the cavernous room from which the gigantic juggernaut had rumbled, they found a bearded man with his lower body pressed flat by the enormous treads that had cruelly rolled over him.

All around the room stood great empty drums with radiation warning signs and symbols plastered on them.

Matt Brophy decided that securing the room and getting the hell out was the safest option possible. Having a career train wreck was one thing, but going radioactive was another kind of career setback entirely.

THE PRESIDENT GOT the word within ten minutes.

"Mr. President, we've found something at the mosque site."

"Go ahead."

"There are tons of steel barrels for storing nuclear waste—all empty."

Harold Smith got the word minutes later.

"You are certain of this intelligence, Mr. President?" Smith asked tightly.

"That's what I'm told by FBI."

"There is only one conclusion I can draw from this. The Messengers of Muhammad have loaded the Fist of Allah with radioactive waste, effectively turning it into a radiological bomb."

"Oh, God!" the President moaned. "How bad is that?"

"Not as bad as a true nuclear device. They have no doubt packed the machine with a mixture of radioactive waste and conventional explosives. When detonated, the result will be not a true atomic explosion, but an ecological disaster in a contained radius."

"That doesn't exactly sound good, Smith."

"This changes the complexion of the threat but not the threat itself. I will get back to you."

Smith called up a close-up of the route for six miles ahead of the rolling juggernaut that was the Fist of Allah. The system showed him a bridge over the Allegheny River in its path and he picked up the satellite handset.

After listening, the President said, "Consider that bridge history."

I HAVE BUT ONE REGRET," said Yusef as the miles rolled by.

"I do not care about your regrets," said Jihad Jones.

"I regret that I never completed the pilgrimage to Mecca. But I was too busy spreading terror."

"I made my *haj* when I was young because I knew I would die young," Jihad boasted.

"I was too busy killing and driving a taxi," Yusef lamented.

"You would have been turned away or hung as an infidel anyway, Gamal Mahour."

Yusef swallowed the biting retort on his tongue. Being called a camel-nosed infidel was better than being called a Jew. He wound his *kaffiyeh* more tightly around his jutting nose.

They were coming up on a great bridge. They could see it through the bug spatters on their giant windscreen, which unfortunately lacked wipers. It looked substantial enough to accommodate their vehicle. This was a relief. The last bridge had been a tight squeeze.

Then out of the sky screamed three F-16 jets, releasing smoking rockets that made the bridge jump apart and collapse before their astounded eyes.

"The spiteful anti-Islamists have destroyed the bridge to Paradise!" Yusef complained.

"I can see that, fool!"

"What do we do?"

"We will go around it," growled Jihad Jones, throwing all his weight into the wheel.

The Fist of Allah began to grind and shimmy under the sudden strain of its new trajectory.

THE HUEY HELICOPTER was dropping to the green field as Remo shouted into a cell phone, "The bridge is down. Time for Chiun and me to do our thing."

"Do not fail," Smith called back over the rotor roar.

"I can't guarantee this will work, but Chiun swears it will."

Then they were running across the tall grass to intercept the Fist of Allah, which was trying to slide off the highway and into soft earth. It was like a land battleship—easy to propel forward, difficult to steer and impossible to reverse.

"Here goes," said Remo, worry on his face.

They got in front of the behemoth, set themselves at either side and waited poised to get out of the way as fast as they could.

The Fist of Allah came on. Its big front tires were turning slowly, painfully. Behind the windscreen, the two drivers were throwing their upper bodies in the direction of the turn, as if their puny weights would help.

"HELP ME TO STEER," Jihad Jones howled.

"I am trying," Yusef grunted. "Which way?"

"Left. No, the other left, fool!"

"I am steering left. Why are the wheels not responding?"

Then the two figures appeared in the road ahead.

"Jihad, look! Are those not the bugs we squashed before?" Yusef asked.

"Forget them. Steer! In Allah's name, steer!"

"I am steering!" shouted Yusef as the sweat of his struggle beaded his forehead.

ON THE GROUND, Remo set himself. The giant tires hummed toward him like big black Ferris wheels.

Poised, Remo watched the front tires loom over him. Then, kicking hard, he tapped the great lead tire, using the hard rubber to rebound away to safety.

On the other side, the Master of Sinanju performed the exact same maneuver in perfect synchronization.

Then Remo and Chiun were rolling away and into the soft earth just in case the worst happened.

THE FIST OF ALLAH gave a sudden lurch, and in the cockpit Yusef Gamal and Jihad Jones found their faces pressed suddenly into the thick windscreen with such force that their noses flattened and they could not breathe.

The impossible began to happen....

ONLY THE PILOT IN the waiting helicopter saw it clearly. The Fist of Allah, shuddering and veering away from the burning bridge that was no longer there, actually stumbled. Stumbled the way a giant stumbles. Stumbled like a mountain or an avalanche.

The front tires locked, the rear treads pushed and strained and, between the opposing forces and the tremendous momentum of the multiton vehicle, something had to give.

The Fist of Allah dug its blunt nose into the road, lifted its rear deck and in slow motion flipped end over end to go sliding into the burning river below.

It made a tremendous splash, and Remo and Chiun narrowly escaped being soaked by the waterfall that followed.

When no explosion came, they got out of the gullies where they had dropped for safety.

WHEN REMO AND CHIUN RETURNED to the waiting helicopter, the pilot wore a stupefied expression and said, "What the hell happened?"

"We tripped it," said Remo.

"Tripped?"

"That is how war elephants were bested in the days of the great Khans," said Chiun proudly.

"That's impossible. You can't trip something that big."

"You can if you know where to stick your toe," said Remo, stepping aboard. "Come on, we have places to go."

Grasping his stick, the pilot lifted the helicopter off the ground and took a long, hard look at the churning water. Air bubbles the size of Hula Hoops were popping on the surface of the muddy river beside the burning mangle that had been a great span.

IN THE FIST OF ALLAH, the water entered in a flood.

"We are drowning, Jihad," Yusef Gamal sputtered.

"It is your fault."

"My fault! You were at the wheel."

"You were at the wheel, as well. Therefore, it is equally your fault."

They tried the hatch but found it had no inside handle. There was no escaping this watery tomb where the light was shrinking. The thought sunk in.

"Jihad, my brother, we are going to die."

"At least there is that."

"Yes, at least there is that."

"But first we must arm the Fist of Allah so that we die with dignity while inflicting terror upon the godless," said Jihad.

"I will do this great thing," Yusef said, reaching for the holy crank.

"No, I have decided to do this wonderful deed."

But as they clawed and struggled in the upside-down cockpit, they found they could only brush the crank hanging over their heads.

"I will stand on your shoulders to reach it, then," Jihad said.

"No, you will not stand upon my Arabic shoulders. I will stand on your Egyptian back."

"If you do not do as I say, no one will die except us."

In the end, Yusef allowed the Egyptian to climb upon his shoulders. The crank was seized and turned. Three times. Four. To no avail.

"What is wrong?" Yusef sputtered as Jihad jumped down to join him amid the clammy, cold wetness that was now nearly to their shoulders.

"It does not work. The water. The cursed water has no doubt made the arming mechanism useless."

"Then only we will die," Yusef said dejectedly. "This is terrible. I am a suicide pilot-martyr. I must take my enemies with me or I will die unfulfilled."

That horrible thought sunk in, too.

As the water rose to the level of their mouths, Jihad Jones looked to Yusef with agonized eyes.

"Remember, when we get to Paradise, I do not know you."

"When I get to Paradise, I will personally point out your Crusader blood to any who will listen," Yusef spat back.

"And I will partake of your unspoiled *houris*, stealing those I can."

"Pork lover!"

"Cross-kisser!"

Glub-glub-blub.

Bloop!

35

Three days later, Remo and Chiun were in their bell-tower meditation room watching television when the telephone rang.

"I got it," said Remo.

It was Harold Smith. "The autopsy report came in on the Deaf Mullah," he said.

"What'd it say?"

"The FBI pathologist wanted to put down 'cause unknown,' but political pressures forced him to state a definite cause of death. He has it down as 'shaken baby syndrome.'"

"Yeah, before we left the mosque, I took the Deaf Mullah's head in my hand and shook it until his brains pureed like a milk shake."

"It will go down as a consequence of the launching of the Fist of Allah."

"They got it out of the water yet?"

"The Army Corps of Engineers are still working on that. Now that we know it was only a radiological bomb and not a true thermonuclear device, it is not so delicate a task. EPA should be able to contain any radiation leakage."

"Still, if it had gone off, it would have been pretty bad."

"They could have brought down the World Trade Center, crippling the city, killing thousands and making lower Manhattan uninhabitable for decades to come. Except for one minor detail."

"What's that?" asked Remo.

"The Fist of Allah has been measured. It was five feet too wide to fit through the Lincoln Tunnel. It would never have made it onto the island."

Remo laughed. When he was done, he asked, "So where did they get Fist of Allah?"

"It was a NASA surplus missile carrier they converted for the purpose. I am still attempting to trace the radioactive waste they filled it with, but there are many unscrupulous waste-disposal companies perfectly willing to allow such materials to fall into questionable hands for a price.

"The FBI roundup appears to have gotten every remaining Messenger of Muhammad, so that crisis is settled," Smith continued.

"What about the fake Deaf Mullah—the one in solitary?"

"He was willing to serve out the real Deaf Mullah's time for the cause. He will continue to enjoy that privilege."

"Is the mail moving again?"

"Given the current state of the postal service, it may be weeks before anyone can answer that question authoritatively," Smith said without sarcasm.

"That pretty much wraps things up, doesn't it?"

"Until the next crisis," Smith said firmly.

"Still smarting from baby-sitting duty?"

"Abeer Ghula should be drowned like an unwanted kitten," Smith said bitterly.

"Guess you won't be watching her interview tonight."

"Hardly."

"Tamayo Tanaka's going to interview her. Chiun and I are planning to watch because we're the only ones who know who Abeer's blond infidel really is."

"You are welcome to do what you wish," said Harold Smith, hanging up.

After Remo returned to his floor mat, Chiun asked, "Emperor Smith was pleased?"

"Didn't say a word about Osaka."

Chiun nodded. "Then our positions are secure."

"Guess we watch no Woos tonight."

"One night is permissible," allowed Chiun.

"Then it'll be back to the same old Woo."

"The incomparable Woo."

"Somehow I don't think we're talking about the same Woo."

TAMAYO TANAKA'S HEART was pounding. Her latest chance to go national was only ten minutes away, and the wall clock was ticking like a time bomb. She had an exclusive with Abeer Ghula, and all she had had to do was promise a couple of FBI guards a wild midnight dance on a queen-size bed at the Helmsley Park Lane Hotel.

Which she never, ever intended to deliver. She had made the promise as Tammy Terrill.

Alone in the New York–affiliate interview studio, she smoothed her jet black wig and checked to see that her oblique eyes matched.

A technician poked his head in. "Ghula's here."

"All set," Tamayo said. This was it. All she had to do was keep that crazy witch from recognizing her voice, and she was home free.

Abeer Ghula swayed into the studio wearing a Nile green floor-length dress that threatened her modesty at three critical points.

Without a word, she sat down and regarded Tamayo with her baleful eagle's eyes.

"I'm Tamayo," Tammy said as the technician tried to find a safe place to attach Abeer's lavaliere microphone. Her cleavage was threatening to explode free at the slightest disturbance, so he just placed it on her lap while Abeer reached around to pinch his buttocks with her black-nailed fingers.

"Later we will talk about my womanly needs," she told the hastily retreating technician.

Then she noticed Tamayo's outstretched hand.

Coolly she lifted her own, saying, "Have you heard the wonderful news about Um Allaha?"

Tamayo smiled as hard as she could. "I want to hear all about her," she cooed as the director started throwing signals. "But let's save it for on-air."

At that point, Abeer relinquished Tamayo's hand, and suddenly she noticed the black-and-blue bite marks on Tamayo's thumb.

"What is this?" she demanded tightly.

"Caught my thumb in a strange zipper," Tamayo said hastily.

Abruptly, Abeer twisted Tamayo's wrist, bringing the wounded thumb closer.

"Teeth marks! I know these. I set such marks on the helpless tools of both my husbands. Where did you get these? How could you have these upon your body? I have never tasted you. I have never sampled any Japanese infidel.''

One eye on the threatened cue and the other on the still-dead tally light, Tamayo started to protest when under the hot lights her right eye popped back into its naturally round shape.

This was not lost on Abeer Ghula, who said, ''What is wrong with your eye, woman?''

''Oh, damn,'' said Tamayo, clawing at her face. A brown contact lens dropped into her lap, and this brought Abeer Ghula out of her chair and into Tamayo's hair.

''You have blue eyes! And yellow hair!'' Abeer shrieked, whipping the wig away. ''You are my infidel!''

''And I'll be your faithful slave if you just sit still long enough to do this interview,'' Tamayo said frantically just before the hard slap knocked her off her chair.

''Deceiver! Um Allaha will punish you after you are dead!''

When the tally light came on, Abeer Ghula was already out of the studio and in hot pursuit of the pinched technician.

THE IMAGE BROADCAST to the nation lasted only ten seconds. But it was long enough for Remo and Chiun to absorb the indelible image of a blond Tamayo Tanaka trying to fumble her black wig onto her head while simultaneously sucking on her thumb.

''That's the biz,'' laughed Remo as Chiun reached for the remote control.

**A downed American superplane throws
Stony Man into a new war against an old enemy.**

STONY MAN™ 25

SKYLANCE

When the Air Force's pride and joy, America's advanced
top-secret reconnaissance plane, is shot down in western
New Guinea, Stony Man is dispatched to do the impossible:
recover the plane or destroy it. Caught in the cross fire of a
raging civil war, Bolan's army goes up against the shock
troops of a first-world industrialist fighting his private war
against America....

Available in November at your favorite retail outlet.

Or order your copy now by sending your name, address, zip or postal code, along
with a check or money order (please do not send cash) for $5.50 for each book
ordered ($6.50 in Canada), plus 75¢ postage and handling ($1.00 in Canada), payable
to Gold Eagle Books, to:

In the U.S.	In Canada
Gold Eagle Books	Gold Eagle Books
3010 Walden Avenue	P.O. Box 636
P.O. Box 9077	Fort Erie, Ontario
Buffalo, NY 14269-9077	L2A 5X3

Please specify book title with your order.
Canadian residents add applicable federal and provincial taxes.

SM25

MILLION DOLLAR SWEEPSTAKES

No purchase necessary. To enter, follow the directions published. For eligibility entries must be received no later than March 31, 1998. No liability is assumed for printing errors, lost, late, nondelivered or misdirected entries. Odds of winning are determined by the number of eligible entries distributed and received.

Sweepstakes open to residents of the U.S. (except Puerto Rico), Canada and Europe who are 18 years of age or older. All applicable laws and regulations apply. Sweepstakes offer void wherever prohibited by law. This sweepstakes is presented by Torstar Corp., its subsidiaries and affiliates, in conjunction with book, merchandise and/or product offerings. For a copy of the Official Rules (WA residents need not affix return postage), send a self-addressed, stamped envelope to: Million Dollar Sweepstakes Rules, P.O. Box 4469, Blair, NE 68009-4469.

SWP-M96

**Exiles from the future in the
aftermath of the apocalypse**

JAMES AXLER

DEATH LANDS®

Stoneface

In 2001, the face of the earth changed forever in a nuclear
firestorm. Generations after the apocalypse, Ryan Cawdor leads
the courageous struggle for survival in a brutal world, striving to
make a difference in the battle raging between good and evil.

In the Deathlands, the war is over...but the fight has just begun.

Available in November at your favorite retail outlet, or order your copy now by
sending your name, address, zip or postal code, along with a check or money order
(please do not send cash) for $5.50 for each book ordered ($6.50 in Canada),
plus 75¢ postage and handling ($1.00 in Canada), payable to Gold Eagle Books, to:

In the U.S.	In Canada
Gold Eagle Books	Gold Eagle Books
3010 Walden Ave.	P.O. Box 636
P.O. Box 9077	Fort Erie, Ontario
Buffalo, NY 14269-9077	L2A 5X3

Please specify book title with your order.
Canadian residents add applicable federal and provincial taxes.

DL34

**Don't miss out on the action in these titles featuring
THE EXECUTIONER®, and STONY MAN™!**

SuperBolan

#61445	SHOWDOWN	$4.99 U.S.	☐
		$5.50 CAN.	☐
#61446	PRECISION KILL	$4.99 U.S.	☐
		$5.50 CAN.	☐
#61447	JUNGLE LAW	$4.99 U.S.	☐
		$5.50 CAN.	☐
#61448	DEAD CENTER	$5.50 U.S.	☐
		$6.50 CAN.	☐

Stony Man™

#61904	TERMS OF SURVIVAL	$4.99 U.S.	☐
		$5.50 CAN.	☐
#61905	SATAN'S THRUST	$4.99 U.S.	☐
		$5.50 CAN.	☐
#61906	SUNFLASH	$5.50 U.S.	☐
		$6.50 CAN.	☐
#61907	THE PERISHING GAME	$5.50 U.S.	☐
		$6.50 CAN.	☐

(limited quantities available on certain titles)

TOTAL AMOUNT	$	
POSTAGE & HANDLING	$	
($1.00 for one book, 50¢ for each additional)		
APPLICABLE TAXES*	$ _____	
TOTAL PAYABLE	$ _____	
(check or money order—please do not send cash)		

To order, complete this form and send it, along with a check or money order for the total above, payable to Gold Eagle Books, to: **In the U.S.:** 3010 Walden Avenue P.O. Box 9077, Buffalo, NY 14269-9077; **In Canada:** P.O. Box 636, Fort Erie, Ontario L2A 5X3.

Name:_____

Address:_____ City:_____

State/Prov.:_____ Zip/Postal Code: _____

*New York residents remit applicable sales taxes.
Canadian residents remit applicable GST and provincial taxes.

GEBACK15A